To renew or order library books visit
www.lincolnshire.gov.uk
You will require a Personal Identification Number.
Ask any member of staff for this

INEVITABLE

LOUIS COUPERUS

INEVITABLE

Translated from the Dutch by
Paul Vincent

PUSHKIN PRESS
LONDON

For Simon

English translation © Paul Vincent and Pushkin Press 2005

First published in Dutch as
Langs Lijnen van geleidelijkheid in 1900

This edition first published in 2005 by
Pushkin Press
12 Chester Terrace
London NW1 4ND

British Library Cataloguing in Publication Data:
A catalogue record for this book is available
from the British Library

ISBN 1 901285 59 6

Cover: *Girl in White c* 1889 by William de Zwart
(1862–1931)
Haags Gemeentemuseum The Hague Netherlands
The Bridgeman Art Library

Frontispiece: Louis Couperus photograph by ED Hoppé
London 1921 Collection Letterkundig Museum The Hague

Set in 10 on 12 Baskerville
and printed in Britain
by Sherlock Printing, Bolney, West Sussex
on Legend Laid paper

**The translation of this book is funded by the
Foundation for the
Production and Translation of Dutch Literature**

INEVITABLE

I

THE MARCHESA BELLONI'S *pensione* was situated in one of Rome's most salubrious, if not most poetic, quarters: half the house formed part of a villa from the ancient Ludovisi gardens, those beautiful old gardens lamented by everyone who knew them before the apartment blocks had risen where the exclusive Roman residential area had once extended. The *pensione* was in Via Lombardia; the old villa section had retained a certain antique charm for the *marchesa*'s guests, and the newly-built extension offered spacious rooms, running water and electric light. The *pensione* had something of a reputation for being good, cheap and pleasantly appointed; a few minutes' walk from the Pincio, and high up so that one need have no fear of malaria, and the price one paid for an extended stay, which was just over eight lire, was exceptional for Rome, well-known for being more expensive than any other Italian city. Consequently the *pensione* was usually full: travellers arrived as early as October—those who arrived earliest in the season paid least; and apart from a few tourists in a hurry most of them stayed on till Easter, before making their way down to Naples after the great church festivals.

The *pensione* had been warmly recommended by English fellow-travellers to Cornélie de Retz van Loo, who was travelling alone through Italy and had written to the Marchesa Belloni from Florence. It was the first time she had travelled in Italy; it was the first time she had alighted at the great, cavernous Termini station close to the baths of Diocletian, and in the square, in the golden Roman sunshine, while the great Acqua Marcia fountain babbled and the coachmen cracked their whips and clicked their tongues (to catch her attention), she had her "precious Italian sensation" as she had imagined, and was glad to be in Rome.

She saw a little old man with 'Hôtel Belloni' written on his cap limping towards her, with the instinct of a veteran porter who immediately recognises his travellers, and she signalled to him with a smile. He greeted her like a long-lost friend, at once familiar and respectful, as if pleased to see her, asked whether she had had a pleasant journey, whether she was tired, accompanied her to the victoria, adjusted her travel-rug and her valise, asked for the ticket for her cases, and said that she should go on ahead: he would follow in ten minutes with the luggage. She found it fun, being looked after by the old fellow with the limp and gave him a friendly nod as the coachman drove off. She felt light and airy, with just a tinge of melancholy at the unknown things that were to happen to her, and looked left and right, taking in the streets of Rome: she saw nothing but houses and houses, apartment blocks; then a great white palace: the new Palazzo Piombino—where she knew the Ludovisi *Juno* was—and then the coachman pulled up, and a bell boy came up to her. He took her to the lounge, a dark room with a table in the centre covered in magazines, arranged in a neat, still unread circle; two ladies, obviously English, and of the aesthetic sort—grubby hair, loose blouses—were sitting in a corner studying their Baedekers before going out. Cornélie nodded briefly, but received no acknowledgement; she did not take it amiss, being familiar with the ways of English travellers. She sat down at the table and picked up the *Roman Herald*, the paper that appears fortnightly and gives information about everything there is to do in Rome, and at that point one of the ladies addressed her aggressively from a corner,

"I'm sorry, but you will be sure not to take the *Herald* to your room, won't you?"

Cornélie turned her head loftily and languidly towards the corner where the ladies were sitting, looked vaguely past their grubby heads, said nothing and looked back at the *Herald*, found herself a seasoned traveller and smiled inwardly, because she knew how to behave with this kind of English lady.

The *marchesa* came in and welcomed Cornélie in Italian and in French. She was a fairly plump matron, in a vulgar way; her ample bosom was contained in a silk cuirasse or spencer that shone at the seams and was bursting under the arms: her grey coiffure gave her a lion-like appearance; the large eyes, lined with yellow and blue, were opened unnaturally wide by belladonna; in her ears huge crystals created a rainbow effect, and bands of nameless precious stones girded her podgy fingers. She spoke very fast, and Cornélie found her phrases as pleasantly homely as the welcome of the crippled porter on the station square. She allowed the *marchesa* to escort her to the lift, and got in with her: the hydraulic lift, a barred cage that ascended past the staircase, climbed at a stately pace and came to a sudden halt between the second and third floors.

"Third floor!" the *marchesa* called down.

"*Non c'è acqua!*" the bellboy called back calmly, meaning—as seemed quite natural—that there was insufficient water to start the lift moving.

The *marchesa* barked a number of orders; two *facchini* appeared, hoisted themselves up with the bustling bellboy on the cable of the lift, and in fits and starts the cage rose higher and higher till it finally, almost, reached the third floor.

"A little higher!" ordered the *marchesa*.

But flex their muscles as the *facchini* might, the lift would not budge.

"We can still get out!" said the *marchesa*. "Wait a moment."

With a long stride, baring her huge white calf, she stepped on to the floor, smiled and extended her hand to Cornélie, who copied her gymnastics.

"We're here!" sighed the *marchesa* with a satisfied smile. "This is your room."

She opened a door and showed Cornélie a room. Although it was bright and sunny outside, the room was as dank as a cellar.

"*Marchesa*," said Cornélie at once, "I wrote to you that I wanted two rooms facing south."

"Really?" asked the *marchesa* in a naïve, innocent tone. "I really couldn't remember. Yes, foreigners are always so set on south-facing rooms … I can assure you this is a lovely room."

"I'm sorry, but I can't take it, *marchesa*."

'La Belloni' grumbled a little, then went down the corridor and opened another room.

"What about this room, *signora* … What do you think of this … ?"

"Is it south-facing?"

"Almost."

"I must have due south."

"This faces west: you'll see the most wonderful sunsets from your window."

"I absolutely must have a south-facing room, *marchesa*."

"I have some most charming east-facing rooms: the most beautiful sunrises."

"No, *marchesa* … "

"Have you no feeling for natural beauty?"

"A little, but I'm a lot more concerned about my health."

"I sleep in a north-facing room myself."

"You're Italian and you're used to it, *marchesa*."

"I'm very sorry, but I have no south-facing rooms."

"Then I'm sorry too, *marchesa*, but in that case I shall have to look elsewhere."

Cornélie turned away, as if to go. The choice of a room can be the choice of a lifetime …

The *marchesa* took her hand and smiled. She abandoned her cool tone and her voice was soothing as balm.

"*Davvero*, foreigners are so set on south-facing rooms! I still have two cubby-holes. Here … "

And she quickly opened two doors: two small, cosy, sunny long and narrow rooms, and from the open windows a lofty, wide panorama over the streets and roofs below and in the distance the blue dome of St Peter's.

"These are my last south-facing rooms," lamented the *marchesa*.

"I'll take them, *marchesa* … "

"Sixteen lire," smiled 'la Belloni'.

"Ten, as you wrote."

"I could put two people up in these."

"I'll be staying—if it's to my liking—the whole winter."

"You're a brave one!" the *marchesa* suddenly exclaimed in her most charming voice, the voice of defeat. "You can have the rooms for twelve lire. No more discussions. The rooms are yours. You're Dutch, aren't you? We have another Dutch family; a mama with two daughters and a son. Would you like to sit next to them at table?"

"No, I'd prefer it if you would seat me somewhere else; I don't like my compatriots when they're travelling … "

The *marchesa* left Cornélie alone. She looked out of the window, her mind empty of thoughts, happy to be in Rome, with a touch of melancholy at the unknown things that were about to happen to her. There was a knock at the door and her suitcases were brought in. She saw that it was eleven o'clock and started unpacking. One of her rooms was a small sitting room, like a birdcage in the air, looking out over Rome. She rearranged the furniture herself, draped the faded chaise-longue with a length of cloth from the Abruzzi and with drawing pins fixed a number of portraits to the distempered wall which was broken up by crude fresco arabesques. And she smiled at the border of purple hearts pierced by arrows that surrounded the frescoed section of the wall.

An hour's work and her sitting-room was organised: a home of her own with a few of her own bits of material, a cover so, a side table so: cushions on the chaise-longue, books to hand. When she had finished and sat down, she suddenly felt very lonely. She thought of The Hague, of what she was leaving behind. But she did not want to think, picked up her Baedeker and read about the Vatican. She could not concentrate and turned to Hare's *Walks through Rome*. A bell rang. She was tired, felt nervous, looked in the mirror, saw her hair that had lost its curl, her blouse smudged with coal and dust, unlocked a second suitcase and changed. As she did her hair she cried, sobbed. The second bell rang and after powdering her face she went downstairs.

She thought she was late but there was no one in the dining-room and she had to wait to be served. She resolved not to come so promptly in future. Some lodgers looked in through the open door, saw that no one was at table yet except for a new lady and disappeared again.

Cornélie looked around and waited.

The dining-room was the antique banqueting room of the old villa section with a ceiling by Guercino. The waiters were just strolling about. An old grey-haired head waiter surveyed the table from afar to make sure everything was in order. He became impatient when no one came and gave orders for Cornélie to be served with the macaroni. Cornélie noticed that, like the porter, he was lame in one leg. But the waiters were very young, scarcely sixteen or eighteen and lacked the usual waiterly aplomb.

A fat gentleman, lively, self-important, pock-marked, badly shaven, in a threadbare black jacket without much linen on show, came in, rubbed his hands, and sat down opposite Cornélie.

He greeted her politely and also had some macaroni.

And it seemed to be a sign that it was time to eat, because numerous guests, mostly ladies, now entered, sat down and had portions of the macaroni being served by the young waiters under the supervision of the grey-haired head waiter. Cornélie smiled at the amusing manners of these travelling types and when she looked involuntarily at the pock-marked gentleman opposite, she noticed that he was smiling too.

He hurriedly ate a little more bread with tomato sauce, leant a little further across the table and in a near-whisper said in French:

"Amusing, isn't it?"

Cornélie raised her eyebrows.

"How do you mean?"

"A cosmopolitan company … "

"Oh, yes … "

"Are you Dutch?"

"How do you know?"

"I saw your name in the register, and it said The Hague after it … "

"That's true … "

"There are some other Dutch ladies here, they're over there … they're charming."

Cornélie ordered a cheap wine from the head waiter.

"That wine is no good," said the lively gentleman, in an animated tone. "I'm having Genzano," he said, pointing to his carafe. "I pay a small corkage and drink my own wine."

The head waiter brought Cornélie her half bottle: it was included with her board.

"If you like, I can give you the address for my wine: Via della Croce 61 … "

Cornélie thanked him. The unusual ease and vivacity of the pock-marked gentleman amused her.

"You're looking at the head waiter?" he asked.

"You're very observant," she smiled.

"Quite a character, our head waiter, Giuseppe. He used to be head waiter at the palace of an Austrian archduke. He did something, I don't know what. Stole perhaps. Or was impertinent. Or dropped a spoon. He came down in the world. Now he's in our humble Pensione Belloni. But what dignity … "

He leant forward.

"The *marchesa* is thrifty. All the staff here are either old or very young. Less in wages."

He bowed to two German ladies, mother and daughter, who had come in and sat down next to him.

"I've got the permit I promised you, to see the Palazzo Rospigliosi, Guido Reni's *Aurora*," he said in German.

"Is the prince back then?"

"No, the prince is in Paris. The palace is closed, except to you."

He bowed gallantly.

The German ladies exclaimed that he was so sweet, that he could do everything, find a solution to every problem. The trouble they had gone to bribe the concierge of Rospigliosi! With no success.

A thin English lady had sat down next to Cornélie.

"And for you, Miss Taylor, I have a ticket for an early mass in his Holiness's own chapel … "

Miss Taylor beamed with joy.

"Have you been sightseeing again?" the pock-marked gentleman continued.

"Yes, the Kircher Museum," said Miss Taylor. "But now I'm exhausted … It was most exquisite."

"I'm prescribing you an afternoon at home, Miss Taylor, and some rest."

"I've arranged to see the Aventine … "

"You mustn't go. You're tired. You're looking worse every day and getting thinner. Rome is too tiring for you. You must rest, otherwise I shan't give you the ticket for morning mass."

The German ladies laughed. Miss Taylor promised, flattered, delighted. She looked at the pock-marked gentleman, as if waiting for his words of wisdom.

Lunch was over: the steak, pudding and dried figs. Cornélie got up.

"Can I pour you a glass from my bottle?" asked the fat gentleman. "Try my wine. Do you like it? If so, I'll order you a flask in the Via della Croce … "

Cornélie did not like to refuse and drank. The wine was wonderfully pure. She thought it would be good to drink a pure wine in Rome and as she thought this the fat gentleman seemed to read her rapid train of thought.

"It's good," he said, "if you drink a fortifying wine in Rome, where life is exhausting."

Cornélie agreed.

"This is Genzano, two lire seventy-five a flask. It will last you a long time, as the wine doesn't go off." He bowed to all the ladies with a circular motion and left.

The German ladies bowed to Cornélie.

"Always so obliging, that Mr Rudyard … "

"What can he be?" thought Cornélie. "French, German, English, American?"

II

AFTER LUNCH she had hired an open carriage and taken a drive through Rome, a first taste of the city she had so yearned for. That first impression had been a great disappointment. Her lively imagination, her reading, even the photographs she had bought in Florence and pored over with the devotion of a novice sightseer, had given her a vision of a city from an ideal antiquity, an ideal Renaissance and she had forgotten that, especially in Rome, life has moved on inexorably and that the ages do not appear in buildings and ruins as separate periods but every period is linked to the next by a tight-knit succession of days and years.

So she had found the dome of Saint Peter's small, the Corso narrow, Trajan's Column a column like any other; she had not seen the Forum as she drove past and on the Palatine she had not been able to call a single emperor to mind.

Now she was back home and tired, resting and thinking, melancholy yet savouring her vague thoughts, the silence around her and the big boarding-house, to which most guests had not yet returned. She thought of The Hague, of her large family, father, mother, brothers and sisters, to whom she had said farewell for a considerable time in order to travel. Her father, a retired colonel of hussars, not being a man of means, had not been able to help satisfy her whim, as he put it, and she would not have been able

19

to indulge that whim, of starting a new life, without a small legacy left her years ago by a godmother. She was glad to have a degree of independence, although she felt the selfishness of that independence …

But what good would she have been to her circle, after the commotion surrounding her divorce? She was weak—selfish—and she knew it; but she had suffered a blow to which she had at first thought she would succumb. And when she survived after all, she had gathered together her remaining energy and told herself that she could not go on living in the same tight circle of sisters and friends, and she had forced her life to take a different direction. She had always had a flair for turning an old dress into an apparently new outfit, of transforming last year's hat into a new creation, and she had done the same with her diffuse and miserable life, storm-tossed and broken as it was: she had scraped together, frugally as it were, what remained and was still serviceable, and from those remnants she had made herself a new life. Yet in the old atmosphere this new life had no room to breathe: it was aimless and alien there, and she had managed to force it into a new path, despite the resistance of family and friends. Perhaps she would not have been quite so resolute in this if her life had not felt quite so fractured. Perhaps she would not have been quite so aware of her energy if she had suffered only a little. She had her strength and she had her weakness; there was a great wholeness in her, but great diversity too, and perhaps that complexity had been the salvation of her youth.

Besides, she *was* very young, twenty-three, and at that age there is an unconscious resilience, for all the apparent

weakness. And her contradictions constituted her equilibrium, so that she did not gravitate towards the abyss …
All of that passed through her, vague and cloud-like, not
with the concision of words, but with the mistiness of
weary dreams. Lying there she did not look as if she had
ever exerted the power of giving her life a new direction.
A pale, delicate woman, slim and with disjointed movements, lying on a chaise-longue in a no longer pristine
dressing gown with its faded pink and crumpled lace. Yet
she was surrounded by the poetry of herself, despite those
tired eyes, the limp lines of her garment, despite the
rented room, with the hastily improvised air of comfort,
which owed more to flair than to reality and could be fitted
into any suitcase. With her fragile figure, her pale features,
more refined than beautiful, she was surrounded by a
halo of individuality, an atmosphere that she emanated
unconsciously, that travelled from her eyes to the things
she gazed at, from her fingers to the things she stroked.
For those unsympathetic to her that atmosphere was odd,
eccentric, unbefitting for a young lady from The Hague,
and was censured. For those who were sympathetic it had
an element of talent, soul, something special that almost
resembled genius, though in an enervated form, and was
enchanting and thought-provoking and promised much:
perhaps too much to contain. This woman was a child of
her time but particularly of her environment, which was
why she was so immature: conflict against conflict, a
balance of contradiction, which might be either her
downfall or her salvation, but was certainly her fate.

She felt lonely in Italy. She had lived for weeks in
Florence, and had tried to construct a life rich in art and

history. Though she forgot much about herself, she still felt lonely. She had spent two weeks in Siena, but had found it oppressive with its gloomy streets and funereal palaces, and had longed for Rome. But that afternoon she had not yet found Rome. And though she felt tired, most of all she felt lonely, totally alone and futile in the great wide world, in a great city, a city where one perhaps feels greatness and futility more intensely than anywhere else. She felt like a tiny atom of suffering, like an ant, an insect, battered and half-crushed among the vast cupolas of Rome that she sensed were outside.

Her hand wandered idly over her reading-matter, which in her conscientious way she had piled up on a side table near her, a few translated classics: Ovid, Tacitus, then Dante, Petrarch and Tasso. Dusk was falling in her room, not a light to read by, and she was too unsure of herself to ring for a lamp; a chill drifted through her room, now that the sun had completely set, and she had forgotten to have them light a stove that first day. Wide acres of loneliness surrounded her, her suffering pained her, her soul longed for another soul, her lips for a kiss, her arms for the man who had once been her husband, and as she tossed about on her cushions, wringing her hands, indecision rose from deep within her:

"Oh God, tell me what I'm to do!"

III

THERE WAS A BUZZ of voices at dinner; the three or four long tables were full; the *marchesa* sat at the head of the centre table. Now and then she beckoned impatiently to Giuseppe, the old head waiter, who had dropped a spoon at an archducal court, and youthful waiters trotted about breathlessly. Sitting opposite her Cornélie found the benevolent fat gentleman whom the German ladies had called Mr Rudyard, and by her place setting her flask of Genzano. She thanked him with a smile, and talked to Mr Rudyard—the usual chit-chat: how she had been for a tour that afternoon, her first taste of Rome, the Forum, the Pincio. She talked to the German ladies and with the Englishwoman, who was always so tired from 'sightseeing', and the German ladies, an old baroness and her daughter, a young baroness, laughed with her at the two aesthetes whom Cornélie had encountered in the drawing-room that first morning. They were sitting some distance away; tall and angular, with unwashed hair, in strangely cut evening dresses that revealed bosoms and arms, comfortably covered by grey woollen vests, over which they had calmly draped strings of large blue beads. Both of them surveyed the long table, as if pitying anyone who had travelled to Rome to become acquainted with art, since they alone knew what art in Rome was. While eating, which they did unappetisingly, almost with their fingers, they read aesthetic works, frowning and occasionally looking up crossly because people were talking at table. With their pedantry, their impossible manners, their appalling taste in clothes, together with their great pretentiousness, they were typical English ladies on their travels, of the kind one finds nowhere but in Italy. The criticism of them at table was unanimous. They came to Pensione Belloni every winter, and painted watercolours in the Forum or on the Via Appia. And they were so extraordinary in their unprecedented originality, in their angular scruffiness, with their evening dresses, the woollens, the blue necklaces, the aesthetic books and their fingers busily picking meat apart, that all eyes were drawn to them by a Medusa-like attraction. The young baroness, a type from a fashionable magazine, incisive, quick-witted, with her round little German face and high sharply drawn eyebrows, laughed with Cornélie, and was showing her a sketchbook containing a drawing she had dashed off of the two aesthetic ladies, when Giuseppe led a young lady to the end of the table where Cornélie and Rudyard were sitting opposite each other. She had obviously just arrived, wished the assembled gathering a good evening, and sat down with a great rustle of material. All eyes turned from the aesthetic ladies towards this newcomer. It was immediately obvious that she was American, almost too beautiful, too young to be travelling alone, with a smiling self-assurance, as if she were at home, very white, with very lovely dark eyes, teeth like a dentist's advertisement, her full bust sheathed in mauve linen with silver trimmings full of arabesques, on her heavily permed hair a large mauve hat with a cascade of black ostrich feathers, attached by an over-large paste clasp. Her silk underskirts rustled at every movement, the plumes waved, the paste glittered. And despite this showy appearance she was like a child, no more than twenty, with a naïve look: she immediately addressed Cornélie and Rudyard; said she was tired, had come from Naples, had danced at Prince Cibo's the night before, that her name was Miss Urania Hope, that her father lived in Chicago. That she had two brothers who, despite papa's fortune worked on a ranch way out West, but that she had been brought up like a spoilt child by her father, who nevertheless wanted her to stand on her own feet and so let her travel alone, and wanted to arrange joint outings in the Old World, in 'dear old Italy'. She was overjoyed to hear that Cornélie was also travelling alone, and Rudyard teased the ladies about their new-fangled notions, and the two baronesses applauded them. Miss Hope took an immediate liking to her Dutch fellow-traveller, but Cornélie, hesitant, gently declined, saying that she was busy and wanted to study in the museums. "My, my, so serious?" inquired Miss Hope respectfully, and the underskirts rustled, the plumes waved and the paste sparkled. She struck Cornélie as a multicoloured butterfly, nimble and unthinking, that was in danger of crashing into the conservatory glass of a confined existence. Though she felt no attraction to the strange creature that looked at the same time like a coquette and a child, she did feel pity, why she did not know. After supper Rudyard suggested a short walk to the two German ladies. The young baroness came over to Cornélie and asked her to join them, to see Rome by moonlight, nearby, around the Villa Medici. She was grateful for the kind words, and was going to put on a hat when Miss Hope ran after her.

"Stay with me in the drawing-room … "

"I'm going for a walk with the baroness," replied Cornélie.

"That German lady?"

"Yes."

"Does she belong to the nobility?"

"I fancy she does."

"Are there many people from the nobility in this *pensione*?" asked Miss Hope eagerly.

Cornélie laughed.

"I don't know. I only arrived here this morning."

"I think there are. I've heard that there are lots of members of the nobility here. Are you a member of the nobility?"

"I was!" laughed Cornélie. "But I had to relinquish my title."

"What a shame!" cried Miss Hope. "The nobility is so sweet. Do you know what I have? An album of coats-of-arms, of all sorts of families, and another album of samples—silk and brocade of every ball gown of the queen of Italy … Would you like to see it?"

"I'd love to," laughed Cornélie. "But now I must put my hat on."

She went off and returned in her hat and cape: the German ladies and Rudyard were already waiting in the vestibule and asked why she was laughing. She told them about the album of samples of the queen's evening gowns, which caused great merriment.

"Who is he?" she asked the baroness, as they walked on ahead down the Via Sistina; the young baroness followed with Rudyard.

She found the baroness charming, but was struck, in this German woman from an aristocratic military background, by a cold, cynical view of life not exactly typical of her Berlin environment.

"I don't know," replied the baroness with some indifference. "We travel a lot. At the moment we have no house in Berlin. We want to enjoy our trip. Mr Rudyard is very nice. He helps us with all kinds of things: tickets for a papal mass, introductions here, invitations there. He appears to have considerable influence. What do I care who or what he is? Else feels the same. I take what he has to offer here and apart from that I don't delve too deeply into him … "

They walked on.

The baroness took Cornélie's arm.

"My dear child, don't think us too cynical. I scarcely know you, but I like you. Odd, isn't it, on our travels, suddenly to be sitting down to a *pensione* set menu with scrawny chicken. Don't think us bad, or cynical. Oh, perhaps we are. Our cosmopolitan, dissolute life free of duty makes one like that: ignoble, cynical and selfish. Very selfish. Rudyard does us many favours. Why shouldn't I accept them? I couldn't care less who or what he is. I'm not putting myself under an obligation to him."

Cornélie looked round involuntarily. In the street, almost completely dark, she saw Rudyard and the young baroness, almost whispering and acting mysteriously.

"And does your daughter feel the same?"

"Oh yes. We're not under any obligation to him. We don't even care greatly for him, with his pock-marked face and black nails. We simply accept his introductions.

27

Do likewise. Or … don't. Perhaps it would be nobler of you not to. I, I've become very selfish, through our travelling. What difference does it make to me … "

The dark street seemed to invite confidences, and Cornélie understood a little of that cynical indifference, unusual in a woman brought up amid narrow concepts of duty and morality. It was not noble; but was it not weariness at life's tribulations? Whatever the case, she had a vague understanding of that indifferent tone, that nonchalant shrug of the shoulders …

And they turned past Hôtel Hassler and approached the Villa Medici. The full moon poured out its flood of white light, and Rome was bathed in the blue-white nocturnal glow. From the full basin of the fountain, beneath the black holm oaks, whose foliage provided an ebony frame for the painting of Rome, the abundant water splashed noisily down …

"Rome must be beautiful," said Cornélie softly.

Rudyard and the young baroness had caught up, and heard Cornélie's words.

"Rome *is* beautiful," he said earnestly. "And Rome is more. Rome is a great consolation to many people."

In the bluish moonlit night his words struck her. The city seemed to be undulating mystically at her feet. She looked at him: he stood before her, with his black coat, without much linen on show: always a fat, polite gentleman. His voice was very piercing, with a rich tone of conviction. She looked at him for a long time, unsure of herself and vaguely sensing an approaching suggestion, but mutely hostile.

Then he added, as if not wanting her to dwell too long on what he had said:

"A great consolation, for many people … since beauty consoles … "

And she found his last remark an aesthetic truism, but he had meant her to find it so.

IV

CORNÉLIE FOUND THE FIRST DAYS in Rome extremely exhausting. She did too much, as everyone does who has just arrived; she wanted to embrace the whole city at once, and the distances, though covered in a carriage, wore her out. In addition she was constantly disappointed, in paintings, in statues, in buildings. At first she did not dare admit those disappointments to herself, but one afternoon, dog-tired, after a painful disappointment in the Sistine Chapel, she admitted it. Everything she saw and already knew from her studies was a disappointment. She decided not to see anything else for the time being. And after her gruelling days of going out in the morning, out in the afternoon, it was a luxury to abandon herself to the subconscious stream of days. She stayed home in the mornings in a *peignoir*, in her cosy, lofty birdcage of a sitting-room, wrote letters, dreamed a little, her arms folded round her head, read Ovid, Petrarch, listened to some street musicians, who with trembling tenor voices, to the plaintive twang of their guitars filled the quiet street with the sobbing passion of music. At lunch she felt she had been fortunate in her choice of *pensione*: in her corner at table she found the Baroness Von Rothkirch with her nonchalant condescension towards Rudyard interesting, as she saw how travel can uproot someone from their narrow circle. The young baroness, who did not worry at all about life and just painted and sketched, interested her when she whispered to Rudyard, so that Cornélie did not understand. Miss Hope was so naïve, so childishly scatterbrained, that Cornélie could not see how Hope Senior, the rich stocking-manufacturer over there in Chicago, simply let this girl travel alone with her excessive monthly allowance and total lack of worldliness and understanding of people; and Rudyard himself, although she was sometimes repelled by him, fascinated her despite that repulsion. So although she had not struck up a deeper friendship with any of these table companions, there were people around her to whom she could talk, and the table conversation was a diversion from the whole day's loneliness.

For in these days of weariness and disappointment she took only a short afternoon walk down the Corso or the Pincio, then returned home, made tea for herself in her silver teapot, and daydreamed in front of the wood fire till it was time to dress for dinner.

And the well-lit dining-room with the Guercino ceiling was cheerful. The *pensione* was full: the *marchesa* was sleeping in the bathroom, having given up her own room. There was a constant buzz of voices at table, the waiters trotted about and spoons and forks clattered. The melancholy mood of so many restaurants with set menus was absent here. People knew each other and the bustle of Roman life, the oxygen of Roman air, seemed to have injected vitality into their gestures and conversations. Amid that vitality the two scruffy aesthetic ladies stood out with their unchanging attitude: always in evening dress, the woollens, the beads, the reading of the thick tome; the angry looks because people were talking.

And after dinner people sat in the drawing-room, in the hall, getting to know this person and that, and talking of Rome, Rome, Rome … There was always great excitement about the music in the various churches: people consulted the *Herald*, asked Rudyard, who knew everything, and surrounded him, while he smiled, fat and polite, and distributed tickets, telling them the days and times when there was an important service in such and such church. Now and then, in passing, he gave English ladies who were not *au fait*, information about the complex formalities and hierarchies of Catholic worship: he told them the nationalities indicated by the various colours of the seminarists whom one met in hordes on the Pincio in the afternoon, staring at St Peter's, in ecstasy at the mighty symbol of their mighty religion; he told them the difference between a church and a basilica; he told intimate stories about the life of Leo XIII. He talked about all this in a fascinating, insinuating tone: the English ladies, eager for information, hung on his every word, found him most charming, asked him for a thousand details.

These days, then, were a time of recuperation for Cornélie. She recovered from her exhaustion, and became indifferent to Rome. But she had no thought of leaving early. Whether she was here or somewhere else, it was the same: she had to be somewhere. Apart from that the *pensione* was good, and her table companions were excellent company. She no longer read Hare's *Walks through Rome* or Ovid's *Metamorphoses*, but reread Ouida's *Ariadne*. She did not like the book as much as when she had found it in The Hague three years before, and read nothing else. But she enjoyed herself for a whole evening with the Von

Rothkirch ladies looking at Miss Hope's collection of seals and sample album. How keen those Americans were on nobility and royalty. The baroness magnanimously stamped her coat-of-arms in the album. The samples were much admired, gold brocade, silk as heavy as silver, foliage-patterned tulle. Miss Hope told them how she had acquired them: she knew one of the queen's lady's maids through her having previously served an American lady and for a high price that maid was able to provide her with the samples: a precious scrap, picked up while the queen was having a fitting, sometimes even cut from a wide seam. The child was prouder of her collection of samples than an Italian prince of his paintings, said Baroness Von Rothkirch. But despite that ridiculousness, that vanity, the beautiful American girl appealed to Cornélie because of the spontaneity and honesty of her nature. In the evenings she looked utterly charming, in a black low-cut dress or a red chiffon blouse. For that matter, it was different every evening. It was a kaleidoscope of outfits, blouses, jewels. She wandered through the ruins of the Forum in a tailored off-white linen suit, lined in orange silk, and her white lace petticoat tripped airily over the foundations of the Basilica Julia or the temple of Vesta. Her busily designed hats provided a dash of the colours of the Avenue de l'Opéra or Regent's Street amid the tragic earnestness of the Colosseum or in the palace ruins of the Palatine. The young baroness teased her about her orange silk lining, so in keeping with the Forum; about her hats, so in keeping with the seriousness of a site of Christian martyrdom, but she never became angry. "But it's a lovely hat!" she would reply in her Yankee accent, giving a splendid view of her fine teeth, but opening her mouth wide, as if she were cracking hazelnuts. And the child was delighted, delighted with the 'old baroness' and the "young baroness", delighted at being in a *pensione* run by a down-at-heel Italian *marchesa*. And the moment she caught sight of the grey lion's mane of the Marchesa Belloni, she would leave the others, rush up to her— according to Mrs Von Rothkirch, because a marchioness is above a baroness—pull 'la Belloni' into a corner and monopolise her, if possible for the whole evening. Rudyard joined the two of them, the marchioness and Miss Hope, and seeing this Cornélie again wondered what Rudyard was, who he was, and what he was after. But it did not interest the baroness, who had just obtained a ticket to mass in the Papal chapel, and the young baroness said only that he was a good raconteur of saints' legends, which helped explain some paintings in Doria and Corsini.

V

O N ONE OF THOSE EVENINGS Cornélie made the
acquaintance of the Dutch family, next to whom
the *marchesa* had first wanted to seat her: Mrs Van der
Staal and her two daughters. They were also staying in
Rome for the whole winter, they had friends there and
went out. The conversation flowed easily, and Mrs Van
der Staal invited Cornélie up to her sitting-room for a
chat. The following day she went to the Vatican with her
new friends, and heard that Mrs Van der Staal was
expecting her son from Florence, who was to come to
Rome to pursue his archaeological studies.

Cornélie was glad to find a Dutch element in the hotel
that was not uncongenial. She enjoyed being able to
speak Dutch and freely admitted it. In the space of a few
days she was on intimate terms with Mrs Van der Staal
and the two girls, and the first evening after the arrival of
Mr Van der Staal Jr, she revealed more of herself than
she had ever thought herself capable of doing to strangers
who she had known just a few days.

They were in the Van der Staals' sitting-room, Cornélie
in an easy chair, by the tall blazing wood fire, as it was a
chilly evening.

She had talked about The Hague, about her divorce,
and now she talked about Italy, about herself.

"I can't see anything any more," she confessed. "My
head is spinning from Rome. I can't see any more colours,

any more shapes. I don't recognise people any more. They swirl about me so. Sometimes I feel a need to sit alone for hours in my birdcage, upstairs, in order to recover. This morning in the Vatican, I can't remember it, I didn't retain a thing. Things are always dull and grey around me. Then the people in the *pensione*. The same faces every day. I see them and yet I don't see them. I see … Mrs Von Rothkirch and her daughter, then the beautiful Urania, Rudyard and the English lady, Miss Taylor, who is always worn out with sightseeing, and finds everything 'most exquisite'. But my memory is so bad that in my solitude I have to work it out: Mrs Von Rothkirch is tall, stately, with the smile of the German empress, whom she resembles slightly, talkative yet indifferent, as if her words were just falling indifferently from her lips … "

"You're very observant … " said Van der Staal.

"Oh, don't say that!" said Cornélie, almost annoyed. "I can't see anything, can't retain anything. I have no impressions. Everything around me is grey. I don't really know why I travel … When I'm alone I think of the people I meet … I've got Mrs Von Rothkirch now and I've got Else. A round witty face with tall eyebrows, and always a witticism or a 'punch line': I sometimes find it tiring, it makes me laugh so much. But still, they are nice. Then there's the beautiful Urania. She tells me everything: she is as communicative as I am at this moment. And Rudyard too, I can see him in front of me."

"Rudyard!" smiled Mrs Van der Staal and the girls.

"What is he?" asked Cornélie, curious. "He's always so polite, he recommended a wine to me; he's always able to get tickets."

"Don't you know what Rudyard is?" asked Mrs Van der Staal.

"No, and neither does Mrs Von Rothkirch."

"Then beware," laughed the girls.

"Are you Catholic?" asked Mrs Van der Staal.

"No ... "

"And nor is the beautiful Urania? Or the Von Rothkirchs?"

"No ... "

"Well, that's why 'la Belloni' put Rudyard on your table. Rudyard is a Jesuit. In every *pensione* in Rome there's a Jesuit who has free board and lodging, if the owner is on good terms with the church, and with great charm tries to win souls ... "

Cornélie found this hard to believe.

"Believe me," Mrs Van der Staal went on. "In a *pensione* like this, an important, reputable *pensione*, a great deal of intrigue goes on ... "

"'La Belloni' ... ?" asked Cornélie.

"Our *marchesa* is a born intriguer. Last winter three English sisters were converted."

"By Rudyard?"

"No, by another priest. Rudyard came here this winter."

"Rudyard walked along with me for quite a way this morning in the street," said young Van der Staal. "I let him talk, and sounded him out."

Cornélie fell back in her chair.

"I'm tired of people," she said with the strange honesty that she had in her. "I'd like to sleep for a month without seeing anyone." And after a little while she got up, said good night and went to bed, with her head swimming ...

VI

S HE STAYED IN for a few days, and ate in her room. One morning, however, she went for a walk in the Borghese gardens and bumped into the young Van der Staal on his bicycle.

"You don't cycle?" he asked, jumping off.

"No … "

"Why not?"

"It's a kind of movement that doesn't agree with my kind of person," replied Cornélie, annoyed at meeting someone who disturbed the solitude of her walk.

"May I walk with you?"

"Of course."

He left his bicycle in the charge of the gateman, and walked along beside her, naturally, without saying much.

"It's so beautiful here," he said.

His words sounded simple and sincere. She looked at him closely, for the first time.

"You're an archaeologist, aren't you?" she asked.

"No," he said defensively.

"What then?"

"Nothing. Mama says that to excuse me. I'm nothing and a quite useless member of society. And not even all that rich."

"But you're studying, aren't you?"

"No. I read a bit here and there. My sisters call that studying."

"Do you like going out, as your sisters do here?"

"No, I think it's dreadful. I never go with them."

"Don't you enjoy meeting and studying people?"

"No. I like paintings, statues and trees."

"Poet?"

"No. Nothing. Really, nothing."

She looked at him more and more attentively. He was walking beside her as if it were the most natural thing in the world, a tall thin fellow of maybe twenty-six, still more a boy than a man in his build and his face, but on the other hand with a certainty and calm that made him older than his years. He was pale, he had dark, cool, almost accusing eyes, and there was something nonchalant about his tall, thin figure in his dishevelled cycling suit, as if he cared nothing about his arms and legs.

He said nothing more, but walked beside her, easily, companionably, without finding it necessary to talk. But Cornélie became nervous and did not know what to say.

"It's so beautiful here," she stammered.

"Oh, it's very beautiful here," he replied calmly, without seeing that she was nervous. "So green, so wide, so peaceful: those long avenues, those perspectives of avenues, an ancient arch over there, and there, look, so blue, so distant, St Peter's, always St Peter's. Shame about all those funny things further on; that cafeteria, that milk stand … They spoil everything these days … Let's sit down here: it's so beautiful :.. "

They sat down on a bench.

"It's so marvellous when something is beautiful," he went on. "People are never beautiful. Things are beautiful: statues, paintings. And so are trees, clouds!"

"Do you paint?"

"Sometimes," he admitted reluctantly. "A bit. But actually everything's already been painted, and I can't really say I paint."

"Do you write too perhaps?"

"Even more has been written than has been painted. Perhaps not everything has been painted yet, but *everything* has been written. Every new book that has no particular scholarly importance is superfluous. All poetry has been said and every novel has been written."

"Don't you read much?"

"Almost nothing. I sometimes leaf through ancient writers."

"But what do you do then?" she asked suddenly, in irritation.

"Nothing," he said calmly, and looked at her humbly. "I do nothing, I exist."

"Do you think that a good approach to life?"

"No ... "

"But why don't you try a different one?"

"Like buying a new jacket, or a new bicycle?"

"You're not being serious," she said crossly.

"Why are you so angry with me?"

"Because you irritate me," she said in annoyance.

He got up, took his leave very politely, and said:

"Then I'd rather go and cycle a bit."

And he slowly walked off.

"Idiotic fellow!" she thought petulantly.

But she was upset at having squabbled with him, because of his mother and his sisters.

VII

IN THE HOTEL, however, he talked politely to Cornélie as if there had been no edgy exchanges or petty tiff between them, and he even asked her quite naturally –since Mama and his sisters had a call to make that afternoon—if they could go to the Palatine together.

"I was there recently," she said nonchalantly.

"And aren't you going to visit the ruins?"

"No."

"Why not?"

"They don't interest me. I just can't see anything of the past in them. All I see are ruins."

"But then why did you come to Rome?" he asked in annoyance.

She looked at him, and could have burst out sobbing.

"I don't know," she said humbly. "I could have gone elsewhere … But I had expected so much of Rome, and Rome is a disappointment."

"How's that?"

"I find Rome hard and relentless, and without feeling. I don't know why, but that's the impression I get. And at present I'm in the sort of mood where on the contrary I need something sensitive and soft."

He smiled.

"Come on," he said. "Come with me to the Palatine. I must show you Rome. Rome is so beautiful."

She felt too sad to be alone, and she quickly dressed

41

and left the hotel with him. Outside the coachmen cracked their whips. "*Vuole, vuole?*" they cried.

He chose one.

"This is Gaetano," he said. "I always take him, He knows me, don't you, Gaetano?"

"*Si, signorino. Cavallo di sangue, signorina!*" said Gaetano, pointing to his horse.

They set off.

"I'm always afraid of those coachmen," said Cornélie.

"You don't know them," he replied, smiling. "I like them. I like ordinary people. They're nice people."

"You like everything about Rome."

"And you are giving in unreservedly to a false impression."

"Why false?"

"Because that initial impression of Rome, of hardness and insensitivity, is always the same and always wrong."

"I find Rome difficult."

"Oh yes. Look, we're passing the Forum."

"When I see it, I think of Miss Hope and her orange lining."

He said nothing, angry.

"And here is the Palatine."

They got out of the carriage and went through the entrance.

"This wooden staircase takes us to the palace of Tiberius. Above this palace, above these arches, is a garden, from where we have a view of the Forum."

"Tell me about Tiberius. I know there were good and bad emperors. We learned that at school. Tiberius was a bad emperor, wasn't he?"

"He was a morose monster. But why must I tell you about him?"

"Because otherwise I have no interest in those arches and chambers."

"Then let's go and sit upstairs, in the garden."

And that was what they did.

"Can't you feel Rome here?" he asked.

"Everywhere I feel myself," she replied.

But he did not seem to hear her.

"It's the atmosphere," he went on. "You should forget our hotel for a change, Belloni and all our fellow-guests, and yourself. When someone first arrives, they have all the fuss of a hotel, rooms, restaurants, vaguely sympathetic or uncongenial people. That's what you had. Forget it. And try to just feel the atmosphere of Rome. It's as though the atmosphere has stayed the same here, despite the fact that the centuries are piled one on top of the other. Once the Middle Ages covered the antiquity of the Forum, and now it is hidden everywhere by our nineteenth-century mania for tourism. That is Miss Hope's orange lining. But the atmosphere has remained the same throughout. Or am I imagining it? … "

She said nothing.

"Perhaps," he continued. "But what do I care? Our life is imagination, and imagination is beautiful. The beauty of our imagination belongs to us, who are not people of substance, our life's consolation. How marvellous to dream all one's life, dream about what happened in the past. The past is what is beautiful. The present is not real, does not exist. And the future doesn't interest me."

"Don't you think about modern issues then?" she asked.

"Feminism?" he asked. "Socialism? Peace?"

"For example."

"No," he smiled. "I think of them sometimes, but not about them."

"What do you mean?"

"I can't get on with them. That's the way I am. My nature is to dream, and the Past is my great dream."

"Don't you dream about yourself?"

"No. About my soul? My innermost core? No. It doesn't interest me much."

"Have you ever suffered?"

"Suffered? Yes, no. I don't know. I suffer about my complete uselessness as a human being, as a son, as a man, but when I dream, I'm happy."

"How do you come to be speaking so frankly to me?"

He looked at her in astonishment.

"Why should I hide?" he asked. "I either don't talk, or I talk as I am talking now. Perhaps it's a bit peculiar."

"So do you speak so confidentially to everyone?"

"No, to almost no one. I used to have a friend, but he's dead. Tell me, I expect you find me a pathological case?"

"No, I don't think so."

"It wouldn't matter to me if you did. Oh, how beautiful it is here. Are you breathing in the spirit of Rome?"

"What Rome?"

"The Rome of antiquity. Below us is the palace of Tiberius. I can see him walking along with his prying eyes—he was very strong, very morose, and he was a monster. He had no ideals. Further that way is the palace of Caligula, a brilliant madman. He built a bridge over the Forum to be able to speak to Jupiter on the Capitol.

You couldn't do that today. He was brilliant and crazy. If you're like that, you have much that is wonderful."

"How can you find an age of emperors who were monsters and mad, wonderful?"

"Because I can see their age before me, in the past, as a dream."

"How can you possibly not see the present before you, and the issues of this age, especially that of eternal poverty?"

He looked at her.

"Yes," he said. "I know, that is the rottenness in me, the sin. The notion of eternal poverty doesn't affect me."

She looked at him, almost with contempt.

"You are not of your age," she said coolly.

"No ... "

"Have you ever been hungry?"

He laughed and shrugged his shoulders.

"Have you ever put yourself in the place of a worker, or factory girl, working till they're exhausted, old, half dead for scarcely a crust of bread?"

"Oh, those things are so gruesome and so ugly: don't talk about them!" he begged.

Her eyes were cool, her lips pursed with disgust and she got up.

"Are you angry?" he asked meekly.

"No," she said softly. "I'm not angry ... "

"But do you despise me for being a useless creature full of aestheticism and daydreams?"

"No. Who am I to blame you for your uselessness?"

"Oh, if only we could find something!" he exclaimed, almost in rapture.

"What?"

"A goal. But mine would always remain beauty. And the past."

"And if *I* had the strength to devote myself to a goal, then the main aim would be: bread for the future."

"How awful that sounds!" he said, impolite in his honesty. "Why on earth didn't you go to London or Manchester, or some black industrial hole?"

"Because I didn't have the strength and think too much about myself, about the unhappiness I've just been through. And I thought I would find some distraction in Italy."

"And that's your disappointment … But perhaps you'll gradually grow stronger, and you'll devote yourself to your goal: bread for the Future. I shan't envy you, though: Bread for the Future … "

She was silent, and he said coolly,

"It's getting late. Let's go home … "

VIII

Dᴜᴄᴏ ᴠᴀɴ ᴅᴇʀ sᴛᴀᴀʟ had rented a large, cavernous studio in Via del Babuino, three flights up, north-facing and chilly. Here he painted, modelled, studied, here he gathered together everything beautiful and ancient he could find in the shops along the Tiber or in the Mercato dei Fiori. It was his passion: hunting through Rome for a portion of an old triptych or an ancient fragment of sculpture. In this way his studio had not remained the great, cold, echoing workplace that testifies to diligent and serious study, but had become a refuge for a vaguely coloured past and classical art, a museum for his dreamy spirit. Even as a child, as a boy he had felt this passion for antiquity growing in himself, had nosed around in the shop of an old Jew, had learned to haggle when he was short of cash, and collected at first worthless trinkets, later, slowly, objects of artistic and financial value. He was a devotee: it was his only vice: he spent all his pocket money on it, and later, without reservations, the little he earned. Because sometimes, very occasionally, he completed something and sold it. But usually he was too dissatisfied with himself to finish things, and it was his humble idea that everything had already been created, and that *his* art was useless.

This idea sometimes paralysed him for months, without making him unhappy. As long as he had a little money to keep body and soul together—and his needs were extremely few—he felt rich and was happy in his studio or wandered happily through Rome. His tall, nonchalant, sinewy and slim body would be dressed in his oldest suit, which, without affectation, revealed a slovenly sports shirt and a tie like a length of string; a hat of indeterminate colour and bedraggled shape was his favourite headgear.

His mother and sisters did not usually consider him presentable, but had given up trying to transform him into the elegant son and brother that they would have loved to take into the drawing-rooms of their Roman acquaintances. Happy to breathe in the atmosphere of Rome he wandered for hours among the ruins, and saw—a dazzling vision of dreamy columns—ethereal temples and palaces of marble rising transparently in a shimmering sunny twilight, and tourists following a trail taken from their Baedeker who passed this tall, skinny young man sitting nonchalantly on the foundations of the temple of Saturn, would never have believed his illusions about architecture: harmoniously rising lines, crowned with a theory of sculpture of noble, divine gestures, high in the blue sky.

He saw them in front of him. He sent the shafts of the columns soaring upwards, he fluted the severe Doric column, he bent the soft Ionic capital around it, and made the Corinthian acanthus spread its leaves; and the temples shot upwards on their columns in a trice; the basilicas arched upwards as if by magic, the statues gestured white against the elusive depth of the sky, and the Via Sacra was alive. He found it beautiful, he was living in his dream, his Past. It was as if he had had a previous existence in ancient Rome, and did not see the modern houses, the modern Capitol and all of them surrounding the grave of his Forum, before his eyes. He could sit like that for hours, or wander, or sit down again and be happy. In the intensity of his imagination he evoked history, it rose like a cloud from the past, at first like a fog, a magic mist, from which the figures soon emerged clearly, against the marble background of ancient Rome. The gigantic dramas were enacted before his dreaming eyes as if on an ideal stage, which extended from the Forum to the hazy sun-drenched blues of the Campagna; with wings that were submerged in the depths of the sky. Roman life came alive in gestures, in the movement of an arm in a toga, a line of Horace, a sudden vision of the assassination of an emperor or a gladiatorial contest in the arena. And just as suddenly the image faded, and he saw the ruins, just the ruins, as the tangible shadow of his unreal illusion: he saw the ruins as they were, discoloured brown and grey, eaten away with age, crumbling, tortured, mutilated by sledgehammers, until only a few columns still stood shaking under the weight of a trembling architrave, and threatened to collapse. And the brown and grey was so richly gilded by streaks of sunlight, the ruins were so splendid as they crumbled, so melancholy in the unconscious randomness of their broken lines, cracked arches and defaced sculpture, that it was as if he himself, after his airy vision of radiant dream architecture, had tortured them with his artist's hand, and caused them to crack, and shake and tremble, for the sake of the melancholy afterglow. Then his eyes would grow moist, his heart would overflow and he would walk away, under the arch of Titus past the Colosseum, on through Constantine's arch, and hurry past the Lateran to the Via Appia and the Campagna, and his stinging eyes would drink in the blue of the distant Alban hills, as if that could cure them of too much gazing and dreaming …

Neither in his mother nor in either of his sisters could he find any trace of sympathy for his eccentric inclinations, and after that one friend who had died, he had never found another and as if by predestination that never allowed him to encounter sympathy, he had borne an inner and outer solitude. But he had populated his solitude so densely with his dreams that he had never felt unhappy, and just as he enjoyed wandering alone among ruins and along byways, he also loved the intimacy of his solitary studio, with a multitude of silent silhouettes on an old fragment of triptych, on a tapestry or on the many sketches fixed to the wall close together, all around him, all with the charm of their lines and colours, all with the silent gesture of their movement and emotion, and merging with the gloom of crannies and the shade of ancient cabinets. And among these dwelt his porcelain and bronze and antique silver, and the tarnished gold braid of an ecclesiastical robe shone dully, and the leather bindings of old books stood in a cheerful row, books from which, opened in his hands the many figures rose up in a mist, living out their love and pain in those muted browns and golds of the silent atmosphere of the studio. Such was his simple life, without much self-doubt, since he did not demand too much of himself, and without the melancholy of a modern artist, because he was happy in his reflections. He had never met many people, despite the hotel existence he shared with his mother and sisters—he slept and ate at

INEVITABLE

Belloni—or dealt with strangers, and by nature he was rather wary of tourists with Baedekers, of English ladies in short skirts, with their identical exclamations of identical admiration, and felt entirely out of place in the circle—half Italian, half cosmopolitan—of his quite worldly mother and elegant sisters, who danced and cycled with Italian princes and young dukes.

And now that he had met Cornélie de Retz he had to admit how little he knew about people and how he could never have conceived of the nature of such a woman—in a book perhaps, but not in reality. Her very appearance—her pallor, the fragile charm, her weariness, had astonished him—and what she said astonished him even more: the conviction and at the same time hesitancy, the artistic sensibility yet the striving to speak in a voice appropriate to her age: an age that he had not yet been able to see as an artist, infatuated as he was with Rome and the Past. And her words astonished him, with their congenial sound, and irritated though he often was by that often bitter, cutting, and then again dull and discouraged tone, until he thought about them again and again, until in his mind he heard them again from her own lips, until she joined the heads and torsos of his studio, and loomed up before him in the soft lily-like presence of her perceived reality, amid the Pre-Raphaelite stiffness of lines, and Byzantine golds of the angels and Madonnas, in canvases and tapestries.

His heart had never known love and he had always regarded it as imagination and poetry. In his life there had never been anything but the natural urge of his manhood and the usual affair with a model. And his ideas about

51

love wavered in too broad and too unreal an equilibrium, without transition or gradation, between a woman who would strip naked for a few lire and Laura; between the desire for a beautiful body and exultation over Beatrice, between flesh and dream. He had never thought of a meeting of soulmates; had never longed for affection, love in the full, burgeoning sense of the word and the concept. And he was not aware that he was now thinking, a great deal, about Cornélie de Retz. In the past he had thought for days, a week about a woman in a poem; never yet about a woman in real life.

And the fact that, though annoyed by some of her words, he nevertheless saw her image with its lily-like out-line against his Byzantine triptychs, like a phantom in his dreamer's solitude, almost frightened him, since it had deprived him of his peace of mind.

IX

IT WAS CHRISTMAS and on the occasion of this festival the Marchesa Belloni offered her guests a tree in the drawing-room, and afterwards a ball in the historical Guercino dining-room. Giving a ball and a tree was the custom with many hoteliers, and those *pensioni* where there was no ball or tree were well known and harshly criticised by foreigners for this break with tradition. Examples were known of very good *pensioni*, to which many travellers—especially ladies—would not go, because there was neither a tree nor a ball at Christmas.

The *marchesa* thought her tree expensive and her ball not cheap either and would happily have found some pretext for making both vanish as if by magic, but she did not dare: the reputation of her *pensione* rested precisely on its worldliness, its chic: dinner in the beautiful dining-room, where one dressed for the occasion, and a splendid party at Christmas. And it was fun to see how keen all those ladies were to receive on top of their bill for the winter a vulgar Christmas present and the opportunity to dance with free almond drink and a cake, a sandwich and a broth. The old, nodding head waiter, Giuseppe, looked down on these festivities with contempt: he remembered the galas of his archducal evenings and found the ball inferior and the tree a sorry sight; the limping doorman, Antonio, used to his relatively peaceful existence—meeting a guest or taking them to the station—calmly sorting the

53

post a couple of times a day, and apart from that lazing around in and near his cubicle and the lift—hated the ball because of all the people invited by the guests—each of them was allowed three invitations—because of all the tiring fuss about carriages, when on top of that the guests managed to get quickly into their fiacre without paying him a tip. Consequently around Christmastime, the mood between the *marchesa* and her two senior dignitaries was far from harmonious, and during those days a torrent of orders and curses beat down on the backs of the old chambermaids, who with their kettles of hot water in their trembling hands clambered laboriously up and down the stairs, and the youthful milksops of waiters who in their reckless keenness charged into each other and broke plates. And only now that the whole staff had been set to work was it apparent how old the chambermaids were, and how young all the waiters, and people found the *marchesa*'s thrifty policy, of employing only old crocks and children 'a shame and shocking'. The only muscular *facchino*, required to lug suitcases, cut an unexpected figure of masculine maturity and robustness. But the *marchesa* was hated mainly for the large number of her serving staff, realising that now, at and around Christmas, they had to give them all a tip. No, they had not known there were so many staff. Not that many were needed anyway! If the *marchesa* were to take on a few strapping young girls and menservants! And there were silent conspiracies in the corners of corridors and agreements on how much they would give as a tip: people were anxious not to spoil the staff, yet they were staying all winter, and so one lire was too little, and so people were hesitating between one lira twenty-five and one lira fifty. But when people worked out on their fingers that there were at least twenty-five staff and so one was spending close to forty lire, they found it alarming and organised subscription lists. Two lists circulated, one of one lira, and one of twelve lire per guest, for the whole staff. On the latter list some, who had come a month earlier or were intending to leave, signed for ten lire, and some for six lire. Five lire was generally considered too little, and when it became known that the scruffy aesthetic ladies wanted to pay five lire, they were regarded with the utmost contempt.

Emotions ran high and commotions were the order of the day. Christmas approached and people flocked to the cribs, constructed by painters in Palazzo Borghese—a panorama of Jerusalem; and the shepherds, the angels, the Three Kings, and Mary with the Christ child in the stall with ox and ass. In Ara Coeli they listened to the sermons of little girls and boys, who climbed in turn on to a platform and acted out the story of the birth: some shyly reciting a verse, prompted by an anxious mother; others, mainly girls, declaiming with Italian tragic pathos and rolling eyes like little actresses and ending with a religious moral. The common people and countless tourists listened to the sermons: a pleasant atmosphere prevailed in the church, where the shrill young children's voices orated; there was loud laughter at gestures and effects; and the clergy walking around were wreathed in unctuous smiles, so sweet and touching was the scene. And in the chapel of the Santo Bambino the miraculous wooden idol was radiant with gold and jewels and the dense throng milled about in front of it.

All the guests at Belloni bought holly branches on Piazza de Spagna and decorated their rooms, and some, for example, Baroness Von Rothkirch, set up a private Christmas tree in their own room. The evening before the great festival everyone went to admire these private trees; they walked in and out of rooms, and all the guests, however much they sometimes squabbled and intrigued against each other, wore benevolent seasonal smiles and received everyone. There was general agreement that the baroness had gone to great trouble and that her tree was magnificent, and that her bedroom had been nicely transformed into a boudoir; the beds draped to become sofas, the washbasins concealed, and the trees radiant with light and gold. And the baroness, in a rather sentimental mood this evening, threw open her doors to everyone, and even offered the two aesthetic ladies sweets, when the *marchesa* also appeared smiling at her door, her bosom wreathed in sky-blue satin, and wearing even larger pendant crystal earrings than usual. The room was full; there were the Van der Staals, Cornélie, Rudyard, Urania Hope, other guests walking in and out, with the result that one could not budge, and was crammed together on the draped beds of mother and daughter. The *marchesa* brought in at her side an unknown young person: small, slim, with a pale olive complexion, with vivaciously sparkling dark eyes, in tails, and with the nonchalant good manners of an indifferent and weary man of the world; distinguished, yet supercilious. And she proudly approached the baroness, who was constantly and charmingly dabbing her moist eyes and arrogantly introduced him:

"My nephew, *duca di San Stefano, principe di Forte-Braccio* … "

The widely known Italian name was deliberately trumpeted loudly into the crowded, far from spacious room and all eyes focused on the young man, who bowed to the baroness and looked vaguely and ironically round the room. The *marchesa*'s nephew had not yet been seen in the hotel that winter, but everyone knew that the young Duke of San Stefano, Prince of Forte-Braccio, was a nephew of the *marchesa*, and one of the advertisements for her *pensione*. And while the prince spoke to the baroness and her daughter, Urania Hope stared at him as if he were a wondrous being from another world. She had grasped Cornélie's arm as if for support, as if she were about to faint at the sight of so much Italian aristocratic grandeur. She found him very handsome, very distinguished: small, and slim and pale, with eyes like carbuncles, with his languid distinction, and the white orchid in his buttonhole. And she would have loved to ask the *marchesa* to introduce her to her chic nephew, but did not dare, thinking of her father's stocking factory in Chicago.

The following evening was the festival of the tree and the ball. It was known that the *marchesa*'s nephew would be coming that evening, and emotions ran high all day long. The prince came after the presents had been taken off the tree and distributed, and by the side of his aunt, the *marchesa*, he made a kind of triumphal entry into the room where the ball had not yet begun but where guests were already seated here and there, with everyone's eyes glued to his ducal and princely presence.

Cornélie was walking with Duco van der Staal, who to the great amazement of his mother and sisters had dug out his coat and tails and appeared in the spacious hall, and both saw the triumphal procession of 'la Belloni' and her nephew and laughed at the star-struck looks of the English and American ladies. They—Cornélie and Duco—sat down in the hall on two chairs in front of a group of palms masking one of the doors of the room, while the ball began inside. They were talking about the statues in the Vatican that they had seen together a few days earlier, when close to their ears they heard a voice that they recognised as the *marchesa*'s imperious boom trying vainly to muffle itself in whispers. They looked round in surprise and noticed the hidden door clearly ajar, and through the chink glimpsed part of the slim hand of the prince and a section of the blue bosom of Belloni, both of them seated on a sofa in the room. They were therefore back to back, divided by the fractionally opened door. For amusement they listened to the *marchesa*'s Italian; the prince's answers were lisped so faintly that they could not follow. And they heard only a few words and phrases. They listened despite themselves when they heard Rudyard's name mentioned, clearly articulated by the *marchesa*.

"And who else?" asked the prince softly.

"An English miss," said the *marchesa*. "Miss Taylor, she's sitting over there, in that corner alone … A simple soul … Then the baroness and her daughter … The Dutch woman; a divorcée … And the beautiful American girl."

"And what about those two nice Dutch girls?" asked the prince.

The music blared more loudly and Cornélie could not hear a thing.

"And the divorced Dutch woman?" the prince continued.

58

"No money," answered the *marchesa* abruptly.

"And the young baroness?"

"No money," repeated Belloni.

"So no one but that stocking seller?" asked the prince wearily.

'La Belloni' became angry, but Cornélie and Duco could not follow the short sentences she rattled off; the music was still booming out.

"She's beautiful," they heard the *marchesa* say. She's worth a fortune. She could be in a top hotel, but she is here, because she was recommended to me as a young girl travelling alone and because it's cosier here. She has the large drawing-room all to herself and pays fifty lire a day for her two rooms. It makes no difference to her. She pays three times as much for her wood as the others and I even charge her for the wine.'

"She sells stockings," murmured the prince reluctantly.

"Rubbish," said the *marchesa*. "Remember that there's no one else at the moment. Last winter we had rich English people from the nobility, with a daughter, but she was too tall for you. You always find something. You mustn't be so fussy."

"I like the look of those two little Dutch darlings."

"They've got no money. You're always attracted to the wrong thing."

"How much has papa promised you, if you … "

The music swelled.

" … Wouldn't matter … If Rudyard talks to her … Taylor is easy … Miss Hope … "

"I don't need that many stockings … "

" … very witty. If you don't want … "

59

" … no … "

" … then I'll withdraw … Rudyard will say … How much?"

"Sixty or seventy thousand: I don't know exactly."

" … Urgent?"

"Debts are never urgent!"

"Are you prepared?"

"All right then. But I'm not selling myself for less than ten million … And … you'll … get … "

They both laughed and again the names of Rudyard and Urania rang out.

"Urania?" he asked.

"Urania … " replied 'la Belloni'. "Those Americans are capable. Think of the Countess de Castellane, the Duchess of Marlborough; aren't they doing honour to their husband's names? They cut an excellent figure. They are mentioned in every fashion magazine and always with appreciation."

" … very well then. I'm tired of all those fruitless winters. But no less than ten million … "

"Five … "

"No, ten … "

The prince and the *marchesa* had got up. Cornélie looked at Duco. Duco laughed.

"I couldn't follow them very well. It's a joke of course." Cornélie started.

"A joke, you think, Mr Van der Staal?"

"Yes, they're fantasising."

"I don't think so."

"I do."

"Do you understand people?"

"Oh no, not at all."

"I'm slowing beginning to. I think Rome can be dangerous and that a *marchesa* with a hotel, a prince and a Jesuit … "

"What then?"

"Can also be dangerous, if not for your sisters, since they have no money, then for Urania Hope … "

"I don't believe a word of it … It was all nonsense. And it doesn't interest me. But what do you think of Praxiteles' *Eros*? Oh, I think it's the most divine sculpture I've ever seen. Oh, the *Eros*, the *Eros* … ! That is love, true love; the inescapability, the fatality of love that begs forgiveness for the suffering it inflicts … "

"Have you ever been in love?"

"No. I don't understand people and I've never been in love. You're always so decisive. Dreams are beautiful, statues are wonderful and poetry is everything. Eros is everything, in love. I would never be able to love in reality as beautifully as Eros the symbol of love … No, knowing people doesn't interest me, and a dream of Praxiteles, still surviving in a torso of mutilated marble, is more noble than anything that calls itself love in the world."

She frowned and looked sombre.

"Let's go into the ballroom," she said. "We're all by ourselves here."

X

THE DAY AFTER THE BALL, Cornélie had a strange feeling; suddenly, as she savoured her superb Genzano, ordered by Rudyard, she realised that it was no coincidence that she was sitting with the baroness and her daughter, Urania and Miss Taylor; realised that the *marchesa* definitely had an ulterior motive with that arrangement. Rudyard, always polite, thoughtful, always attentive, always with a ticket or an introduction in his pocket that was difficult to obtain, or at least so he led them to believe, and talked the whole time, recently mainly with Miss Taylor, who went faithfully to listen to all the lovely church music and always came home in raptures. The pale, simple, skinny English lady, who was at first enthralled by museums, ruins and sunsets on the Aventine or Monte Mario, and was always tired from her wanderings through Rome, henceforth devoted herself entirely to the hundreds of churches, viewed and studied every one, and especially attended religiously all musical services and was ecstatic about the choir of the Sistine Chapel and the trembling glories of the male sopranos.

Cornélie talked to Mrs Van der Staal and Baroness Von Rothkirch about what she had caught of the conversation between the *marchesa* and her nephew through the chink in the door but neither of them, although intrigued, took the words of the *marchesa* seriously, and regarded them as simply a frivolous ball conversation between a scatterbrained woman, who was keen to match-make, and her reluctant nephew. It struck Cornélie how unwilling people are to believe in seriousness, but the baroness was very nonchalant, said that Rudyard would not do her any harm and still always gave her tickets, and Mrs Van der Staal, who had been long in Rome and used to *pensione* intrigues, thought that Cornélie was getting too worked up about the fate of the beautiful Urania. However, Miss Taylor had suddenly disappeared from table. People thought she was ill, when it emerged that she had left the Pensione Belloni, but after a few days it was common knowledge through the whole *pensione* that Miss Taylor had converted to Catholicism and moved into a *pensione* recommended to her by Rudyard: a boarding-house frequented by many *monsignori* and where there was a spiritual atmosphere. Her disappearance gave something forced to the conversation between Rudyard, the German ladies and Cornélie and the latter, during a week that the baroness spent in Naples, changed her place and joined her compatriots at table. The Rothkirchs also changed—because of the draught, as the baroness assured the management; new guests took their places: and among those new elements Urania was left alone at table with Rudyard for lunch and dinner. Cornélie blamed herself and on one occasion had a serious talk with the American girl and warned her. But she did not dare tell her what she had overheard at the ball, and her warning made no impression on Urania. And when Rudyard had obtained the privilege of a private audience with the Pope for Miss Hope, Urania refused to hear another bad word said about Rudyard and found him the kindest man she had ever met, Jesuit or not.

But a pall of mystery continued to cloak Rudyard in the hotel, and people could not agree whether he was a Jesuit or even whether he was a priest or a layman.

XI

"WHAT DO YOU CARE about those strange people?" he asked.

They were sitting in his studio, Mrs Van der Staal, Cornélie and the girls, Annie and Emilie. Annie poured tea and they talked about Miss Taylor and Urania.

"I'm a stranger to you too!" replied Cornélie.

"You're not a stranger to me, to us … But I couldn't care less about Miss Taylor or Urania. Hundreds of ghosts haunt our lives: I don't see them and feel nothing for them … "

"And aren't I a ghost?"

"I've talked to you too much in Borghese and on the Palatine to think you a ghost."

"Rudyard is a dangerous ghost," said Annie.

"He has no hold over us," replied Duco.

Mrs Van der Staal looked at Cornélie. She understood the look and said, with a laugh,

"No, he has no hold over me either … Yet, if I had had need of religion—I mean church religion—I'd rather be Roman Catholic than Calvinist. But now … "

She did not finish her sentence. She felt safe in this studio, in this soft, multi-coloured swirl of beautiful objects, in their sympathetic presence: she felt in harmony with all of them: with the charming and worldly air of the rather superficial mother and her two beautiful girls: a little doll-like and vaguely cosmopolitan, quite vain about young marquesses with whom they danced and cycled, and with the son, the brother, so completely different from the three women and yet visibly related in a movement, a gesture, the occasional word. It also struck Cornélie that they accepted each other lovingly as they were; Duco his mother and sister with their stories about the Princesses Colonna and Odescalchi; Mrs Van der Staal and the girls, him, with his old jacket and dishevelled hair. And when he began talking, especially talking about Rome, when he put his dream into words, in words that were almost fit for a book, but which flowed so gradually and naturally from his lips, Cornélie felt harmonious, felt safe, interested, and lost a little of the urge to contradict that his artistic indolence sometimes awakened in her. And apart from that his indolence suddenly seemed to her only apparent, and perhaps affectation, since he showed her sketches, watercolours, none of them finished, but each watercolour vibrant with light, especially with light, with the light of all Italy: the pearly sunsets across the fluid emerald of Venice; Florence's towers drawn with dreamy vagueness in tender rose-coloured skies; fortress-like Siena blue-black in bluish moonlight; orange sunflares behind St Peter's, and especially the ruins and in every light: the Forum in fierce sunlight, the Palatine in the evening twilight, the Colosseum mysterious in the night, and then the Campagna: the dream skies and hazy light of the cheerful and sad Campagna, with soft pink mauves, dewy blues, dusky violet, of the brash ochres of pyrotechnic sunsets, and fanning clouds like purple phoenix wings. And when Cornélie asked him why nothing was finished, he replied that nothing was any good. He saw the skies as dreams, visions and apotheoses, and on paper they were water and paint, and paint could be finished. And then he lacked self-confidence. And then he abandoned his skies, he said, and copied Byzantine Madonnas.

When he saw that his watercolours nevertheless interested her, he went on talking about himself, telling her how he first enthused about the noble and naïve Primitives, Giotto and especially Lippo Memmi ... How subsequently, spending a year in Paris, he had found that nothing compared with Forain: dry, cool satire in two or three lines; how then, in the Louvre, Rubens had revealed himself: Rubens, whose unique talent and unique brush he had traced among all the imitation and apprentice work of his numerous pupils, until he was able to say which cherub was by Rubens himself in a sky full of cherubs painted by four or five pupils.

And then, he said, he did not think about painting for weeks, and did not pick up a paintbrush, and went to the Vatican every day and was totally absorbed by the noble marbles.

Once he had spent a whole morning sitting dreaming in front of *Eros*, once he had dreamed up a poem accompanied by a very faint monotonous melody, like a devout incantation: at home he had wanted to put down the poem and the music on paper, but had not been able. He could no longer stand Forain, found Rubens disgusting and coarse, and had remained loyal to the Primitives.

"And suppose I painted a lot and sent a lot to exhibitions? Would I be happier? Would I feel satisfaction at having done something? I don't think so. Sometimes I finish a watercolour, sell it, and I can survive for a month without troubling mama. I don't care about money. Ambition is totally alien to me! But don't let's talk about me. Are you still thinking about the future and … bread?"

"Perhaps," she replied, smiling sadly, and around her the studio darkened, the silhouettes of his mother and sisters faded, as they sat quietly and languidly uninterested in easy chairs, and all colour dissolved silently into shadow. "But I am so weak. You say you are no artist, and I, I am no apostle."

"Giving direction to one's life is the difficult thing. Every life has a line, a direction, a way, a path: it is along that line that life must flow into death and what comes after death; and *that* line is difficult to find. I shan't find my line."

"I can't see my line before me either … "

"Do you know, a restlessness has come over me. Mama, do you hear, a restlessness has come over me. In the past I used to dream in the Forum, I was happy and didn't think about my line. Mama, do you think about your line, and do my sisters think about theirs?"

His sisters, in the dark, sunk in the deep chairs like cats, giggled a little. Mama got up.

"My dear Duco, you know, I can't follow you. I admire Cornélie for being able to appreciate your watercolours and for understanding what you mean by that line. My line is the way home now, as it's getting very late … "

"That is the line of the next moment. But I feel restlessness about my line of the days and weeks afterwards. I'm not living the right way. The Past is very beautiful, and so peaceful because it's over. But I have lost that calm. The Present is really very small. But the Future …

Oh, if only we could find a goal! For the Future … ”

They were no longer listening to him; they groped their way down the dark stairs.

“Bread?” he wondered.

XII

ONE MORNING when she stayed home, Cornélie reviewed the reading matter that was scattered about her room. And she decided that it was useless for her to read Ovid in order to study a few Roman customs, some of which had alarmed and shocked her; she decided that Dante and Petrarch were too difficult for studying Italian, when it was enough to pick up a few words to make oneself understood in a shop or with the serving staff; she decided Hare's *Walks* was too exhausting as a guidebook, since every last stone in Rome did not excite the same interest in her as it had obviously done in Hare. Then she admitted to herself that she would never be able to see Rome the way Duco van der Staal saw it. She never saw the light in the skies and the scudding of clouds as he had in his unfinished watercolour studies. She never saw the ruins glorified as he did in his hours spent dreaming in the Forum and on the Palatine. She saw a painting only with the eyes of a layman; a Byzantine Madonna meant nothing to her. She did like sculpture; passionate love for a lump of mutilated marble such as he felt for the *Eros*, seemed pathological to her, she thought at the time, but "morbid"—though the word made her smile—expressed her view better. Not pathological, but morbid. And she considered an olive a tree that resembled a willow, though Duco had told her that an olive was the loveliest tree in the world.

She did not agree with him, either about the olive or about *Eros* and yet she felt that from some mysterious perspective that was inaccessible to her, he was right, since it was like a mystical hill amid unbridgeable mystical circles, which he passed through as emotional spheres that were not hers, just as the hill was an unknown throne of feeling and perspective. She disagreed with him and yet she was convinced that he was right in a superior way, had a superior vision, a nobler insight, a deeper feeling; and she was certain that her way of seeing Italy—in the disappointment of her dream—was not noble or good, that the beauty of Italy was escaping her; while for him it was like a tangible and embraceable vision. And she cleared away Ovid, Petrarch and Hare's guidebook, and locked them in her case and took out the novels and pamphlets that had appeared that year on the Women's Movement in Holland. She was interested in the issue and it made her feel more modern than Duco, who suddenly appeared to her as if belonging to a past era. Not modern. Not modern. She repeated the word with relish and suddenly felt stronger. Being modern would be her strength. One remark of Duco's had made a deep impression: that exclamation "Oh, if only we could find a goal! Our life has a line, a path that you must travel . . . " Being modern, wasn't that a line? Finding a solution to a modern question, was that not a goal? He, he was right, from his point of view, from which he viewed Italy, but was not the whole of Italy a past, a dream, at least the Italy that Duco saw, a dream paradise of nothing but art. It could not be good to stand and see and dream like that. The Present was there: on the grey horizons there was the rumble of an approaching storm and the modern questions flashed like lightning. Was it not that that she must live for? She felt for Women and Girls: she herself had been a Girl, brought up with nothing but a drawing-room education, in order to shine, beautifully and charmingly, and then to marry. And she had been beautiful, and charming, she had shone and had married, and now she was twenty-three, divorced from that husband, who had once been her only goal: now she was alone, lost, in despair and mortal desolation: she had nothing to cling to, she was suffering. She still loved him, blackguard, wretch that he was; and she had thought she was being very strong by setting off on a trip, for the sake of art, to Italy. Oh, how clearly she saw, after those conversations with Duco, that she would never understand art, though she had drawn a little in the past, although she had once had an unglazed terracotta group after Canova in her bedroom: *Amor and Psyche*, so sweet for a young girl. And how certain she was now that she would not understand Italy, since she did not find an olive tree that beautiful, and had never seen the sky of the Campagna as a fanned phoenix's wing. No, Italy would never be her life's consolation …

But what then? She had been through a lot, but she was alive and very young. And again at the sight of those pamphlets, that novel, the longing reawakened in her heart: to be modern, to be modern! To tackle modern problems. To live for the Future! To live for Women, for Girls …

She did not dare look deep inside herself, afraid she might waver. To live for the Future … It separated her a little more from Duco, that new ideal. What did she care, did she love him? No, she didn't think so. She had loved her husband and did not want to fall immediately for the first nice young man who came along, whom she happened to meet in Rome …

And she read the pamphlets. *On the Women's Question* and *Love*. Then she thought of her husband and then of Duco. And wearily she dropped the pamphlet, thinking how sad it was. People, women, girls. She, a young woman, an aimless woman, how sad she was in her life. And Duco, was he happy? But still he sought the line in his life, still he was on the lookout for his goal. A new restlessness had come over him. And she cried a little, and tossed and turned restlessly on her cushions, and wrung her hands, and prayed unconsciously, to whom she knew not.

"Oh God, tell me what we're to do!"

XIII

IT WAS SOME DAYS after that Cornélie had the idea of leaving the *pensione* and taking rooms. Hotel life interfered with her emerging thoughts, like a wind of vanity that kept scorching scarcely formed blossoms, and despite a torrent of abuse from the *marchesa*, who accused her of having rented for the whole winter, she moved into the room, which she had found after much searching and climbing of stairs with Duco van der Staal. It was in Via dei Serpenti, many flights up, a suite of two spacious but almost completely unfurnished rooms: there were only the bare necessities, and though the view stretched far and wide across the massed houses of Rome to the circular ruin of the Colosseum, the rooms were bleak and cheerless, bare and uninhabitable. Duco had not liked them and said they made him shiver, although they faced the sun, but there was something about the awkwardness of this room that struck Cornélie in her new mood as harmonious. When they parted that day, he thought of her: how little of the artist there is in her; and she thought of him: how un-modern he is! They did not see each other again for days, and Cornélie was very lonely, but did not feel her loneliness, because she was writing a pamphlet about the Social Position of the Divorced Woman. That idea had come to her after she had read a few sentences in a pamphlet on the Women's Movement, and suddenly, without having thought much about it, she wrote her

74

sentences in a succession of bursts and intuitive leaps, awkward, cool and clear; she wrote in an epistolary style, artlessly, but with conviction and experience, as if to warn girls against having too many illusions about Marriage. She had not made her rooms comfortable; she sat there, high above Rome, looking over the rooftops towards the Colosseum, writing, immersing herself in her suffering, revealing herself in her recalcitrant sentences, bitter, but pouring the gall within her into her pamphlet. Mrs Van der Staal and the girls, who came to visit her, were astonished, at her slovenly appearance, at her bleak rooms, the dying embers in the grate, not a flower, no books, no tea, and no cushions, and when they left after a quarter-of-an-hour, on the pretext of having to go shopping, they looked at each other in amazement as they tripped down the endless staircase, utterly confused and mystified by her metamorphosis: from an interesting, elegant young woman, with an aura of poetry about her, and a tragic past—into a 'free woman', writing frantically at a pamphlet, with bitter imprecations against society. And when Duco visited her again after a week, and sat with her for a moment, he sat absolutely still, stiff as a board on his chair, without speaking, while Cornélie read him the opening of her pamphlet. He was moved by what he glimpsed of personal suffering and experience, but he was irritated by the lack of harmony between that slim, lily-like woman, with her fractured movements, and the surroundings, in which she now felt at home, totally absorbed in her hatred of society, especially Hague society, which had become hostile to her, because she had not stayed with a blackguard who abused her. And as she read Duco thought: she would not write this way if she were not writing everything from the perspective of her own pain. Why doesn't she turn it into a novella … ? Why that generalising of one's own suffering, and why that admonitory tone … He did not find it beautiful. He found the sound of her voice so harsh, those truths so personal, that bitterness unsympathetic and that hatred of convention so petty. And when she asked him something, he did not say much, shook his head in mild approval, and sat there uncomfortably stiff. He did not know what to reply, he did not know how to admire, he found her un-artistic. And yet a great pity welled up in him, he saw how sweet she would be, what a noble woman, once she had found the line in her life and moved harmoniously along that line with the music of her own movement. Now he saw her taking a wrong path; a path pointed out to her by others, and not taken on an inner impulse. And he felt a deep pity for her. He, as an artist, but especially as a dreamer, sometimes saw things with great clarity, despite his dreams, despite his all-embracing feeling for line and colour and haziness; he, the artist and dreamer, often saw as if clairvoyant the emotion glimpsed beneath people's pretence, saw the soul, like a light shining through alabaster, and he suddenly saw her lost, searching, wandering; searching for she knew not what; wandering through she knew not what labyrinth; far from her line, her lifeline and the direction in which her soul was moving, which she had never yet found.

She sat excitedly in front of him, having read her final pages, face flushed, voice resonating, her whole being feverish. It was as if she wanted to fling those pages full of bitterness at the feet of her Dutch sisters, at the feet of all women. Lost in his reflections, melancholy in his pity for her, he had scarcely listened, and shook his head in vague approval. And suddenly she spoke about herself, gave herself completely, told the story of her life: her young lady's existence in The Hague, the upbringing designed to make her shine a little and be pleasant and beautiful, without one serious look at her future, simply awaiting a good match, with a flirtation here, and a crush there until she was married; a good marriage in her own circle; her husband a lieutenant in the hussars, a handsome strapping fellow, good distinguished family, a little money, with whom she had fallen in love because of his handsome face, and the dashing figure he cut in uniform, which suited him; who had fallen in love with her, as he might have fallen in love with another girl, because she had a pretty face: then, the revelation of those very first days: the immediate eruption of disharmony between their characters. She, spoiled at home, fine, delicate, sensitive, but egoistically sensitive, but irritable about her own spoiled ego; he, no longer paying court, but immediately and crudely the husband with rights to this and rights to that, now with curses, now with fulminations; she, without any tact, without any of the patience needed to make the best of their lives that were headed for disaster: nervous, passionate, pitching passion against coarseness, which made his violence flare up to the point where he abused her, swore at her, hit her, shook her and slammed her against the wall …

Then her divorce; he at first unwilling, despite everything happy to have a home, and in that home a wife, a little woman for the master of the house, and not want-ing to return to the wretchedness of living in rooms, until she simply left, went to her parents, to friends out of town, inveighing against the law, so unjust to women … He had finally given in, allowed himself to be charged with adul-tery, which was not far from the truth. Then she was free, but she stood as if alone, looked at askance by everyone she knew, unwilling to bow to their conventional insis-tence on that kind of semi-mourning that according to their conventional notions should surround a divorced woman, and returning immediately to her earlier young girl's glittering existence. But she had felt that it could not go on like that, neither for her friends nor for herself: the friends looking askance at her, and she disgusted by them, their receptions and their dinners, until she had become deeply unhappy, lonely, lost, without anything, without anybody, and had experienced the pressure that weighs on the divorced woman. Deep down she had occasionally thought that with great patience and tact she might have been able to control her husband, that he was not bad, just coarse, that she still loved him, or at least his handsome face and strong body. It wasn't love, but had she ever thought about love, in the way she now had occasional premonitions of it? And didn't everyone com-promise more or less in their lives, adapting to what they had been given? But she scarcely admitted that regret to herself, did not even admit it to Duco, though she did admit her bitterness, her hatred for her husband, for marriage, convention, people, the world: for all the great abstractions, generalising her own feeling into a single curse against life. He listened to her, with pity. He felt that there was something noble in her, but that it had been stifled from the outset. He forgave her for not being artistic, but it pained him that she had never found herself, that she did not know who she was, what her life should be like, where the line of her life was winding to, the only path that she must follow, as every life follows one path. Oh, how often, if people simply let themselves go, like a flower, like a bird, like a cloud, like a star, which orbited obediently, they would find their happiness and their life, as the flower and the bird found them, as the cloud drifted in the sun and the star followed its orbit. But he told her nothing of what he was thinking, knowing that particularly in her mood of bitterness she would not understand and would derive no support from it, that it would be too vague for her, and too alien to her own thoughts. She was thinking of herself, but she *thought* that she was thinking of Women, Girls and their movement towards the Future. The lines of women … But did not each woman have her own line? But how few knew it, their direction, their path, their lifeline, its meandering course through the twilight of the future. And perhaps, because they did not know for themselves, they were now looking for a wide path for all of them, a main highway, along which hosts of them could advance, a surging throng of women, regiments of women, with slogans and banners and war cries, a broad path, parallel to the men's movement, until the paths merged into one, till the hosts of women mixed with the hosts of men, with equal rights and freedom to live as they chose …

He said nothing of this to her. She noticed his silence, and did not see how much was going on inside him, how deeply he was thinking about her, how deeply he pitied her. She thought she had bored him. And suddenly, she saw around her the bare room with the light fading, the fire extinguished, and her enthusiasm deflated, her fever cooled, and she thought her pamphlet inferior, without force or conviction. How much a word from him would have meant! But he sat there without a word, seemingly uninterested: probably he did not like her style. And she felt sad, desolate, alone, alienated from him, and bitter about that alienation, she felt ready to cry, to sob, and— strangely—in her bitterness she thought of him, her husband, with his handsome face. And she could not stop herself: she wept. He went up to her, laid his hand on her shoulder. She felt something of what was going on inside him, and that his silence was not cold. She told him that she would not be able to stay alone that evening, too awful, too awful … He comforted her; said that there were a lot of good and true things in her pamphlet, that he was not a good judge of such modern questions; that he was only clever when talking about Italy; that he cared so little for people and so much for statues; so little for the new things that were being built for centuries to come, and so much for the ruins that remained of previous centuries. He said this as if apologising. She smiled through her tears, but repeated that she could not stay alone, and that she was going with him to Belloni, to his mother and sisters. And they went out together and walked around together; and he told her, in order to take her mind off things, about his own thoughts, told her anecdotes about Renaissance masters. She did not hear what he was saying, but his voice soothed her. The was something so gentle about his indifference to the modern, which interested her: he had such calm, soothing as balm, in the calm of his soul, which abandoned itself to the golden thread of his dreams—as if that thread were the direction of his life—such calm and softness, that she too became calmer, and looked up at him and smiled.

And however far they were from each other, he following his dream line, she lost in a dark labyrinth—they felt themselves coming closer together, felt their souls coming closer, while their bodies moved side by side along a real street, across Rome in the evening. He put his arm through hers, but despite that gesture supported *her*.

And as they approached Belloni, she thanked him, without knowing exactly why: for his eyes, for his voice, for their walk, for the comfort that she felt inexplicably, but distinctly emanating from him, and she was glad to have to have gone with him that evening, and to feel the distraction of Belloni's set dinner around her.

But at night, alone, alone in her bleak rooms, her wretchedness washed over her like a black sea, and looking out at the Colosseum—a dimly discernible arch in the dark night—she sobbed, feeling herself sinking into death-like depths, being washed away, abandoned and alone, sinking and being washed away so high above Rome, above the rooftops, above the dim lights of the nocturnal city, under the clouds of the dark night, as if drifting like a shipwrecked mariner on an ocean that was drowning the whole world and was roaring in lament at the inexorable sky.

XIV

STILL, A CALM CAME OVER CORNÉLIE now that her pamphlet was written. She unpacked her cases, made her rooms a little more comfortable and, feeling calmer, she copied out the pamphlet and as she did so improved her style, and even her ideas. After she had worked in the morning, she usually lunched in a little *osteria* and almost always met Duco van der Staal there, and ate with him at the same table. Usually she dined at Belloni, with the Van der Staals, as a distraction for the evening. At first the *marchesa* had not acknowledged her, though she tolerated her for dinner at three lire an evening, and slowly she began saying hello to Cornélie, with a bitter-sweet smile, having meanwhile re-let the two rooms on more favourable terms. And Cornélie, in her calmer mood, enjoyed dressing up in the evenings, going to Belloni, seeing Mrs Van der Staal and the girls, hearing stories about the drawing-rooms of Rome, and running her eye over the long tables. And she saw that the guests were different ones, as in a kaleidoscope of transient people. Rudyard had disappeared, owing the *marchesa* money, no one knew where. The Rothkirchs had gone to Greece, but Urania Hope was still there and sat next to the Marchesa Belloni and with on her other side the nephew, the Prince of Forte-Braccio, Duke of San Stefano, who dined regularly at Belloni. And Cornélie saw that it was like a conspiracy: the *marchesa* and the prince beleaguering the vain little

American from both sides. On a later occasion Cornélie saw two *monsignori* sitting at the *marchesa's* table in animated conversation with Urania, while the *marchesa* and the prince nodded in agreement. All the guests were talking about it, all eyes were looking in that direction, everyone spied on the manoeuvring and enjoyed the romance.

Only Cornélie was not amused; she had wanted to warn Urania about the *marchesa*, the prince and the *monsignori* who had taken Rudyard's place, but especially about Marriage, even to a prince-duke. And becoming excited she talked to Mrs Van der Staal and the girls, repeating the words of her pamphlet, glowing, bright red with her young hatred against society and the world and people.

Dinner had ended; still talking animatedly she accompanied the Van der Staals—Mrs Van der Staal and the girls and Duco—to the drawing-room, sat down in a corner, continued her conversation, burst out at Mrs Van der Staal, who contradicted her, until she suddenly saw a fat lady—the girls had already nicknamed her the satin frigate—approaching and saying from a distance,

"I beg your pardon, but I wanted to say something … Look, I've been coming regularly to Belloni every winter for ten years, from November to Easter, and every evening after dinner—but only after dinner—I sit in this corner, at this table, in this place. So please excuse me, but would you mind if I sat in my usual place … "

And the 'satin frigate' smiled sweetly, but when the Van der Staals and Cornélie got up in speechless amazement, she flopped on to the couch with a rustle of satin, bobbed up and down on the springs for a moment, put her crochet work on the table as if planting an English flag on a colony, and said with her most charming smile:

"Very much obliged, thank you very much."

Duco burst out laughing, the girls giggled, but the 'satin frigate' smiled benevolently at them. And still not quite aware what was happening, astonished but cheerful, they sat in another corner, the girls with irrepressible giggles. The two aesthetic ladies, in evening dress and woollens, who were sitting reading at the centre table closed their two books simultaneously, got up and left indignantly, because of all the laughter and talking in the drawing-room.

"It's shameful!" they said aloud, and angular, arrogant and shabby they flounced out.

"Strange pair!" thought Duco smiling: ghosts of people " … their lines swirl through ours like arabesques. Why do they cross our lines with their petty movements, and why do those who might be most welcome to our soul never cross our path … "

He always accompanied Cornélie back to Via dei Serpenti in the evenings. They walked slowly through the silent deserted streets. Sometimes it was late, sometimes it was immediately after dinner, and then they walked down the Corso and he usually asked her to sit for a while at Aragno's. She agreed and they had a cup of coffee together, in the cheerful, brightly-lit café, looking out at the evening bustle in the street. They said little, distracted by the passers-by and the customers in the café, but they both enjoyed being together for a moment, and felt in tune. Duco obviously did not give a thought to their liberal behaviour, but Cornélie thought of Mrs Van der Staal, and of how she would not approve and would not let either of her daughters do it: sit alone in a café with a gentleman at night. And Cornélie thought too of The Hague and smiled at the thought of her Hague acquaintances. And she looked at Duco ... He sat calmly, happy to be sitting with her, and drank his coffee, said the occasional word and pointed out a passing character or beautiful woman ... One evening, after dinner, he suggested going to the ruins; there was a moon, it was enchanting ... But Mrs Van der Staal was frightened of malaria, and the girls of robbers; so they went alone, Duco and Cornélie. The streets were abandoned, the Colosseum loomed up like a black fortress in the night, but they went in, and through the open arches shone the moonlit blue of the night: in the circular pit of the arena, on one side black, in shadow, while on the other the moonlight poured in, like a white flood, like a waterfall, and it was as if the night were full of ghosts as though the Colosseum and the whole of Rome's past were full of ghosts: emperors, gladiators and martyrs; shadows slunk around like prowling wild animals, a patch of light was like a naked woman, and the galleries seemed to roar with the throng ... And yet there was nothing and they were alone, Duco and Cornélie, in the depths of the lofty gigantic ruin, half in shadow and half in light, and though she was not afraid, she was awed by the vast ghostly presence of the past, and moved closer to him and squeezed his arm and felt small, very small. He squeezed her hand for a moment, in his simple, easy way, as if to reassure her. And the night frightened her, the ghostliness oppressed her, the moon seemed to be at a dizzy height in the sky and to be growing to gigantic proportions and to be revolving like a silver wheel. He said nothing, he was in his dream, he saw the past before him … And silently they left, and he led her into the Forum through the arch of Titus. On the left rose the ruins of the imperial palaces, and around them stood the black fragments, the few remaining columns pointed upwards and the white moon stream flowed down like a ghostly sea from the sky. They met no one, but she was afraid and gripped his arm tighter. When they sat down for a moment on a piece of the foundations, she shivered with the cold. He was startled, said she must be sure not to catch cold, and they went on and left the Forum. He took her home, and she went up the stairs alone, striking a match to give some light in the dark stairwell. In her room she reflected that it was dangerous to go wandering through the ruins at night. She thought of how little Duco had said, not thinking of danger, lost in his nocturnal dream, peering into the awesome ghostly depths … Why … had he not gone alone? Why had he asked her along? She fell asleep after her thoughts had churned chaotically: the prince and Urania; the fat satin lady, the Colosseum and the martyrs, and Duco and Mrs Van der Staal … His mother was so ordinary, his sisters sweet but banal, and he … so odd! So simple, so without pretension, giving himself as he was; and for that reason so odd … He would be impossible in The Hague, among her friends … She smiled when she thought what he had said and how he had said it and he could be calmly silent, for minutes at a time, with a smile playing round his mouth, as if he were thinking of something beautiful …

But she must warn Urania.

And, exhausted, she fell asleep.

XV

CORNÉLIE'S SUSPICION about Mrs Van der Staal's opinion of her relationship with Duco proved true: Mrs Van der Staal had a serious talk with her, saying that if she went on in this way she would compromise herself, and added that she had spoken to Duco in the same vein. But Cornélie answered quite haughtily and stated nonchalantly that after having respected convention and nevertheless having become deeply unhappy, henceforth she no longer bothered about it, and that she enjoyed Duco's conversation without allowing herself to be prevented by what 'one' did and thought. And anyway, she asked Mrs Van der Staal, who was 'one'? The three or four people they knew at Belloni? Who else knew her? Where else did she go? What did she care about The Hague? And she laughed sarcastically, loftily parrying Mrs Van der Staal's arguments. As a result their relationship cooled: she did not come to Belloni to dine that evening, stung in her easily-offended over-sensitivity. The next day, meeting Duco at their table in the *osteria*, she asked what he thought about his mother's reprimand. He smiled vaguely, eyebrows raised, obviously not realising the mediocre truth of his mother's words, saying that those were mama's ideas, naturally perfectly good and current in the circles mama and his sisters moved in, but which he did not delve into too deeply, and which did not bother him, unless Cornélie thought that mama was right. And Cornélie erupted sarcastically, shrugging her shoulders and asked in the name of whom and what they should allow themselves to be prevented from continuing their friendly relations. They ordered half a flask between them, and had a protracted and enjoyable meal, like two comrades, two students. He said that he had thought about her pamphlet; he spoke— to please her—about the position of modern woman, about girls. She criticised the upbringing Mrs Van der Staal was giving his sisters, the insubstantial, glittering education and that eternal going out and looking for a husband. She spoke from experience, she said. That day they walked along the Appian Way and visited the Catacombs, guided by a Trappist. Then they took a carriage, drove back to Rome and had tea at Razotti's patisserie. When Cornélie got home, she felt in a pleasant mood, light-hearted and cheer- ful. She did not go out again, banked up her fire with wood for the night, which was becoming chilly, and dined alone on some bread and jelly so as not to have to go out to a restaurant. In her *peignoir* with her hands behind her head, she stared into the nicely burning wood, and let the evening glide past. She was happy with her life, so free, free of every- thing and everyone. She had a little money, and could go on living like this. She did not have many needs. Her life in rooms and modest restaurants, did not cost much. She did not need outfits. She felt content. Duco was a good friend; how lonely she would be without him. But, her life must acquire a purpose … What? What? The Women's Move- ment … ? But how, abroad? Working on it was so difficult … She would send her pamphlet to a new women's maga- zine, recently founded. But what then? The fact was that she was not in Holland and did not want to go to Holland:

and yet it would definitely be easier to become active there, and exchange views with others. But here in Rome … A languor came over her, in the warmth of her snug room. Duco had helped her arrange her sitting-room. He really was a cultured person, even if he was not modern. He knew a lot about history, about Italy, and talked really well. The way he explained Italy to her, she found the country interesting after all.

The only problem was that he was not modern. He had no sense of the politics of Italy, nor of the battle between the Quirinal and the Vatican; nor of anarchism, which was rearing its head in Milan, nor of the turbulence in Sicily … A goal; so difficult to have a goal …

And in her evening languor after a pleasant day, she did not feel the lack of a goal, she savoured the gentle delight of letting her thoughts glide along with the languorous evening hours, in selfish contentment. She looked at the pages of her pamphlet, strewn over her large desk: a table for working at: they lay there yellow in the light of her reading lamp: none of them had yet been copied out, but she did not feel like doing it now: she threw a log into the hearth, and the fire smoked and revived. It was so cosy abroad using logs of wood for fires … And she thought of her husband. Sometimes she missed him. Would she not have been able to manage him with a little tact and patience? He had after all been very nice to her at the time of their engagement. He was coarse, but he was not evil. He sometimes swore at her, but perhaps he had not really meant it. He waltzed beautifully, he spun you round with him so firmly … He was a handsome fellow, and she admitted she was in love with him, only because of his handsome face, his handsome body. There was something in his eyes and his mouth that she could not resist. When he spoke she had been unable to resist looking at his mouth. Anyway, it was over now … Perhaps life in The Hague had been too monotonous for her nature. She liked travel, seeing new people, developing new thoughts, and she had never been able to put down roots in her coterie. And now she was free, free of all bonds, all people. What did she care if Mrs Van der Staal was angry … And Duco was modern after all in his indifference to convention. Or was it just the artist in him; or was it indifferent to him, as an un-modern man, as it was to her, a modern woman? A man had more lee-way. It was not as easy for a man to compromise himself. Modern woman … She repeated it proudly. A sense of pride pierced her languor. She stood up, stretched her arms, saw her slim figure in the mirror, her delicate face, rather pale, eyes large, grey and shining beneath strikingly long lashes; her dark blond hair in a loose, dishevelled bun; her fractured lily-like figure extremely appealing in the crumpled folds of her old *peignoir*, pale-pink and faded. Where was her path? She felt not only a worker and a striver, she felt very complex; she felt a woman too, she felt a great deal of femininity in herself, like a languor, that threatened to paralyse her energy. And she wandered round the room, unable to decide whether to go to bed, and staring into the glowing embers of the fire that had died down, she thought of her future, of who and what she would become, and how and where she would go, along which of life's arabesques, wending her way through what woods, winding down what avenues, crossing what other arabesques of what other questing souls?

XVI

FOR SOME TIME it had been an *idée fixe* of Cornélie's that she must speak to Urania Hope, and one morning she wrote a note asking to see her that afternoon. Miss Hope agreed and at five o'clock Cornélie found her at home in her beautiful, expensive apartment at Belloni: a blaze of light, flowers everywhere; Urania, hammering on the piano, in a house-dress of Venetian lace, while a sumptuous tea of cakes, sandwiches and sweets had been laid out. Cornélie had written in her note that she wished to speak to Miss Hope alone on an important subject and asked immediately if they would be alone, undecided now that Urania received her so grandly. But Urania put her mind at rest: she was only at home to Mrs De Retz and was very curious to know what Cornélie wished to talk to her about. Cornélie reminded Urania of her first warning and when Urania laughed she took her hand and gave her such a serious look, that she made an impression on the American's girl's light-hearted nature and Urania became intrigued. Now she suddenly found it very important—a secret, an intrigue, a danger in Rome!—and the two whispered together. And Cornélie, no longer afraid in this atmosphere of increasing famil-iarity, confessed to her what she had overheard at the Christmas ball through the chink in the door: the machi-nations of the *marchesa* and her nephew, whom she was determined to marry off to a rich heiress for the sake of

91

the prince's father, who appeared to have promised her a considerable sum for such a marriage. Then she spoke about the conversion of Miss Taylor, engineered by Rudyard, who seemed unable to exert his influence on her, Urania— being unable to gain a hold over her unsuspecting but airy butterfly nature, and—as Cornélie suspected—as a result had incurred the disapproval of his clerical superiors, and had disappeared, without being able to pay what he owed the *marchesa*. Now he seemed to have been replaced by the two *monsignori*, who looked more distinguished, more worldly, and were more emollient, with more smiles. And Urania, staring this danger in the face, at those layers hidden beneath her feet, which Cornélie suddenly revealed to her, was now truly alarmed, went pale and promised to be on her guard. In fact she would have preferred to tell her chambermaid to pack at once in order to leave Rome as soon as possible, and go to another town to another *pensione*, where the nobility was well represented: the nobility was so adorable! And Cornélie, seeing that she had made an impact, went on, talked about herself, talked about marriage, and said that she had written a pamphlet against marriage and about the Social Situation of the Divorced Woman. And she talked of the unhappiness she had been through, and of the Women's Movement in Holland. And once she got into the swing, she could no longer hold herself in check, and became more and more impassioned and intense, until Urania found her very clever—a very clever girl— to be able to reason like that and write about a '*question brûlante*'. She put a heavy emphasis on the first syllables of the French words and admitted that she would like to have the vote, and as she spoke unfolded the long train of her lace tea-gown. Cornélie spoke of the injustice of the law, which leaves a woman nothing, but takes everything from her, forces her completely into the power of the man, and Urania agreed with her and offered her the dish of fine sweets. And over a second cup of tea they talked excitedly, both at the same time, the one not hearing what the other was arguing, and Urania said that it was a shame. From a general discussion, they returned to their own interests: Cornélie described the character of her husband, too coarse to understand a woman's nature, unable to accept that a woman should stand alongside him and not below him. And again she returned to the Jesuits, on the dangers lurking in Rome for rich girls on their own, to that crone of a *marchesa*, and to that prince: titled bait, cast out by the Jesuits, to win a soul and to improve the finances of an impoverished Italian house—one that had remained loyal to the Pope and did not serve the king. They were both so heated and excited that they did not hear a knock at the door, and only looked up when the door slowly opened. They started, looked up, and both went pale when they saw the Prince of Forte-Braccio enter. He apologised with a smile, said that he had seen the light on in Miss Urania's drawing-room, that the doorman had tried to bar his way but that he had forced his way in. He sat down and despite everything they had just discussed, Urania was delighted that the prince was sitting there and had accepted a cup of tea and consented to eat a cake.

Urania showed them her album of coats-of-arms—the prince had already printed his own in it—and then her album of samples of the queen's evening gowns. The prince laughed and produced an envelope from his pocket: he opened it and carefully took out a scrap of blue brocade decorated with silver pearls. "What was it?" asked Urania in delight. And he said that he was bringing her a sample of Her Majesty's most recent outfit; his cousin, not Black like himself but White; not a Papist, but a Monarchist lady-in-waiting—had been able to secure this scrap for Urania's album. Urania would see for herself: the queen would wear this outfit at the court ball in a week's time. He was not going, he did not even go officially to see his cousin, nor to their reception, but he still saw her because of the family tie, out of friendship. Now he begged Urania not to betray him: it might harm his career (what career? Cornélie wondered), if it were known that he saw his cousin a lot, but he had visited her frequently recently, for Urania, to get hold of that sample.

And Urania was so grateful that she forgot all about the social position of girls and women, married or unmarried, and she would willingly have sacrificed her vote for such a sweet Italian prince. Cornélie was annoyed, got up, greeted the prince with a cool nod of the head, and pulled Urania with her towards the door.

"Don't forget our conversation," she warned. "Be on your guard."

And she saw the prince, while they were whispering, looking at them sarcastically, suspecting, that they were talking about him, suspecting a dislike in that Dutch woman, but proud of the power of his personality and his title and his attentions over the daughter of an American stocking manufacturer.

XVII

THERE WAS AN ESTRANGEMENT between Mrs Van der Staal and Cornélie, and Cornélie no longer came to dine at Belloni. She did not see the mother and her daughters for weeks, but she saw Duco every day. Despite their essential difference in character, they were so used to meeting that they missed each other if they went a day without contact, and gradually they had naturally come to breakfast and dine with each other every day: in the mornings in the *osteria*, in the afternoons in some little café, usually very simply. So as not to have to settle up between them, Duco and Cornélie would take turns to pay. Usually they had lots to talk about; he taught her Rome, took her round churches and museums after lunch, and under his guidance she began to understand, to appreciate and find things beautiful. Unconsciously, he communicated some of his ideas to her: painting she found very difficult, but she understood sculpture much more quickly. And she began to find him more than merely 'morbid'; she looked up to him, he spoke simply to her from his lofty vantage point of sentiment and knowledge, about exalted things, which she as a young girl and later as a young woman had never seen in the noble light of glorification, that he lit for her like the first glow of a dawn; a new day, in which she contemplated new things in life, created from the most noble part of the artist's soul. He regretted not being able to show her Giotto in Santa Croce in Florence, the Primitives in the Uffizi, and that he had to teach her about Rome at once, but he guided her through all the exuberant artistic life of the Papal Renaissance, until, through his words, she experienced for a single intense moment, and Michelangelo, Raphael, stood before her as if alive. He thought, after one such day: she is not really all that unartistic, and she thought of him with respect, even when the spell was broken, and she thought things over and, actually deep inside, no longer understood as well as that morning, because she lacked love for those things. And yet so much radiance and colour and times past still swirled before her eyes, that her pamphlet seemed dull, that the Women's Movement did not interest her, and she could not care less about Urania Hope.

He admitted to himself that he had completely lost his composure, that the figure of Cornélie was present in his thoughts, coming between him and his ancient triptychs; that his life, solitary, without friends, naïve and simple, content to wander through and around Rome, reading, dreaming, and now and then painting, had changed completely in habit and line, now that the line of his life had crossed her lifeline and they seemed to be following a single path; he did not really know why. He could not call the feeling that attracted him to her, love … And only very vaguely, deep inside, unconsciously did he suspect, still inarticulately, and not even thought out, that it was the line of her body, almost something Byzantine; the frailty of the figure, the long arms, the broken lily line of the woman of sorrow, the melancholy in her grey eyes, shaded by the eyelashes that were almost too long; that it was the nobility of her hand, small and dainty for a tall woman; that it was a movement of hers, like a bending stalk, a swan that was tired and looked round behind it. He had never met many women, and those that he had met had always seemed very ordinary, but she was strange to him, in the contradictions of her character, with its vagueness and elusiveness, in all the semi-tones which escaped his eye, though it was accustomed to half-tints … What was she like? … He had always seen a woman in a book, a heroine in a poem in her character. What was she like, a living woman, flesh and blood? She was not artistic; she had no energy, yet she was not lacking in vitality, she was not highly educated, and she wrote, on impulse and with intuition, a pamphlet on one of the issues of the moment, and she finished and it became a text, no worse than any other. She had a breadth of thought and hated the narrowness of coteries, no longer felt at home in her circle in The Hague after her sorrow, and here in Rome she listened at a door to some innocent intrigue—scarcely an intrigue, he thought—and had gone to Urania Hope, to become involved in the confused twists and turns of inferior lives, without importance, of people whom she despised for their lack of line, colour, dream, of aura, of everything that was dearest to him and made life worthwhile for him … What was she like? He did not understand her, but the twists and turns of *her* life mattered to him. She did not lack a line, either an artistic line or a lifeline; she moved through the dream of her own vagueness before his peering eyes, and she loomed up from the haze, from the gloom of his studio atmosphere, and stood before him like a phantom. He

could not call it love, but she was precious to him as a revelation, which constantly veiled itself in mystery. And his
life of a lonely wanderer had certainly changed, but she
had not brought any unharmonious habits into his life: he
liked eating in a little café or *osteria*, with the ordinary
people of Rome around him, and she shared that with
him easily and simply, not acting as if it were beneath her
but companionable, harmonious, adapting with great
ease, with the same natural grace with which she dined at
Belloni. All that, the interplay of oddness, contradiction,
and that living vision of vagueness, that elusiveness of her
individuality, that hiding of her soul, that merging of her
essences, had come to enchant him: a restlessness, a need,
a nervousness in his life, usually so peaceful, with his
modest contentedness and calm—but most of all enchantment, indispensable everyday enchantment.

And without worrying about what Mrs Van der Staal
thought of it, they sometimes went to Tivoli together for
the day; on another day they walked from Castel-Gandolfo
to Albano, and drove to the lake of Nemi, and break-
fasted with an ancient capital as a table in Villa Sforza-
Cesarini. They rested together in the shade of the trees,
they admired the camellias, looked silently at the glassy
clarity of Lake Nemi, the mirror of Diana—and drove
back via Frascati. In the carriage they were silent, and
smiling he thought how everywhere that day they had
been taken for man and wife. She also thought about their
growing intimacy, and thought also that she would never
remarry. And she thought of her husband and compared
him to Duco. So young facially, but eyes full of depth,
soul, dream, his voice so measured, what he said so

98

clever, so knowing, and then his calm, his naivety, his
lack of passion, as if his nerves had been formed only for
feeling the calm of art, in the dreamlike haze of his life.
And she admitted to herself, there in the carriage beside
him—around them the gently rolling hills, fading purple
into the evening, ahead of them the fading, mauvish pink
of a scarcely golden sunset—that he was precious to her
because of that calm, that lack of passion, that naivety,
that knowingness: a clear voice resounding from dreamy
twilight—and that she was happy sitting beside him,
hearing that voice, and accidentally feeling his hand …
happy that her lifeline had crossed his, and both lines
seemed to form a single path, towards the dimly looming
outline, every day brighter, of their immediate future …

XVIII

CORNÉLIE NO LONGER saw anyone but Duco. Mrs Van der Staal had fallen out with her and no longer wanted her daughters to see Cornélie socially. Relations had also cooled between mother and son. Cornélie saw no one but Duco, and occasionally Urania Hope. The American girl visited her from time to time and told her about Belloni: there was much talk about Cornélie and Duco and many comments on their relationship. Urania was glad to feel above hotel gossip, but still wanted to warn Cornélie. There was something spontaneous and friendly in her words, which Cornélie found sympathetic. But when Cornélie asked about the prince she fell silent and obviously did not want to say much. Then, after the court ball—where the queen really had worn the sequined brocade!—Urania visited Cornélie again and admitted over a cup of tea that she had promised the prince that morning to visit him at his residence. She said it quite simply, as if it were the most natural thing in the world. Cornélie was alarmed and asked how on earth she could have promised such a thing …

"Why not?" replied Urania. "What's wrong with it? I receive his visits … why should I, if he asks me to come and see his rooms—he lives in Palazzo Ruspoli—if he wants to show me some paintings, miniatures and antique lace … why should I refuse to go? Why should I make such a fuss about it? I'm above such petty-mindedness.

We American girls behave very freely with our gentlemen. And what about you? You walk with Mr Van der Staal, you dine and breakfast with him, you go on excursions with him, you go to his studio … "

"I've been married," replied Cornélie. "I don't have to answer to anyone. You have your parents … What you're contemplating is rash and reckless … Tell, is the prince thinking … of marriage?"

"If I become a Catholic … "

"And … ?"

"I think … I will … I've written to Chicago," she said hesitantly.

She closed her lovely eyes for a moment and went pale as she had a vision of the title of princess-duchess.

"It's just … " she began.

"What … ?"

"Life won't be much fun. The prince is one of the Blacks. They are in permanent mourning for the Pope. Scarcely anything happens in their coterie, no balls or parties. If we got married, I'd like him to come to America with me. His father is very proud, inaccessible and taciturn. I've heard that from various sides. What am I to do, Cornélie? I love Gilio very much; his name is Virgilio. And you know the title is an old Italian one: *principe di Forte-Braccio, duca di San Stefano* … But you see, that's all there is, all. San Stefano is a hole. That's where his papa lives. They sell wine and that is what they live on. And olive oil: but they don't make any money from it. My father manufactures stockings but he has made a fortune from it. They haven't many family jewels. I've made inquiries … His cousin, the Countess di Rosavilla,

101

the queen's lady-in-waiting, is sweet … but we would not see her officially. I wouldn't be able to go anywhere. It seems to me a rather boring prospect … "

Cornélie responded vehemently, burst out and repeated her slogans: against marriage in general and against this marriage in particular, purely for the sake of a title. Urania agreed: it was just a title … but it was also Gilio: he was sweet and she loved him. But Cornélie didn't believe a word, and told her straight. Urania wept: she did not know what to do.

"And when were you supposed to visit your prince?"

"Tonight … "

"Don't go."

"No, no, you're right, I won't go."

"Do you give me your word?"

"Yes, yes."

"Don't go, Urania."

"No, I won't go. You are a dear girl. You're right: I won't go. I swear to you I won't go … "

XIX

BUT THERE HAD BEEN SUCH VAGUENESS in Urania's assurances, that Cornélie felt uneasy and that evening talked to Duco about it in the restaurant where they met. But he was not interested, in Urania, what she did or did not do, and shrugged his shoulders indifferently. But she was silent and withdrawn and did not hear what he said: a side panel of a triptych, definitely by Lippo Memmi, which he had discovered in a shop down by the Tiber: the angel of the Annunciation, almost as beautiful as the one in the Uffizi, kneeling in the last sweep of his flight, with the lily stalk in his hands. But the shopkeeper wanted two hundred lire for it and he was only prepared to offer fifty. And yet the dealer had not mentioned the name of Memmi: he had no idea that the angel was by Memmi …

Cornélie had not been listening and suddenly she said,

"I'm going to Palazzo Ruspoli … "

He looked up in surprise.

"Why?"

"To ask for Miss Hope."

He was speechless with amazement and stared at her open-mouthed.

"If she's not there … " Cornélie went on, "then it's all right. If she's there … if she went after all, then I'll ask to speak to her urgently … "

He did not know what to say, finding her impulse so strange, so eccentric, so futile a twisting arabesque to cross the arabesques of insignificant, indifferent people, that he was at a loss for words. Cornélie looked at her watch.

"It's past eight-thirty. If she goes after all, she'll go about this time."

She motioned to the waiter and paid. She buttoned her coat and got up. He followed her.

"Cornélie," he began, "isn't what you're proposing to do rather odd? It'll get you into all sorts of trouble."

"If we were always deterred by a bit of trouble, no one would ever do a good deed."

They walked on in silence, he angry at her side. They did not talk: he thought what she was planning was simply crazy: she thought he was weak for not wanting to protect Urania. She thought of her pamphlet, of Women, and she wanted to protect Urania from marriage, from that prince. And they walked down the Corso, towards Palazzo Ruspoli. He became nervous, made a last attempt to restrain her, but she was already asking the guard:

"Is the *signore principe* at home?"

The man looked at her suspiciously.

"No," he said brusquely.

"I have a feeling he is. If so, please ask whether Miss Hope is with his Excellency. Miss Hope was not at home; I have a feeling that she is coming to visit the prince this evening and I need to speak to her urgently … on a matter that cannot be put off. Here … *la signora* De Retz … " She presented her card. She spoke with such aplomb, portrayed Urania's visit with such calm and simplicity, as if it happened every evening that American girls visited Italian princes, and as if she were convinced that the guard was acquainted with the custom. The man was completely non-plussed, bowed, took the card and with-drew. Cornélie and Duco waited in the gateway.

He admired her calm. He found what she was doing eccentric, but there was a certainty about her eccentric-ity that showed in a quite different light. So would he never understand her, never grasp anything or know any-thing for certain, in the shifting and intangible vagueness of her self? He would never have been able to say those few words to the guard. How had she found the tact, that lofty, serious tone in addressing that imposing doorman with his cane and three-cornered hat! She did it with the same ease, the same familiar amiability with which she ordered dinner from the waiter in their little restaurant … The guard returned.

"Miss Hope and His Excellency would like you to come upstairs … "

She looked at Duco with a smile, triumphantly, amused at his confusion.

"Are you coming?"

"No," he stammered. "I'll wait for you here."

She followed a lackey upstairs. The wide corridor was hung with family portraits. The door of the drawing-room was open. The prince came to meet her.

"Forgive me, your highness," she said calmly, putting out her hand: his eyes were as small as squeezed carbun-cles, he was white with rage, but he controlled himself and pressed his lips briefly on the hand she proffered.

"Forgive me," she continued. "I must speak to Miss Hope urgently … "

She entered the drawing-room; Urania was there, blush-ing, embarrassed.

"You understand," smiled Cornélie "I wouldn't have dared disturb you, had it not been a matter of great importance. A matter between women … but important nonetheless!" she joked and the prince said something cloyingly gallant in reply. "May I speak to Miss Hope alone for a moment?"

The prince looked at her. He suspected antipathy, even enmity in her. But he bowed, with his cloying smile, and said that he would leave the ladies alone for a moment. He withdrew into another room.

"Cornélie, what's wrong?" asked Urania hectically.

She grasped both of Cornélie's hands and looked at her anxiously.

"Nothing's wrong," said Cornélie severely. "I've nothing to talk to you about. I just had a suspicion and was sure you wouldn't keep your promise. I wanted to be certain whether you were here or not … Why did you come?"

Urania began crying.

"Stop crying!" whispered Cornélie unrelentingly. "For God's sake stop crying. What you've done is as reckless as can be … "

"I know … " admitted Urania nervously, drying her tears.

"Why did you do it then?"

"I couldn't help it."

"Alone with him, here, in the evening … ! A well-known good-for-nothing … "

"I know!"

"What do you see in him?"

"I love him … "

"You only want to marry him for his title. You're

106

compromising yourself for the sake of his title. What if he does not respect you as his wife-to-be this evening? What if he forces you to be his mistress?"

"Cornélie … quiet … !"

"You're a child, a reckless child. And your father lets you travel alone. To see 'dear old Italy' … You're American, liberal, fine; you go boldly travelling round the world on your own: fine, but you're not a woman yet, you're a child!"

"Cornélie … "

"Come with me; say you're going with me. For some urgent reason. Or no … best say nothing. Stay. But I'll stay too … "

"Yes, you stay too … "

"We'll call him."

"Yes."

Cornélie rang and a lackey appeared.

"Tell his Excellency that we are awaiting him."

The man left. After a while the prince entered. He had never been treated like this in his own house. He was seething with rage, but remained extremely courteous and outwardly calm.

"Has the important matter been dealt with?" he asked with a hypocritical smile in his small eyes.

"Yes, thank you for your discretion in leaving us alone for a moment," said Cornélie. "Now I have spoken to Miss Hope, I am reassured about her opinion … Oh, I expect you would like to know what we were talking about?!"

The prince raised his eyebrows. Cornélie had spoken coquettishly, wagging her finger, smiling, and the prince looked at her and suddenly saw that she was beautiful.

Not with the striking beauty and freshness of Urania
Hope, with a more complex attractiveness: that of a married woman, divorced, but very young, that of a woman
of the *fin de siècle*, with a touch of perversity in her deep
grey eyes, operating beneath very long eyelashes, that of
a woman with an exceptional grace in the fractured lines
of her tired, languid, morbid charm: a woman who knew
life, a woman who—he was sure of it—saw through him;
who spoke to him—for whom she felt antipathy—coquettishly in order to please him, win him over, unconsciously, out of pure femininity. He saw her as beautiful
and perverse, and he admired her, sensitive as he was to
different types of women. He suddenly found her more
beautiful and less banal than Urania, and much more distinguished, and not so naively susceptible to his title,
something he found so absurd in Urania. He was suddenly
at ease with her, his rage subsided: he enjoyed having two
beautiful women with him instead of one, and he joked in
return, said he was burning with curiosity, had listened at
the door, but had unfortunately not caught anything …
Cornélie laughed merrily, behaved coquettishly in return
and looked at her watch. She mentioned leaving, but at
the same time sat down, unbuttoned her coat and said to
the prince:

"I've heard so much about your miniatures; now the
opportunity presents itself: may I see them?"

The prince was willing, enchanted as he was by her
eyes, her voice, on fire, aflame in a moment.

"But … " said Cornélie, "my escort is waiting outside
at the gate. He did not want to come up, he does not
know you … It is Mr Van der Staal … "

The prince smiled at her. He knew the rumours at Belloni. He had no doubt that there was a liaison between Van der Staal and *signora* De Retz. He knew that they cared nothing for convention. And he conceived a great liking for Cornélie.

"But I'll have Mr Van der Staal invited up at once."

"He's waiting in the gateway," said Cornélie. "He won't want … "

"I'll go myself," said the prince, in a lively, helpful manner.

He went. The two ladies were left behind. Cornélie took off her coat, but kept her hat on, since her hair would be a mess. She looked in the mirror.

"Have you got your powder with you?" she asked Urania.

Urania took her ivory case out of her pocket and gave it to Cornélie. And while Cornélie quickly powdered her face, Urania looked at her friend, uncomprehending. She remembered the serious impression Cornélie had immediately made on her, making a study of Rome … later writing a pamphlet on the Women's question and the Condition of the Divorced Woman … Then her warnings against Marriage and against the prince. And now she suddenly saw her as a charming, fickle woman, irresistibly attractive, more enchanting than really beautiful, full of coquetry in the depths of her grey eyes whose gleam moved up and down beneath the curling eyelashes, dressed simply in a dark silk blouse and linen skirt, but with such style and undeniable coquettishness, such distinction and yet a fragile line of charm, that she scarcely recognised her …

But the prince had come in and brought Duco with him, reluctant, nervous, not knowing what had happened, not understanding how Cornélie had acted. He saw her sitting there calmly, smiling and immediately explaining to him that the prince was to show her his miniatures.

Duco said frankly that he was not interested in miniatures. His angry tone led the prince to suspect he was jealous. And this suspicion spurred the prince on to woo Cornélie. And he acted as if he were showing the miniatures only to her, as if he were showing *her* his antique lace. She particularly admired the lace, and rubbed it with her delicate fingers. She asked him to tell them about his grandmothers, who had worn the lace. Had they had adventures? He told her of one that made her laugh heartily: he repeated a few anecdotes, spirited, catching fire under her gaze, and she laughed. In the atmosphere of that large drawing-room, the prince's study—his desk stood there—with the candles lit, flowers arranged for Urania, a tingle of perverse merriment and airy *joie de vivre* was born. But only between Cornélie and the prince. Urania had fallen silent, and Duco did not say a word. Cornélie was a revelation to him too. He had never seen her like this—not at the Christmas ball, not at dinner, not in his studio, not on their excursions, or in their restaurant. Was she one woman, or ten?

And he admitted to himself that he loved her, loved her more with each revelation, more with every woman he saw in her, as another facet that she made gleam. But he could not speak, he could not join in the repartee, alien in that atmosphere, alien in that element of so much airy *joie de vivre,* about nothing but aimless words, as if French and Italian were sparkling, as they mixed them at will, as if their humour glittered like fools' gold, and their ambivalent puns shone like rainbows ... The prince regretted that his tea was no longer drinkable, but had champagne brought in. He considered his evening partly a failure for his plans—since afraid of losing Urania, he had planned to force the issue; since seeing her hesitation, he had determined on taking the irrevocable step—but his nature was so lacking in seriousness—he would marry more for the sake of his father and the Marchesa Belloni than for himself; he lived just as pleasantly with debts and without a wife as he would do with a wife and millions in the bank, so that he began to find the failed evening exceedingly amusing, and he had to laugh to himself about it when he thought of his aunt the *marchesa,* his father: of their machinations, which had no hold over Urania because an attractive coquettish woman did not want them to. Why did she not want them to, he thought, pouring the foaming champagne, which spilled over the sides of the glasses; why is she placing herself between me and that American stocking-seller? Is she looking for an Italian title herself? But he could not really care less: he found the intruder attractive, beautiful, very beautiful, coquettish, seductive, enchanting. He focused on her. He neglected Urania. He scarcely filled her glass. And when it finally got late and Cornélie got up and put her arm in Urania's and gave the prince a triumphant look, which they both understood, he whispered in her ear "I thank you most sincerely for your visit to my humble abode: you have *conquered* me: *I surrender* ... "

The words seemed to be just an allusion to their joking, to their banter about nothing, but between the two of them—the prince and Cornélie—they were heavy with significance and in her eye he saw a smile of victory …

He remained in his room alone and poured himself the last of the champagne. And putting the glass to his lips, he said aloud,

"*O, che occhi! Che belli occhi … ! Che belli occhi … !!*"

XX

T HE NEXT DAY, when Duco met Cornélie in the *osteria*, she was very excited and merry: she announced that she had already had a reply from the women's magazine to which she had sent her pamphlet a week ago, and that her work had been accepted and she would even be paid a fee. She was so proud at the prospect of earning her first money, and she was as bubbly as a child. She did not talk about the previous evening, seemed to have forgotten about the prince and Urania, but had a need to talk exuberantly.

She had all kinds of ambitious plans: travelling as a journalist, immersing herself in the ebb and flow of city life, chasing up every new item of news, having herself sent to conferences and festivities by a magazine. The mere thought of the few guilders she would be earning, made her drunk with industriousness, and she would want to earn a great deal and do a great deal and pay no attention to weariness. He found her simply adorable: in the half-light of the *osteria*, eating her gnocchi at the small table, the half flask in front of her, full of pale country wine, her usual languor gained a new vitality that surprised him; her outline, on the right semi-dark and on the left lit by the light from the street, acquired a new grace as if in a drawing, which reminded him of French draughtsmen: the pale, even-coloured face with the delicate features, illuminated by her smile, sketchily visible

113

under her matelot, which was deep over her eyes; her
hair with golden highlights, or dark dusky blond; the
white veil lifted and crinkling hazily on top of her head;
her figure, slim and graceful in the simple coat—unbuttoned—and a corsage of violets tucked into her blouse.

The way she poured her wine, asked the waiter, the only
one—who knew them both well, as regular customers—
for something in a familiar, agreeable tone; the vivacity
that alternated with her languor. Her grand plans, her
happy words—it dazzled him, student-like yet distinguished, free yet feminine, and especially with the same
ease of manner that she had everywhere; with a tactful
assimilation that struck him as especially harmonious. He
thought about the previous evening, but did not talk
about it. He thought about that revelation of her coquetry
but she was not thinking of any such thing. She was never
coquettish with him. She looked up to him, she found
him particularly clever, although not of his time; she
respected what he said and thought, and she was so
natural with him, like one comrade with another, an
older, cleverer comrade. She felt deep friendship for him,
an indescribable feeling of having-to-be together, having-
to-live-together; as if their lines formed a single line. It
was not a sisterly feeling and it was not passion, and she
did not picture it to herself as love, but it was a great sensation of respectful tenderness, of awed longing and of
affectionate joy at having met him. If she were never to
see him again, she would miss him like no one else in her
life. The fact that he was not interested in modern questions, did not lower him in her estimation as a young
modern militant, about to wave her first banner. It might

114

irritate her for a moment, but it was never decisive in her appreciation.

And he saw that she was so simply affectionate with him, without coquettishness. Yet he would never forget how she had been with the prince yesterday. He had felt jealousy and had noticed it in Urania too. But she herself must have acted so spontaneously in accordance with her nature that she was not thinking of that evening now, of the prince, of Urania, of coquetry, or of possible jealousy on his part. He paid—it was his turn—and they got up and she took his arm merrily and said that she wanted to give him a surprise. She wanted to give him something nice. She wanted to give him something, a nice, a very nice souvenir. She would like to spend her fee on the souvenir. But she didn't have it yet … what did that matter! She would be getting it after all … And she wanted to spend it on him.

Laughing, he asked what it could be … She hailed a carriage and whispered an address to the coachman; he did not hear what she said … What could it be? But she refused to say yet … The *vetturino* drove down the Borgo towards the Tiber. There he stopped in front of a dark shop full of junk that was piled up into the street.

"Cornélie … !" he cried, guessing what she had in mind.

"Your angel by Lippo Memmi: I'm buying it for you, sh … "

His eyes filled with tears; they went in.

"Ask how much he wants for it."

He was so moved that he could not speak and Cornélie had to ask and haggle. She did not bargain for long; she bought the panel for a hundred and twenty lire … She

115

carried it out to the victoria herself. They drove to his studio. They carried the angel upstairs together, smiling, as if they were carrying pure happiness into his home. In his study they put the angel on a chair. Noble, with slightly mongoloid features, the eyes long and almond-shaped, the angel was kneeling in the last flourish of his flight, and the golden sash of his gold-purple robe fluttered up, while his long wings, tall and straight, trembled. Duco gazed at his Memmi, full of a double emotion; at the Angel itself and at her ... And quite naturally he opened his arms wide.

"Can I thank you, Cornélie?"

He took her in his arms and she returned his kiss.

XXI

WHEN SHE GOT HOME she found a card from the prince. It was simply a polite gesture after the night before—her impromptu visit to Palazzo Ruspoli—and she gave it no further thought. She was in a pleasant mood, pleasantly content; pleased that her work—at first as an article—had been accepted by *The Rights of Women*; later she would publish it as a pamphlet; pleased that she had given Duco pleasure with the Memmi. She changed into her *peignoir* and sat down by the fire in a reflective attitude and thought about how she could put her grand plans into effect … Who should she turn to? An International Women's Conference was taking place in London and *The Rights of Women* had sent her a programme. She leafed through it. Various women leaders were to speak; numerous social questions were to be dealt with: the psychology of the child; the responsibility of parents, the impact on domestic life of the admission of women to all professions; women in art, in medicine; women in fashion, women in the home, on the stage; legislation on marriage and divorce …

Potted biographies of the speakers, with portraits were attached. There were American and Russian, English, Swedish and Danish women; almost every nationality was represented. There were old and young women; some beautiful, some plain; some masculine, some feminine; some hard and energetic with highly sexual boyish faces;

the occasional one elegant, with a plunging neckline and permed. They could not be divided into groups. What had been the impulse in their lives to join the fight for women's rights? For some it had certainly been inclination, nature; for a few a vocation; for others jumping on the bandwagon … And in herself, what had been the impulse … ? She dropped the programme into her lap, stared into the fire and reflected … Before her appeared her drawing-room education, her marriage, her divorce …

Where was the impulse … ? Where was the trigger … ? She had gradually begun travelling to widen her horizons; to reflect, to get to know art, the modern life of women … She had gradually slid along the line of her life, without wanting much, without fighting much, even without thinking or feeling much … She looked into herself, as if she were reading a modern novel, the psychology of a woman … Sometimes she seemed to have the will, to want to fight, like now, with her great plans … Sometimes she sat, as she had often in the last few days, by her cosy fire. Sometimes she felt, as she did for Duco now … But mostly her life had been a gradual process, gliding along the line she had to follow, gently impelled by the finger of fate … For an instant she saw clearly. There was a great deal of sincerity in her: she was not play-acting, neither for herself, nor for others. There were contradictions in her, but she admitted them all to herself, to the extent that she saw them. But the openness of her soul became clear at this moment. She saw the complexity of her being briefly sparkling with its many facets … She had written, with *élan* and intuition, but was what she had written any good? A doubt rose in her. The Dutch statute book lay on the table, a remnant from the time of her divorce … but had she understood the law? Her article had been accepted, but were the editors of *The Rights of Women* capable of judging it? Again scanning the women's portraits, their biographies, the seriousness and harshness of some of them, she was frightened that her work would not be good—too superficial—and that her thinking was not guided by study and knowledge … But she could also picture her own portrait in that programme with her name below it and the short note: author of 'The Social Situation of the Divorced Woman', published in *The Rights of Women*; with dates, etc. And she smiled: how very convincing it sounded! But how difficult it was to study, to do things and to know and act and negotiate the modern movement of life! Now she was in Rome: she would have liked to be in London. But the journey was not convenient at this moment. She had felt rich when she bought Duco's Memmi, thinking of her fee: and now she felt poor. She would have liked to go to London … But she would have missed Duco; and the conference only lasted a week. She had now settled in here somewhat, she was coming to love Rome, her rooms, the Colosseum over there like a dark arch, like the dark wings of a theatre at the end of the city, and beyond the vague blue mountains … Then she thought of the prince for a moment, and for the first time she thought of yesterday, she recalled the evening, an evening of badinage and champagne: Duco sat silent and sulky, Urania crushed, and the prince, small, vivacious, slim, aroused from the dull routine of being a distinguished man of the world, with his carbuncle-like eyes narrowed. She liked him, she occasionally liked that coquettish, flirting tone, and the prince had understood her. She had saved Urania, she was sure of that: she felt the satisfaction of her good deed …

She was too lazy to get dressed and go to the restaurant. She was not very hungry and just had a light supper made with what she had in the cupboard: a few eggs, bread, some fruit. But she thought of Duco, who was bound to be waiting at their table and wrote him a note that she had delivered by the concierge's little son …

Duco was just coming downstairs on his way out to the restaurant when he bumped into the lad on the stairs. He read the note, and was bitterly disappointed. He felt little, sad as a child. And he went back to his studio, lit a few lamps, threw himself down on a wide sofa, and in the twilight lay peering at Memmi's angel, which, still on the chair, glowed faintly gold in the centre of the room, as a sweet solace, with a gesture of annunciation, as if wanting to announce all the mysterious things that were to happen …

XXII

A FEW DAYS LATER Cornélie was waiting for the visit of the prince, who had asked to see her. She sat at her desk correcting the proofs of her article. A lamp on the desk lit her softly through a yellow silk shade; and she wore a white silk crêpe *peignoir*, with a corsage of violets. Another, standing, lamp gave a second source of illumination from a corner of the room; and the room was duskily cosy and intimate in the third glow of a wood fire—with watercolours by Duco, sketches and photographs, white anemones in vases, violets everywhere, and the occasional large palm. Her desk was strewn with the books and printed sheets that bore witness to her work.

There was a knock and she called out for the visitor to enter, and when the prince came in, she remained seated for a moment, then put down her pen and rose. She approached him with a smile and proffered her hand, which he kissed. He was dressed very smartly in his morning coat, top hat and light-grey gloves; a pearl tie-pin. They sat down by the fire and he paid her a succession of compliments, on her décor, on her outfit and on her eyes. She joined in the repartee and he asked if he was disturbing her.

"Perhaps you were writing an interesting letter to someone close to your heart?"

"No. I was correcting printer's proofs."

"Proofs?"

"Yes … "

"Do you write?"

"This is my first attempt."

"A novella?"

"No, an article."

"An article? What about?"

She told him the long title. He looked at her open-mouthed. She laughed cheerfully.

"You wouldn't have thought it, would you?"

"*Santa Maria!*" he muttered in astonishment, not accustomed in his world to 'modern women', banding together in the Women's Movement. "In Dutch?"

"In Dutch."

"Next time write in French: then I'll be able to read it … "

She promised with a laugh and poured him a cup of tea, and offered him sweets. He nibbled a few.

"Are you so serious? Have you always been like this? You weren't serious the other day, were you?"

"Sometimes I'm very serious."

"So am I."

"I realise that. On that occasion, if I had not turned up, you might have become very serious."

He laughed fatuously and looked at her knowingly.

"You are an exceptional woman!" he said. "Very interesting and very clever. What you want to happen, happens … "

"Sometimes … "

"Sometimes, what I want to happen, happens too … Sometimes I'm very clever too. *When* I want to be, but usually I don't want to be."

"The other day you did … "

He laughed.

"Yes! You were cleverer than I was then. Tomorrow I may be cleverer than you."

"Who knows!"

They both laughed. He nibbled the sweets, one after the other, from the dish, and preferred a glass of port to tea. She poured him one.

"May I give you something?" he asked earnestly.

"What?"

"A souvenir of our first meeting."

"That is charming of you. What can it be?"

He took something wrapped in tissue paper from his inside pocket and handed it to her.

She opened the package and saw a piece of antique Venetian lace, flounced, for a low petticoat.

"Please accept it," he entreated her. "It's a very fine piece. It gives me such joy to make a gift of it to you."

She looked at him with all her coquettishness in her eyes, as if wanting to see through him.

"You must wear it like this … "

He got up, took the lace, draped it across her white *peignoir* from shoulder to shoulder. His fingers fiddled with the pleats, his lips brushed hers for a moment. She thanked him for his gift. He sat down.

"I am glad that you are accepting it."

"Have you given Miss Hope something too?"

He laughed, his triumphant laugh.

"Samples are good enough for her, from the queen's evening gowns. I would not dare give you samples. You I give antique Venetian lace."

"But you nearly ruined your career for that sample?"

"Oh well!" he laughed.

"What career?"

"Oh no!" he said defensively. "Tell me, what is your advice?"

"How do you mean?"

"Should I marry her?"

"I'm against all marriage, between educated people … "

Now he was certain of a liaison between her and Van der Staal, if he had had any lingering doubts.

"And … do you regard me as educated?"

She laughed, coquettishly, with a brief flash of contempt.

"Listen, will you be serious."

"With the greatest pleasure."

"I don't find either you or Miss Hope suited to free love."

"So I am not educated?"

"I don't mean you are not cultivated. I mean modern education."

"So I am not modern?"

"No," she said, a little irritated.

"Teach me to be modern."

She laughed nervously.

"Oh, don't let's talk like this. What do I advise you? *Not* to marry Urania."

"Why not?"

"Because your life together would be a disaster. She is a sweet little American parvenue … "

"I am offering her what I have; she is offering me what she has … "

He nibbled the sweets. She shrugged her shoulders.

"Do it then," she said indifferently.

"Tell me you don't want it to happen, and I won't do it."

"And your papa? And the *marchesa*?"

"What do you know about them?"

"Oh, everything … and nothing!"

"You are a demon!" he exclaimed. "An angel and a demon. Tell me, what do you know about my father and the *marchesa*?"

"For how many millions are you selling yourself to Urania? For no less than ten million?"

He looked at her in stupefaction.

"But the *marchesa* is content with five. It's not bad: five million … Dollars or lire?"

He clapped his hands together.

"You are a devil!" he exclaimed. "You are an angel and devil! How do you know? How do you *know*? Do you know everything??"

She threw herself backwards and laughed.

"Everything … "

"But *how*?"

She looked at him, shook her head, played the coquette.

"Tell me … "

"No. It's my secret … "

"And you don't think I should sell myself?"

"I do not dare advise you on your interests."

"And as far as Urania is concerned?"

"I advise her against it."

"Have you already advised her against it?"

"Now and then … "

"So you are my enemy?" he said angrily.

"No," she said softly, wanting to win him back. "A friend … "

"A friend? To what point?"

125

"As far as *I* want to go."

"Not as far as *I* want to go … ?"

"Oh no, never!"

"But perhaps we both want to go just as far?"

He had stood up, his blood on fire. She sat calmly, almost languidly, with her head thrown back. She did not answer. He fell to his knees, grasped her hand and kissed it before she could push him away.

"Oh angel, angel! Oh, demon!" He muttered as he kissed.

She pulled her hand free, pushed him gently away and said:

"Italians are so quick to kiss!"

She was laughing at him. He got up.

"Teach me what Dutch women are like, even though they are slower than we are."

She motioned him to a chair with an imperious gesture.

"Sit down. I am not a specifically Dutch woman. Otherwise I would not have come to Rome. I pride myself on being cosmopolitan. But we weren't talking about me, we're talking about Urania. Are you seriously intending to marry her?"

"What can I do if you are working against me? Why don't you work with me, as a dear friend … ?"

She hesitated. Neither Urania nor he were ripe for her ideas. She despised them both. Right, let them marry then: he to become rich, she to become princess-duchess.

"Listen!" she said, leaning towards him. "You are marrying her for her millions. But your marriage will be unhappy from the start. She is a fickle young thing; she wants glamour … and you are member of the Blacks."

"We can live in Nice: she can do as she likes. We'll come to Rome now and then, and occasionally San Stefano. And unhappy … "—he pulled a tragic face—"but what do I care. I'm not happy anyway. I shall try to make Urania happy. But my heart … will be elsewhere … "

"Where?"

"With the Women's Movement."

She laughed.

"Now I'm supposed to be nice?"

"Yes … "

"And promise to help you?"

What difference did it make to her?

"Oh angel, demon!" he exclaimed.

He nibbled a sweet.

"And what does Mr Van der Staal think?" he asked roguishly.

She raised her eyebrows.

"He doesn't give it any thought. He thinks only about his art."

"And about you."

She looked at him, and bowed her head, assenting like a queen.

"And about me."

"You dine with him often."

"Yes."

"Why not dine with me for a change."

"Oh, I'd love to."

"Tomorrow evening? Where?"

"Wherever you like."

"At the Grand-Hôtel?"

"Invite Urania too."

"Why not just the two of us?"

"I think it's better to include your wife-to-be. I will chaperone her."

"You're right. You're quite right. And ask Mr Van der Staal if he will do me the honour … "

"I shall."

"Till tomorrow then, at eight-thirty?"

He got up to take his leave.

"I ought to go," he said. "Actually I'd rather stay … "

"Well stay then … or stay some other time, if you have to go now."

"You are so cool."

"You don't think nearly enough of Urania."

"I'm thinking of the Women's Movement."

He sat down.

"You really should go," she said, with a smile in her eyes. "I have to get dressed … to dine with Mr Van der Staal."

He kissed her hand.

"You are an angel and a demon. You know everything. You can do everything. You are the most interesting woman I have ever met."

"Because I correct proofs."

"Because you are who you are … "

And very seriously, still holding her hand, he said, almost threateningly:

"I shall never be able to forget you … "

And he left. When she was alone she opened her windows. She was aware of being something of a coquette, but it was in her nature: she did it so naturally, with some men. Certainly not with all men. Never with Duco.

Never with men she looked up to. She despised that jumped-up prince, with his flaming eyes and his kisses … But he was sufficient to amuse her …

She changed and went out, and she arrived in the restaurant long after the appointed hour, found Duco waiting for her, with his head in his hands, and told him at once that the prince had detained her.

XXIII

AT FIRST Duco had been unwilling to accept the prince's invitation, but Cornélie told him she would enjoy it more if he came. And it had been an excellent dinner in the restaurant of the Grand-Hôtel, and Cornélie had thoroughly enjoyed herself and had looked utterly charming in an old yellow ball gown, a relic from the first days of her marriage, which she had quickly altered a little and draped with the prince's antique lace. Urania had looked very beautiful, white, fresh, sparkling eyes, sparkling teeth, in a very modern, close-fitting outfit of blue-black sequins on black tulle, as if she were in chain mail; the prince's verdict was: a siren with a scaly tail. And there had been much peering from other tables at their table, since everyone knew Virgilio di Forte-Braccio; everyone was aware he was to marry a rich American heiress, and everyone had thought that he was being extremely gallant towards the slim, blond woman whom no one knew … She had been married—it was thought; she was chaperoning the princess-to-be; and she was on very close terms with that young man, a Dutch painter, who was studying in Rome. People soon knew the whole story …

Cornélie had enjoyed people looking at her and had flirted so ostentatiously with the prince that Urania had become angry. And early the next morning, while Cornélie was still in bed, no longer thinking of the previous evening but pondering a phrase in her pamphlet, there was a knock and the maid brought in her breakfast and letters and said that Miss Hope wished to speak to her. Cornélie had Urania shown in, while she remained in bed and drank her hot chocolate. And she looked up in surprise when Urania immediately bombarded her with accusations, burst into sobs, called her names, and made an emotional scene, and said that she now saw through her, admitted that the *marchesa* had warned her to be wary of Cornélie and called her a dangerous woman. Cornélie allowed her to let off steam and replied coolly that she was not aware of any harm having been done, and that on the contrary she had saved Urania; that on the contrary she, as a married woman, had served Urania as a chaperone, not saying that the prince had wanted to dine alone with her, Cornélie … But Urania refused to listen and went on … Cornélie looked at her and found her vulgar in her rage, speaking her American English as if she were chewing hazelnuts, and finally answered coolly:

"Dear girl, you're getting all worked up about nothing. But if you prefer, I shall write to the prince to ask him to stop his attentions … "

"No, no, don't do that: Gilio will think I'm jealous … "

"And what are you then?"

"Why are you monopolising Gilio? Why are you flirting with him? Why do you flaunt yourself with him, like yesterday, in a crowded restaurant?"

"Well, if you don't like it … I won't flirt with Gilio any more and won't flaunt myself with him … I don't give two hoots about that prince of yours … "

"All the more reason."

"It's agreed, dear child."

Her coolness calmed Urania, who asked,

"And we will stay good friends, won't we?"

"But of course, dear girl. Is there any reason for us to fall out? I can't see any … "

The pair of them, the prince and Urania, didn't matter two hoots to her. True, she had preached at Urania at first, but about a general idea: later, when she realised Urania's insignificance, she lost her interest in the girl. And if a little fun and innocent flirting upset her, well, that would be the end of it … Her mind was more on the proofs of her article that had come in the post … She got up, stretched …

"Go into the sitting-room, Urania my dear, and let me have my bath … "

After a while she rejoined Urania in the sitting-room, fresh and smiling. Urania was crying.

"My dear girl, what are you getting so upset about? Your dream has almost come true. Your marriage is a virtual certainty. Are you waiting for a reply from Chicago? Are you impatient? Send a telegram. I would have telegraphed to start with. You surely don't think your father has an objection to your becoming duchess of San Stefano?"

"I don't know if I do myself," cried Urania. "I don't know, I don't know … "

Cornélie shrugged her shoulders.

"You're cleverer than I thought … "

"Are you really a good friend? Can I trust you? Can I trust your advice?"

"I don't want to give you any more advice. I gave you advice. Now you must make up your own mind."

Urania took her hand.

"What do you prefer: that I take Gilio … or … not?"

Cornélie looked her deep in the eyes.

"You're making yourself unhappy for nothing. You think, and the *marchesa* probably thinks with you, that I am trying to take Gilio away from you? No, darling, I would not want to marry Gilio, even if he were king and emperor. I have a bit of the Socialist in me: I won't marry a title … "

"Neither will I … "

"Of course you won't, darling. I would never dare maintain that you were doing it … But you're asking me what I would like to see? Well, I give you a straight answer: I wouldn't like to see anything. It leaves me completely cold."

"And you call yourself my friend … "

"Oh, dear child, and I want to remain your friend. But don't bombard me with so many reproaches, on an empty stomach … "

"You're a flirt … "

"Naturally, sometimes. I promise I won't be any more with Gilio."

"Promise?"

"Yes, of course. What do I care? I find him amusing, but if it upsets you, I shall gladly sacrifice my amusement. It doesn't matter that much."

"You like Mr Van de Staal?"

"Very much … "

"Are you going to marry him, Cornélie?"

"Oh no, my child. I shan't marry again. I know what marriage is like. Will you come for a walk with me? It's nice weather and you've overwhelmed me with so many grievances that I shan't be able to work this morning anyway. It's wonderful weather: come on: let's go and buy flowers in Piazza di Spagna … "

They went, they bought the flowers, and Cornélie saw her back home to Belloni. As she walked on, on her way to the *osteria* for lunch, she heard someone catching her up. It was the prince.

"I saw you from the start of Via Aurora. Urania was just going home?"

"Prince," she said at once, "this has got to stop."

"What?"

"No more visits, no jokes, no gifts, no dinners in the Grand-Hôtel and no champagne."

"Why not?"

"The princess-to-be does not want it."

"Is she jealous?"

Cornélie told him about the scene.

"And you can't even walk beside me."

"Yes I can."

"No, no."

"I'm going to anyway."

"So male rights, might is right?"

"Exactly."

"My vocation is to fight against them. But for today I'm being unfaithful to my vocation."

"You are utterly charming … as always."

"You mustn't say that any more."

"She's a nuisance, Urania … Tell me, what do you advise me? Should I marry her?"

Cornélie burst out laughing.

"You're both asking *my* advice!"

"Yes, yes, what do you think?"

"Of course, marry her!"

He failed to see her contempt.

"Exchange your coat-of-arms for her purse," she went on, amid gales of laughter.

Now he glimpsed it.

"You despise me, both of us perhaps."

"Oh no … "

"Tell me you do not despise me."

"You want to know my opinion. Urania is the sweetest, nicest girl, but should not travel alone. And you … "

"And I?"

"You are a charming fellow. Buy those violets for me, will you … "

"At once, at once."

He bought the bouquet.

"You love violets, don't you … "

"Yes. This must be your second … and last gift. This is the parting of the ways."

"No, I'll see you home."

"I'm not going home."

"Where then?"

"I'm going to the *osteria*. Mr Van der Staal is waiting for me there."

"Lucky man!"

"You really think so?"

"How could it be otherwise?"

"I don't know. Goodbye, your highness."

"Invite me," he begged. "Let me have lunch with you."

"No," she said seriously. "Definitely not. It's better if you don't. I think … "

"What … "

"That Duco is just like Urania … "

"Jealous?... When will I see you again then?"

"Really, it's better if you don't … Goodbye, your highness. *Merci* … for the violets."

He bent over her hand. She made her way to the *osteria* and saw that Duco had seen their farewell through the window.

XXIV

DUCO WAS SILENT and nervous at table. He played with his bread and his fingers were trembling. She felt that something was troubling him.

"What is it?" she asked sweetly.

"Cornélie," he said, full of emotion. "I have to speak to you."

"What about?"

"It's not right."

"In what way?"

"With the prince. You've seen through him, and yet … yet you go on tolerating him, you keep meeting him … Let me finish," he said, looking around: there were only two Italians in the restaurant, at the table furthest from them, and he could speak without fear of eavesdropping. "I want to finish," he repeated, as she was about to interrupt him. "Of course you're free to do as you please. But I'm your friend and I want to advise you. What you're doing isn't right. The prince is a blackguard. Ignoble, base … How can you accept gifts and invitations from him? Why did you force me to go with you yesterday evening? That whole dinner was torture for me. You know how much I love you—why shouldn't I admit it. You know how highly I value you. I can't bear to see you demeaning yourself with him like that. Let me speak. Demean, I said. He's not worthy to tie your shoelaces. And you play with him, you banter with him, you flirt …

137

Let me speak: you flirt with him. What do you care about him, that conceited twit. What is he in your life. Let him marry Miss Hope, what do you care about either of them? What do you care about those inferior people, Cornélie? I despise them and so do you. I know. So why do you cross their path? Let them live in their vain world of titles and money, what do you care? I don't understand you. Oh, I know: you can't be understood, you are every-thing that is woman. And I love everything of you that I see: I love you in everything … It doesn't matter if I don't understand. Yet I feel that *this* isn't right. I'm asking you not to see the prince again. Have nothing more to do with him. Cut him dead … That dinner yesterday was torture … "

"You poor thing," she said softly and filled his glass from their flask. "But why?"

"Why? Why? You're demeaning yourself."

"I'm not that exalted … No, now *I* want to speak. I'm not on a pedestal. Just because I have a few modern ideas, and a few others that are more liberal than those of the mass of women? Apart from that I'm an ordinary woman. If a man is jovial and witty, it amuses me. No, Duco, I'm speaking. I don't find the prince a blackguard, I think maybe he's conceited, but I think he's jovial and witty. You know that I'm very fond of you too, but you're neither cheerful nor witty. You're much more. I won't even compare *il nostro Gilio* with you … I don't want to say any-thing more about you, otherwise you'll get pedantic. But you're not cheerful or witty. And my poor nature some-times needs those things. What is there in my life? Nothing but you, only you. I am very happy to have your friendship, I am happy to have met you. But why can't I be cheerful occasionally. Really, there's a light-hearted side to me, frivolous even … Must I fight against it? Is it bad? Tell me, Duco, am I bad?"

He gave a melancholy smile, a moist sheen lay across his eyes and he did not answer.

"I can fight, if I have to," she continued. "But is this something to fight against? It's a moment's froth. Nothing more. I've forgotten about it instantly. I've forgotten about the prince instantly. And you I don't forget."

He looked at her and beamed.

"Do you understand? Do you feel that I don't flirt and play the coquette with you? Hold my hand, don't be angry any more … "

She stretched out her hand to him across the table and he squeezed her fingers.

"Cornélie," he continued softly. "Yes, I feel that you are genuine. Cornélie, marry me."

She looked earnestly straight ahead, dropped her head a little and stared straight in front of her. They were no longer eating. The two Italians got up, said goodbye and left. They were alone. The waiter had put out some fruit for them and withdrawn.

They were both silent for a moment. Then she spoke in a very soft voice and with such an air of tender melancholy that he could have burst into sobs of adoration.

"Of course I knew you would ask me that one day. It was in the nature of things. A great friendship like ours led naturally to that question. But it's impossible, my dear Duco … It's impossible, my dear boy … I have my ideas … but it's not that. I'm against marriage … but it's not that. In some cases a woman betrays all her ideals in a single instant … What is it then … ?"

She stared wide-eyed, brushed her forehead, as if she could not see clearly … Still, she continued:

"The thing is … that I'm afraid of marriage. I've known it, I know what it is … I can see my husband clearly in front of me right now. I can see that habit, that drudgery in front of me, in which all nuance is erased. That's what marriage is: habit, drudgery. And now I'll tell you frankly: I think marriage is disgusting. I think that habit is disgusting. I think passion is beautiful, but marriage isn't passion. Passion can be noble, and superhuman, but marriage is a human institution of petty human morality and calculation … And I've become afraid of such wise moral bonds. I have promised myself—and I think I shall keep that promise—never to marry again. My whole nature has become unsuitable. I am no longer the young girl from The Hague with her soirées and dinners, on the look-out for a husband, together with her parents … My love for *him* was passion! And in my marriage he wanted to bridle that passion till it became drudgery and habit. I rose up … Don't let me talk about it. Passion is too short-lived to fill a marriage … Respect afterwards, etcetera? There's no need to get married for that. I can respect, even unmarried. Of course, there is the question of children, there *are* all kinds of difficulties … I can't think that through now. I just feel now, very seriously and calmly, that *I* am unsuited to marriage, and never want to marry again. I wouldn't make you happy … Don't be sad, Duco. I love you, you are dear to me. And perhaps … I've met you at the right moment. If I had met you earlier in my

Hague days ... you would certainly have been too high for me to aspire to. I wouldn't have come to love you. Now I can understand you, respect you and look up to you. I'm saying this to you quite simply, that I love you and look up to you, look up to you, for all your softness, in a way that I never looked up to my husband, however much he asserted his masculine rights. And you must believe, with great firmness, that I am telling the truth. Flirting ... is something I do only with Gilio ... "

He looked at her through his silent tears. He got up, called the waiter, paid absent-mindedly, while his eyes were swimming and gleaming. They went out and she hailed a carriage and gave the address of Villa Doria-Pamphili. She remembered that the gardens were open. They drove there in silence, overwhelmed by their thoughts of the future, which opened trembling before them. Sometimes he took deep breaths and shivered all over. Once she squeezed his hand with great emotion. They got out at the gate of the villa, and walked together along its majestic avenues. Down below lay Rome, and they suddenly saw St Peter's. But they did not talk, and she suddenly sat down on an antique bench and in her weakness began softly weeping. He put his arm round her and consoled her. She dried her tears, smiled and embraced him, returned his kiss ... Dusk started to fall and they went back. He gave the address of his studio. She followed him there. And she gave herself to him, in the fullness of her honesty and truth, and with a love so powerful and overwhelming that she thought she would faint in his arms.

XXV

THEY DID NOT CHANGE their life. Duco, though, after a scene with his mother, no longer slept at Belloni, but in a box room, adjoining his studio, which at first had been full of suitcases and junk. Cornélie regretted the scene, since she had always liked Mrs Van der Staal and the girls. But she felt a surge of pride, and despised Mrs Van der Staal for being unable to understand Duco or her. Still, she would have liked to prevent the estrangement. At her suggestion Duco visited his mother again, but she remained cool and rejected him. After that Cornélie and Duco went to Naples. They were not running away, they just did it; Cornélie told Urania and the prince that she was going to Naples for a while and that Van der Staal might follow her. She did not know Naples and would very much appreciate it if Van der Staal could be her guide in and around the city. Cornélie kept on her rooms in Rome. And they spent two weeks of mindless, pure, intense happiness. Their love burgeoned in the golden southern skies of Naples, by the blue waves of Amalfi, Sorrento, Capri and Castellammare, simple, irresistible and calm. They glided gradually along the purple thread of their lives, hand in hand they followed the lines that had merged into a single path, oblivious to people's laws and ideas, and their attitude was so lofty that their situation was not something shameless, although in themselves they despised the world. But their happiness softened all that pride in their soaring souls, as if it were strewing blossoms around them. They were living as if in a dream, at first among the marbles of the museum, later on the flower-covered cliffs of Amalfi, on the beach at Capri, or on the terrace of the hotel in Sorrento: the rush of the sea at their feet; yonder, in a pearly haze, vaguely white, like smudged chalk, Castellammare and Naples and the ghost of Vesuvius, with its hazy plume of smoke.

They kept away from everyone, from all people, all tourists: they ate at a small table and it was generally thought that they were newly-weds. Those who looked them up in the guest book saw their two names and commented in whispers. But they did not hear, they did not see, they were living their dream, looking into each other's eyes or at the opal sky, the pearly sea, and the hazy white mountains in the distance, with the towns set in them like chalk patches.

When they had almost run out of money they smiled and returned to Rome and lived there as they had before; she in her rooms, he in his studio, and they had their meals together. But they pursued their dream among the ruins on the Via Appia, around Frascati: beyond the Ponte Molle, on the slopes of Monte Mario and in the gardens of the villas, among the statues and paintings, mixing their happiness with the atmosphere of Rome: he interweaving his new love with his love of Rome, she falling in love with Rome for his sake. And that enchantment created a kind of halo around them, so that they did not see ordinary life and did not meet ordinary people.

Finally, one afternoon, Urania found them both at home, in Cornélie's room, with the fire lit, she staring smiling into the fire, he sitting at her feet, and she with her arm round his neck. And they were obviously giving so little thought to anything but their own love, that neither of them heard the knock, and both suddenly saw her standing in front of them, as an unsuspected reality. Their dream was over for that day. Urania laughed, Cornélie laughed, and Duco pulled up an armchair. And Urania, happy, beautiful, dazzling, told them that she was engaged. Where on earth had the two of them got to? she asked inquisitively. She was engaged now. She had already been to San Stefano and had seen the old prince. And everything was beautiful, good, and sweet: the old castle 'a dear old house', the old man 'a dear old man'. She saw everything through the glittering curtain of her forthcoming title of princess. The date of the wedding had been set, before Easter, so in just over three months. The ceremony was to be in San Carlo, with all the lustre of a great wedding. Her father was coming over for the occasion with her youngest brother. She was obviously apprehensive about their coming. And she couldn't stop talking; she told them a thousand details about her trousseau, with which the *marchesa* was helping her. They were to live in Nice, in a large apartment. She was crazy about Nice: it was a good idea of Gilio's. And in passing, suddenly remembering, she told them that she had become a Catholic. What a burden! But the *monsignori* were looking after everything, she was being guided by them. And the Pope was to receive her in a private audience, together with Gilio … The problem was her audience outfit, black of course, but velvet or satin? What did Cornélie recommend? She had such good taste. And the black lace veil fastened with diamonds … Tomorrow she was going to Nice with the *marchesa* and Gilio, to see their apartment …

When she left, asking Cornélie to call and admire her trousseau, Cornélie said with a smile:

"She's happy … Happiness means something different to everyone … A trousseau and a title wouldn't make me happy."

"Those are the little people," he said, "whose paths occasionally cross ours. I prefer to avoid them … "

And they did not say, though they both thought it— their fingers intertwined, her eyes gazing into his—that *they* were happy too, but in a higher, nobler way; and pride swelled in them: and as if in a vision they saw the line of their life winding up a steep hillside, and happiness strewed blossoms and holding their proud heads in the blizzard of blossoms, with the smile and eyes of love, they continued onward in their dream, removed from humanity and reality.

XXVI

THE MONTHS PASSED BY in a dream. And their love caused such a summer to blossom in them, that she ripened in beauty, and he in talent; the pride in them burst outward as self-confidence: in her case blossoming, in his creative energy; her languid charm was transformed into proud slenderness; her form swelled into rounded fullness; a gleam shone in her eyes, happiness around her mouth—his hands trembled with nervous emotion when he took up his brushes, and the skies of Italy created vaulted domes before his eyes like firmaments of love and passionate colour. He created and completed a series of watercolours: hazy evocations of a dream atmosphere, reminiscent of the noblest work of Turner: monuments to nature made of nothing but haze: all the milky blue and pearly mistiness of the Bay of Naples, like a goblet full of light, where a turquoise melts into water—and he sent them to Holland, to London, and he had suddenly found his vocation, his work and his fame: courage, strength, goal and triumph.

She also enjoyed a degree of success with her article: it was reviewed, attacked; her name was mentioned. But she felt a certain indifference when she read her name involved in the Women's Movement. She shared rather in his life of observation and emotion and often contributed amid the haziness of his vision, in the excessive haze of his tinted dream, a glow of light, an enclosing horizon, a chink of reality, which gave substance to the mistiness of his ideal. With him she learned to distinguish and feel nature, art, the whole of Rome, and when a wave of symbolism came over him, she followed him completely. He drafted a great sketch of a theory of women ascending the climbing winding lifeline: they seemed to be moving from a collapsing city of antiquity, whose columns, linked by the occasional architrave, were wrapped in a shimmer of dusk; they seemed to be freeing themselves from the shadow of the ruin, which on the horizon was already dissolving in the night of oblivion—and they pushed forward, hailing each other with cries, waving to each other with a great outstretching of hands, above them a waving swirl of banners and blazons; with muscular arms they grasped hammers and pickaxes, and the throng moved upwards, along the line, to where the light became whiter and whiter, to where in a haze of light one could discern in the far distance a new city, whose iron buildings shone tall in the white shimmering light in the distance like central stations and Eiffel Towers with a reflection of glass arches and glass roofs, and high in the sky the musical bars of sound and conductivity …

And so the influences of each worked on the other's soul, so that *she* learned to see and he learned to think; that she *saw* beauty, art, nature, haze and emotion and no longer conceived, but felt; that *he* saw as in his sketch—with its very vague modern city of glass and iron—a modern city rising from his dream haze of Rome's past, and in accordance with his own nature and disposition, thought about a modern question. She learned mainly to see and think as a woman in love, with the eyes and heart of the man she loved: he worked out the question in plastic terms. But whatever imperfections there were in the absolute nature of their new spheres of thought and feeling, the interaction that their love engendered brought them a happiness so great, so unified, that at the moment they could not comprehend or contemplate it, that it was almost like a state of ecstasy, a vague unreality in which they dreamed—though it was pure truth and tangible reality. The way they thought, felt and lived was an ideal of reality: ideally entered and achieved along the gradual line of their lives, along the golden thread of their love, and they scarcely registered or comprehended it, since ordinary life still clung to them. But only to an unavoidably small extent. They lived separately, but she would come to see him in the morning and would find him in front of his sketch, and would sit next to him, lean her head on his shoulder, and they would work it out together. He sketched his figures of the theory of woman separately, and he searched for the features and the modelling of the forms: some had the mongoloid quality of the angel of the Annunciation of Memmi; others the slenderness of Cornélie and her later robust, fuller figure; he searched for the folds: in the folds of their *peplos* robes the women freed themselves from the violet dusk of the ruined city and further on they changed their robes as a masquerade of the centuries: the noble lady's dress with a train, the veils of the sultans, the woollen dresses of cleaning women, the wimple of the sisters of mercy—with the clothing becoming more modern as the wearer embodied a more modern age … And in that grouping the drawing had such an ethereal and sober quality, the transition from falling drapery to practical tight-fitting clothes was so gradual, that Cornélie could scarcely detect a transition and seemed to see a single style, a single style of dress, though every silhouette was dressed in a different cut and material, with a different line … In the drawing there was a purity recalling the Old Masters, a purity of outline, but modern—highly strung and morbid—and yet without a conventional ideal of symbolic bodily shapes; there was a Raphael-like harmony in the grouping; in the watercolour tint of the first studies the haze of Italy: the ruined city glimmered as she saw the Forum glimmer; the city of glass and iron glittered with its Crystal Palace-like construction, out of a white apotheosis of light, as he had seen around Naples from Sorrento. She felt that he was engaged on a great work and had never been so vitally involved in anything as she was now in his concept and his sketches. She sat still and silent behind him and followed his drawing of the swirling banners and winding blazons, and she held her breath when she saw how with a few smudges of white and dabs of light—as if he had light on his palette—he evoked the dreamlike glass city on the horizon. Then he would ask her something about a figure, put his arm round her waist, pull her towards him, and they would peer endlessly and work out line and concept, till evening fell, the evening chill pervaded the workplace and they slowly got up. They would go out and the Corso would bring them back to real life: sitting silently at Argano's, they would survey the bustle; and in their little restaurant, looking deep into each other's eyes, they would eat their simple meal, so visibly harmoniously happy that the Italians, the two who were always at the table furthest from them at the same time, smiled as they greeted them.

149

XXVII

And he felt suffused with energy: so many thoughts kept looming in his mind that he was constantly finding new motifs and symbolising them in another figure. He sketched, life-size, a woman walking, with that mixture of child, woman and goddess that characterised his figures—and she followed a gradually descending line into gloomy depths without seeing or understanding; her staring eyes were drawn magnetically towards the abyss: indistinct hands hovered around her like a cloud and gently pushed and guided; above, on high rocks, other figures with harps, in bright light, called to her, but she went down into the depths, impelled by the hands; in the abyss strange purple orchids blossomed, like amorous mouths …

One morning when Cornélie arrived in his studio, he had suddenly sketched this idea. It was a surprise to her, as he had not talked about it: the idea had arisen suddenly; putting it down on paper, quickly and spontaneously, had taken him less than an hour. He almost apologised to her for it, when he saw her surprise. She found it beautiful, but spine-chilling and preferred *Banners*, the large watercolour, the procession of women advancing towards the fight for life …

And to please her he put the descending woman aside and worked only on the completion of the militant women. But new ideas kept disturbing his work and in her absence he sketched a new symbol, until the sketches piled up and were strewn everywhere. She put them away in portfolios; she removed them from the easel and the shelf; she stopped him from wandering too far from *Banners*, and this was the only work that he completed.

So their life seemed to want to move gently on, along a charming line, in a single golden direction, while his symbols flowered to the side, while the azure of their love was like the firmament above, but she pruned the overabundance of flowers and only *Banners* waved above their path, in the firmament of their ecstasy, just as they waved above the militant women …

There was only one diversion: the wedding of the prince and Urania: a dinner, a ball and the ceremony in San Carlo, in the presence of the entire Roman aristocracy, though they welcomed the rich American with some reserve. But when the Prince and Princess of Forte-Braccio left for Nice, that was the end of distractions and the days again glided past along the same charming golden line. Cornélie had only one unpleasant memory: her encounter during the festivities with Mrs Van der Staal, who had cut her dead, turned her back on her and given her to understand that all friendship between them was over. She had resigned herself; she had understood how difficult it was—even if Mrs Van der Staal had been willing to talk to her—to explain her own proud ideas of freedom, independence and happiness to a woman like that set fast in her social and worldly conventions. And she had also snubbed the girls, sensing that that was what Mrs Van der Staal wanted. She was not angry about this, or offended; she could understand this attitude in Duco's mother: it simply saddened her a little, because she liked

Mrs Van der Staal, and she liked the two girls … But she understood completely: it must be that Mrs Van der Staal knew, or suspected everything. Duco's mother could not act otherwise, although the prince and Urania, out of friendship, denied any relationship between Duco and her, Cornélie—even though the Roman world treated them simply as friends, acquaintances, compatriots— whatever people whispered behind their fans. But the festivities were now over, they had passed that crossroad with the world and people: now their gold course undulated softly and smoothly before them …

It was then that Cornélie, who had no thought of The Hague, received a letter from home. The letter was from her father and was several pages long, which surprised her, since he never wrote. What she read alarmed her greatly, but did not entirely discourage her, perhaps because she did not appreciate the full weight of her father's news. He begged her for forgiveness. He had been in financial difficulties for quite some time. He had lost a great deal. They had to move, to a smaller house. The mood at home was bitter; mama was crying all day, the sisters squabbling; the family was giving advice; their friends were being unpleasant. And he begged her forgiveness. He had speculated and lost. And he had also lost her small amount of capital that he was administering, the legacy from her godmother. He asked her not to blame him too much. It might have turned out differently and then he would have been three times as rich. He admitted that he had acted wrongly—but he was still her father and he asked her, his child, to forgive him and return.

She was badly shaken at first, but soon regained her calm. She was in too happy a mood of harmonious existence for her father's news to destroy it. She received the letter in bed, and stayed there for a little, thought it over, then got dressed, ate as usual and went to Duco. He received her enthusiastically and showed her three new sketches … She reproached him gently for allowing himself to be distracted too easily from his main idea, and said that these digressions would drain his energy and stamina. She urged him in particular to keep working on *Banners*. And she looked intently at the great watercolour, at the ancient, crumbling Forum-like city; the procession of the women towards the Metropolis of the Future, up there in the days of light … And suddenly it dawned on her that her past too had collapsed and that the crumbling arches were hanging threateningly over her head. She gave him her father's letter to read. He read it twice, looked at her in bewilderment, and asked what she was going to do. She said that she had already thought about it, but that for the moment all she was sure of was what she would do immediately. Give up her rooms and move in with him in his studio. She had just enough to pay for her rooms. But then she would be penniless. Completely penniless. She had never wanted alimony from her husband. She was just waiting for the fee from her article. He immediately put out his hands to her, drew her to him, kissed her and said that he had immediately had the same idea. Move in with him. Live with him. He had enough: a trifling inheritance from his father; he was earning on top of that: he would have enough for both of them. And they laughed and kissed and looked around the studio.

Duco slept in a small adjoining cubicle, rather like a long built-in wardrobe. And they looked round to see what they could do. Cornélie had the answer: here, drape a curtain over a cord and put the bed and washbasin behind it. That was all she needed. Just that little alcove; otherwise Duco would not have proper light. They were very cheerful and thought it was a very cosy idea. They immediately went out, bought an iron bed, a washstand, and hung up the curtain themselves. Then they both went to pack cases in Via dei Serpenti—and dined in the *osteria*. Cornélie suggested eating at home occasionally, as it was cheaper … When they got home she was delighted that her construction took up so little space, scarcely a couple of square metres, with the little bed behind it. They were very merry that evening. Their bohemian existence amused them. They were in Italy, the land of sunshine, beauty and *lazzaroni*, beggars dreaming on the steps of cathedrals, and they felt an affinity with that sunny poverty. They were happy, they didn't need anything. They would live on nothing. On very little, at least. They faced the future smiling and lucid. They were closer now, they were living closer together. They loved each other and were happy, in a land of beauty, in an ideal world of symbols and life-embracing art.

The following morning he worked hard, without a word, lost in his dream, his work, and she too, silent, content, happy, carefully checked her blouses and skirts, and worked out that she would not need anything for a whole year, and that her old clothes were sufficient for their life of happiness and simplicity.

And she wrote a very short reply to her father, saying

that she forgave him, felt sympathy for them all, but was not returning to The Hague. She would support herself, by writing. Italy was cheap. That was all she wrote. She did not mention Duco. She took leave of her family, in her mind and in life. She had not found any sympathy among any of them during her sad marriage, or during the agony of her divorce, and now she in turn felt no warmth. And her happiness made her one-sided and self-ish. She wanted nothing but Duco, nothing but their togetherness and harmony. He worked and smiled at her now and then as she lay on the sofa and reflected. She looked at the women marching to battle; she too would not be able to remain lying on the sofa, she too would have to fight. She had a presentiment that she would have to fight: for him. He was now working in the art business, but if that, after a positive result, after a personal and public success, were to slacken off—for a moment—it would be normal and logical and *she* would have to fight. He was all that was noble in both their lives, his art could not support her. His fortune amounted to almost nothing. She would like to work and earn money for both of them, so that he could hold fast to the pure principles of his art. But how, how was one to fight, work, work for their lives and for a living? What could she do? Write? It paid so little. What else? A slight melancholy enveloped her, be-cause there was so little she could do. She had some minor talents and skills: she had a good style, she sang, played the piano, she could make a blouse and she knew a little about cooking, She would cook herself now and then and sew her own clothes. But all of that was so petty, so little. Fight, work? How? Well, she would do what she could. And suddenly she picked up a Baedeker, leafed through it and sat down at Duco's desk, at which she also wrote. And she thought for a moment and began an article. A travel letter for a magazine on the area around Naples: that was easier than starting immediately on Rome. And in the studio, filled with the slight heat of a stove, as it was north-facing and chilly, it became absolutely still: only her pen scratched occasionally, or he rummaged among his crayons and pencils. She wrote a few pages but could not find an ending ... Then she got up and he turned and smiled at her: his smile of affectionate happiness ...

And she read out what she had written to him. It was not the style of her pamphlet. It was not invective: it was a sweet travel letter ...

He quite liked it, but did not think it anything special ... But it didn't have to be, she said defensively. And he hugged her, for her hard work and courage. It rained that day and they did not go out for their lunch; she had some eggs and tomatoes and made an omelette on a paraffin stove. They drank only water and ate lots of bread with it. And while the rain lashed the large, uncurtained studio window, they enjoyed their meal, like two birds huddling close together to avoid getting wet.

XXVIII

IT WAS A COUPLE OF MONTHS after Easter: the spring days of May. The flood of tourists had subsided immediately after the great church festivals and Rome was already very hot and became very quiet. One morning, as Cornélie was crossing Piazza di Spagna, where the sunshine flowed along the creamy yellow façade of Trinità de' Monti, down the monumental staircase, where only a few beggars and a last flower boy sat dreamily blinking in a corner, she saw the prince coming towards her. He greeted her with a happy smile and hastened toward her.

"I am so happy to meet you. I'm in Rome for a few days and I have to go to San Stefano to see my father on business. Such a nuisance, business, especially at this time. Urania is in Nice. But it's hot, we're going away. We've just returned from a trip through the Mediterranean. Four weeks on a friend's yacht. It was wonderful! Why haven't you come to see us in Nice, as Urania asked you in her letters?"

"I really couldn't come … "

"I called on you at Via dei Serpenti yesterday. But I was told you had moved … "

He looked at her with a mocking laugh in his small, sparkling eyes. She said nothing.

"I did not wish to be indiscreet," he concluded meaningfully … "Where are you going?"

"I have to go to the post office."

"I have nothing to do. May I walk with you? Don't you find it too hot to walk?"

"Oh no, I like the heat. Of course you may. How is Urania?"

"Fine, excellent. She's excellent. She's marvellous, simply marvellous. I would never have thought it. I would never have dared hope it. She cuts a brilliant figure. As far as that is concerned, I have no regrets about my marriage. But apart from that, what a disappointment, what deception. *Gesù mio!*"

"Why?"

"You guessed, didn't you—how I still have no idea—the price tag I carried? Not five, but ten million. Oh, *signora mia*, the deceit! You saw my father-in-law at our wedding. What a Yankee, what a stocking-salesman and what a businessman! We can't cope with that. Not I, not my father, and not the *marchesa*. First promises, contracts, oh yes. But then haggling about this, haggling about that. We don't know how to do that. I couldn't. Nor could papa. Only auntie knew how to haggle. But she was no match for the stocking-salesman. She hadn't learnt how in all those years of running a *pensione*. Ten million? Five million? Not even three million! But anyway we've received about that much, plus lots of promises, for our children's children, when everyone's dead. Oh, *signora, signora*, I was richer before I was married! It's true I had debts then, and now I don't. But Urania is so thrifty, so practical. I would never have thought it … It's been a blow to everyone, papa, auntie, the *monsignori*. You should see them together. They could scratch each other's eyes out … Papa almost had a stroke; auntie came to blows with the *monsignori*.

Oh, *signora*, *signora*, I don't like such things. I'm a victim. For whole winters they fished with me as bait. But I didn't want to cooperate, I resisted: I didn't let the fish bite. And now it has finally happened. Less than three million. Lire, not dollars. I was so stupid that at first I thought it would be dollars. And Urania is so thrifty. She gives me my pocket money. She manages everything, she does everything. She knows exactly how much I lose at the club. No, you're laughing, but it's sad. You see, sometimes I could just cry! And then she has the oddest ideas. For example, we have our apartment in Nice now and we're keeping on my rooms in Palazzo Ruspoli, as a *pied-à-terre* in Rome. It's enough: we don't go to Rome much anyway, because we are 'black' and Urania finds that boring. In the summers we had planned to go somewhere or other, to a seaside resort. Exactly, that had been firmly agreed. But now Urania suddenly takes it into her head that she wants San Stefano as a summer residence! San Stefano!!! I ask you. I can't stand it there. It's true it's high up, and cool: the climate is pleasant—fresh mountain air. But I need more to live than mountain air. I need more than that. Oh, you wouldn't recognise Urania. She's so stubborn sometimes. It's now been irrevocably decided: San Stefano in the summers. And the worst thing is that by doing this she's stolen papa's heart. So I've lost out. It's two against one. And the worst thing of all is … that we must be very economical so that we can do up San Stefano. It's a famous historic site but very run down. What do you expect; we've never had much luck. Since a Forte-Braccio was once pope … our star waned and we were never lucky again. San Stefano is a model of grandeur in

159

decline. You should see it. Being economical to do up San Stefano! That's now Urania's ambition. She is determined to do justice to our ancestral home. Anyway, she has won over my father and he has recovered from his stroke. But do you understand now why *il povero Gilio* is poorer than before he had shares in a stocking factory in Chicago?"

The flood of words was unstoppable. He was deeply unhappy, small, chastened, tamed, defeated, devastated and needed to get things off his chest. They had already walked past the post office and were now retracing their steps. He was looking for sympathy from Cornélie, and he found it in the smiling attention with which she listened to his laments. She replied that it spoke well of Urania that she had a feeling for San Stefano.

"Oh, yes," he conceded humbly. "She is very good. I would never have thought it. She's a princess to her fingertips. It's wonderful. But as for the ten million, the dream has gone! But my goodness, how well you look! You are more beautiful every time I see you. Do you know that you are a very beautiful woman? You must be very happy. You are an exceptional woman, I've said so all along. I don't understand you … Can I be frank? Are we good friends? I don't understand you. What you have just done, I find so terrible … It is unheard of in our world."

"Your world is not mine, prince."

"All right, but I expect your world takes the same view. And the calm way, the pride, the happiness with which you calmly do … what you feel like. I find it awesome. I'm amazed … Yet … it's a shame. In my world people are very easy-going … But *that* is beyond the pale!"

"Prince, once again, I have no world. My world is my own circle."

"I don't understand … Tell me, how am I to tell Urania? Because I'd be delighted if you would visit us at San Stefano. Oh, come on, come, come and keep us company. I beg you. Have pity, do a good deed … But first tell me how I am to break it to Urania … "

She laughed. "What?"

"What they told me at Via dei Serpenti: that from now on your address was: Via del Babuino, Mr Van der Staal's studio … "

Smiling, she looked at him almost pityingly.

"It is too difficult for you to tell her," she replied, slightly condescendingly. "I'll write to Urania myself to tell her and explain my behaviour to her."

He was obviously relieved.

"That's wonderful, excellent! And … will you be coming to San Stefano?"

"No, I can't, really."

"Why not?"

"I can no longer venture into the circles you live in, after my change of address," she said, half-laughing, half-serious.

He shrugged his shoulders.

"Listen," he said. "You know our Roman society. Provided certain conventions are observed … everything is permitted."

"Exactly, but it's just those conventions that I am not observing … "

"Then that is very wrong of you. Believe me, I'm saying this as your friend."

161

"I live according to my own laws and do not ask you to enter my world."

He folded his hands.

"Yes, yes, I know that, you are a 'new woman'. You are a law unto yourself. But I beg you, have pity on me. Have mercy on me. Come to San Stefano."

She sensed a seductive edge in his voice and so said:

"Prince, even if it accorded with the conventions of your world ... I would still not want to. I don't want to leave Van der Staal."

"You come first and he can come later. Urania would like to ask his advice on a number of artistic matters to do with her 'refurbishment' of San Stefano. We have many paintings there. From antiquity too. Come on, do it. I'm going to San Stefano tomorrow. Urania will join me in a week. I shall suggest she asks you soon ... "

"Really, prince ... I can't at such short notice ... "

"Why not?"

She looked at him for a long time.

"Shall I be very frank?"

"Of course."

They had already passed the post office a number of times. The street was eerily quiet, and there were no pedestrians. He looked at her quizzically.

"Well then," she said, "we are in serious financial difficulties. At the moment we have nothing. I have lost my capital and the little I have earned from writing an article has gone. Duco works hard, but he is engaged on a large-scale work and is earning nothing. He is expecting money in a few months. But at the moment we have nothing. Nothing at all. That's why I went down to a shop by the

Tiber this morning to ask how much the dealer would give for a couple of antique paintings that Duco wants to sell. He is reluctant to part with them. But there's no alternative. So you see that I cannot come. I would not like to leave him, and than I have no money for the journey or a decent wardrobe ... "

He looked at her. He had first been struck by her burgeoning beauty; he was now struck by the fact that her skirt was rather worn, her blouse was no longer fresh, although she was wearing a couple of roses in her belt.

"*Gesù mio!*" he exclaimed. "And you tell me that so calmly, so serenely ... "

She smiled and shrugged her shoulders.

"What do you want me to do? Whine about it?"

"But you are a woman ... a woman worthy of respect!" he exclaimed. "How is Van der Staal coping with it?"

"He's a little depressed. He has never experienced financial problems. And it is stopping him from working with all his talent. But I hope I am some support to him in this unfortunate period. So you see, prince, that I cannot come to San Stefano."

"But why did you not write to us? Why did you not ask us for money?"

"It is very sweet of you to say that, the idea never even occurred to us."

"Too proud?"

"Too proud, yes."

"But what a situation! What can I do to help you? Can I give you a few hundred lire? I have a few hundred on me. And I shall tell Urania that I have given them to you."

"No, prince, thank you. I am very grateful, but I cannot accept."

"Not from *me*?"

"No."

"Not from Urania?"

"Not even from her."

"Why?"

"I want to earn my money and cannot accept alms."

"A fine principle. But only for now."

"I shall stick to it."

"May I say something?"

"What is it?"

"I admire you. More than that. I love you."

She made a gesture with her hand and frowned.

"Why can't I say that to you? An Italian does not keep his love hidden inside. I love you. You are more beautiful and nobler and loftier than I could ever imagine a woman ... Don't be angry: I am not asking anything of you. I'm a bad lot but at the moment I really feel something inside that you see on our old family portraits. A chance remaining atom of chivalry. I ask nothing of you. I am just saying to you, on behalf of Urania too: you can always count on us. Urania will be angry that you did not write to her."

They went to the post office and she bought a few stamps.

"There go my last few *soldi*," she said with a laugh and showed her empty purse. "We needed them for some letters to an exhibition organising committee in London. Will you walk me home?"

She suddenly saw that there were tears in his eyes.

"Accept two hundred lire from me!" he begged.

She declined with a smile.

"Are you eating at home?" he asked.

She gave him a funny look.

"Yes," she said.

He did not want to ask any more questions, for fear of offending her.

"It would be very sweet of you," he said, "if you would dine with me tonight. I'm bored. At present I have no close friends in Rome. Everyone is away. Not in the Grand-Hôtel, but in a cosy restaurant where they know me. I'll call for you at seven o'clock. Be a darling, and do it! For my sake!"

He could not hold back his tears.

"I'd be delighted," she said softly, with her smile.

They stood in the doorway of the house on Via del Babuino, where the studio was. He raised her hand to his lips, and kissed it fervently. Then he tipped his hat and left hurriedly. She slowly climbed the stairs, fighting back her emotion, before entering the studio.

XXIX

SHE FOUND DUCO lying listlessly on the sofa. He had a bad headache and she sat down beside him.

"Well?" he asked.

"The man was prepared to give eighty lire for the Memmi, he said: but he maintained that the triptych panel was not by Gentile da Fabriano; he remembered seeing the panel at your studio."

"The man's talking nonsense," he replied. "Or he's trying to get my Gentile for nothing ... Cornélie, I really can't sell them."

"Alright Duco, then we'll find some other way," she said, putting her hand on his forehead that was contorted by his headache.

"Perhaps a few smaller things, a few knick-knacks ... " he groaned.

"Perhaps ... Shall I go back again this afternoon?"

"No, no ... I'll go. But really, we can buy such things, but can never sell them.'

"No Duco," she admitted, laughing. "But yesterday I inquired what I could get for a couple of bracelets and I'll sell them this afternoon. And then we'll be able to manage for a month. But I wanted to tell you something. Do you know who I met?"

"No."

"The prince."

He frowned.

166

"I don't like that blackguard," he said.

"I've told you before, Duco: I don't think he's a black-guard. And I don't believe he is. He invited us to dinner tonight, very simply."

"No, I don't feel like it … "

She was silent. She got up, boiled water on a paraffin stove and made tea.

"My dear Duco, I rather neglected lunch. A cup of tea and a sandwich is all I can offer you. Are you very hungry?"

"No," he said evasively.

She hummed as she poured tea into an antique cup. She cut the bread and took him tea on the sofa. Then she sat next to him, also with a cup in her hand.

"Cornélie, would it be better if we had lunch in the *osteria* … ?"

Laughing, she showed him her empty purse.

"Here are the stamps," she said.

Disheartened, he flung himself on the cushions.

"My lovely man," she went on. "Don't be so down. This afternoon I'll have money again, from the bracelets. I should have sold them before. Really, Duco, it's nothing. Why didn't you work? It would have cheered you up."

"I wasn't in the mood and I've got a headache … "

She was silent for a moment. Then she said,

"The prince was angry that we hadn't written to him for help. He wanted to give me two hundred lire … "

"I hope you refused?" he said, furious.

"Of course," she said calmly. "He invited us to stay at San Stefano, where they are spending the summer. I refused that too."

"Why?"

"I wouldn't have any clothes … But you wouldn't want to go anyway, would you?"

"No," he said flatly.

She drew his head to her and stroked his forehead. A broad area of reflected afternoon light shone through the studio window from the blue sky outside and the studio seemed to be alive with dusty light, in which the silhouettes stood out with their immobile gestures and unchanging emotions. The relief embroidery on the chasubles and stoles, the purple and azure blues of Gentile's triptych panel, the mystical luxuriance of Memmi's angel in its robe of heavily creasing brocade, the golden lily stem in the fingers—were like a piled treasure house of colour and shone in that reflected light like handfuls of jewels. On the easel was the watercolour of *Banners*, fine and noble. And as they sat there on the sofa, he with his head leaning against her, both of them drinking tea, they were harmoniously happy against that background of art. And it seemed incredible that they were worrying about a few hundred lire, since he was glowing within with a jewel-like colour, and her smile was like a sheen. But his eyes were discouraged and his hand hung limply.

She went out for a little while that afternoon, but soon returned home, telling him that she had sold the bracelets and that he now need not worry. And she sang and moved cheerfully about the studio. She had bought some things: an almond cake, rusks, half a bottle of port. She had brought them home in a basket and sang as she unpacked them. Her liveliness roused him: he got up and suddenly positioned himself in front of *Banners*. He looked at the light and reckoned that he still had an hour left to work. A wave of delight rose in him as he surveyed the watercolour: there were lots of good, beautiful things in it. It had breath and delicacy; it was modern without the gimmicks of modernism: there was a thought in it and yet a purity of a line and grouping. And the colour had a calm distinction: purple and grey and white; violet and grey and white; dark, dusk, light; night, dawn, day. The day particularly, the day dawning up there on high, was full of a white, confident sun: a white certainty, in which the future became clear. But the streamers, flags and standards and banners were like a cloud, fanning out with heraldic pride over the ecstatic heads of the women fighters … He sought out his colours, sought out his brushes, and worked solidly until there was no light left. And he sat down beside her, happy, content, In the twilight they drank some of the port and ate some of the cake. He had an appetite, he said: he was hungry …

At seven there was a knock at the door. He started, went to the door, and the prince came in. Duco's forehead clouded, but the prince saw nothing in the darkening studio, Cornélie lit a lamp.

"*Scusi*, prince," she said. "I'm embarrassed to say that Duco doesn't feel like going out—he's been working and is tired—I had no one to take a message to you to say we could not accept your invitation."

"But you can't be serious! I had so looked forward to seeing you both. What else am I to do with my evening … ?"

And with his torrent of words, his complaints of a spoiled child wanting its own way, he began to persuade the reluctant, stiff Duco. Duco finally got up, shrugged his shoulders, smiled pityingly, almost insultingly, but gave way. But he could not suppress his feeling of reluctance; his jealousy at the swift repartee of Cornélie and the prince was still intense, like a pain. In the restaurant he was silent at first. Still, he made an effort to join in the conversation, remembering what Cornélie had said to him on that momentous day in the *osteria*: that she loved *him*, Duco; that she looked up to him, that she did not even compare the prince with him; but … that he was not cheerful and witty … And feeling his superiority because of that memory, despite his jealousy he smiled and rather talked down to the prince and tolerated his charm and flirtatiousness, because it amused Cornélie, that quick wordplay and those snappy sentences succeeding each other like the dialogue in a French play.

XXX

THE NEXT DAY the prince was due to go to San Stefano and early in the morning Cornélie wrote him the following note:

Dear Prince,
I come to you with a request. Yesterday morning you were kind enough to offer me your help. At the time I felt able to refuse your friendly offer. But I hope that you will not find it terribly whimsical if today I turn to you to ask you to lend me what you were prepared to offer yesterday.

Lend me two hundred lire. I hope to be able to return them to you as soon as possible. Of course you need not keep it secret from Urania, but do not let Duco know about it. Yesterday I tried to sell my bracelets, but only sold one, for very little. The goldsmith was offering too low a price, but I was forced to part with one for forty lire, as I hadn't a sou! And now I am appealing to your friendship and asking you to put the two hundred lire in an envelope and allowing me to collect them PERSONALLY from the concierge. Please accept my sincerest thanks in advance.

What an entertaining evening you provided us with yesterday. An hour or two of friendly chat over an excellent dinner does me the world of good. However happy I feel, our present situation with its money worries sometimes oppresses me, though I keep up appearances for Duco's sake. Fretting about money disturbs his work and undermines his energy. That is why I talk to him as little as possible about it, and so ask you expressly to keep this small secret from him.

CORNÉLIE DE RETZ

When she went out later that morning she headed immediately for Palazzo Ruspoli.

"Has his highness already left?"

The concierge bowed respectfully, familiarly.

"An hour ago, *signora*. His Excellency left behind with me a letter and a package, to give to you if you should call. Allow me to fetch them … "

He went and soon returned and handed Cornélie the package and letter. She went off down a side street of the Corso, opened the envelope and among a number of banknotes found a letter:

My Dear Madam,

I am so happy that you turned to me and I'm sure Urania will approve. I believe I am acting entirely in her spirit in sending you not two hundred, but a thousand lire, with the most humble request that you accept them and keep them for as long as you choose. Since I do not of course dare say: accept them as a gift. Still, I am bold enough to send you a souvenir. For when I read that you had felt obliged to sell your bracelet, the news pained me so terribly that without a second thought I dropped into Marchesini's and as best I could chose a bracelet, which I beg you on my knees to accept. You must not refuse your friend this. Keep my bracelet secret from both Urania and Van der Staal.

Once again accept my deepest thanks for deigning to accept my help and rest assured that I greatly appreciate this token of your favour.

Your very humble servant,
VIRGILIO DI F B

Cornélie opened the package: in a velvet case she saw a bracelet in Etruscan style: a slim gold band set with pearls and sapphires.

XXXI

IN THE HEAT OF MAY the spacious studio, facing north, was cool, while the city outside was scorching. Duco and Cornélie did not go out before nightfall when they started thinking about going for dinner somewhere. Rome was quiet: Roman society was away, the tourists had gone. They saw no one and their days flowed past. He worked hard; *Banners* was finished: the two of them, arms around each other's waists, her head on his shoulder, sat in front of it, with swelling, smiling pride in those final days before the watercolour was to be sent to the International Exhibition in Knightsbridge, London. There had never been such pure harmony in their feelings for each other, such a unity of like-mindedness as now when his great project was finished. He felt that he had never done such noble work, so sure and unhesitating, with such strength in himself and yet so tender, and he was grateful to her. He admitted to her that he would never have been able to work in this way if she had not shared his thoughts and feelings in the hours spent reflecting, the hours spent staring at the procession, the women's theory that developed from the night that crumbled down in columns to the City of nothing but new whiteness and glowing glass buildings. His soul was at rest now that he had done such great and noble work. And both of them felt pride: pride in their lives, in their independence, in that work of lofty and distinguished art. In their happiness there was a large element of conceit and of looking down at people, the crowd, the world. Particularly for him. In her there was something quieter and more humble, though outwardly she showed herself as proud as he was. Her article on the Social Situation of the Divorced Woman had appeared as a pamphlet and had been a success. Her name was applauded among progressive women. But what she had done did not make her as proud as Duco's art made her, and proud of him, and proud of their life and happiness.

As she read the reviews of her pamphlet in Dutch newspapers and magazines—often disagreeing with her, but never dismissive, and always acknowledging her authority to speak out on this matter—as she re-read her pamphlet, a doubt rose in her about her own conviction. She felt how difficult it is to be pure in fighting for a cause, the way those symbolic women, there in the watercolour, went into battle. She felt she had written fresh from her own suffering, her own experience, and solely from her own suffering and experience; she realised that she had generalised her own feeling about life and suffering, but without a deeper vision of the core of things; not out of pure conviction, but rather out of bitterness and anger; not from reflection, but from sad dreaming about her own fate: not out of love for women, but rather out of petty hate for society. And she remembered Duco's original silence; his silent disapproval, his intuitive feeling that the source of her inspiration was not pure, but full of the bitterness and murkiness of her own experience. Now she respected that intuition; now she realised his true purity; now she felt him—because of his art—to be exalted, noble, without ulterior motives in his actions, creating beauty for its own sake. But she also felt that she had roused him to this. That was her pride and happiness and she loved him even more deeply. But she was humble about herself. She felt her womanly nature, which prevented her from going on fighting for the goal of Women. And again she thought of her upbringing, her husband, their short but unhappy married life … and she thought of the prince. She felt herself to be so many people, and would have liked to be one. She lurched from contradiction to contradiction and admitted to herself: she did not know herself. It created a dusky melancholy in the days of her happiness …

The prince … Had she not asked him with only apparent pride not to tell Urania that she was living with Duco, because she would tell her herself? In fact she was afraid of Urania's opinion … She was annoyed by the dishonesties of petty everyday life: she called the intersection of her line and those of other, petty people: petty everyday life. Why when she came to such an intersection did she feel as if by instinct that honesty was not always sensible? Where were her pride and self-confidence—not apparent, but real—the moment she was afraid of Urania's criticism, the moment she feared that the criticism could harm her in some way? And why did she not mention Virgilio's bracelet to Duco? She did not tell him about the thousand lire, since she knew that money matters oppressed him, and that he did not want to borrow from the prince. Because if he got to know of this he would not be able to work with his usual energy and gusto and concentration … As it was he had worked untroubled and her silence had been for a noble aim. But why did she not mention Gilio's bracelet … ?

She did not know. Several times she had had the impulse to say quite naturally: look what I was given by the prince, because I sold one bracelet … But she could not say it. Why, she did not know. Was it because of Duco's jealousy? She did not know, she did not know. She thought it would create less trouble to say nothing about the bracelet and not to wear it. In fact, she would have preferred to return it to the prince. But she thought that that would be impolite after all his kindness, after all his readiness to help her.

And Duco … thought that she had sold the bracelets for a good price, and he knew that she had received money from her publisher, for her pamphlet. He asked no further questions, and thought no more about money. They lived very simply … Still, it troubled her that he did not know, even though it had been good for his work not to know.

They were small things. Small clouds in the golden skies of their great and noble life: their life of which they were proud. And only she saw them. And when she saw his eyes from which confidence in life shone, when she heard his voice sounding so sure of his new energy and pride, and when she felt his embrace, in which she felt all his happiness in her trembling … she no longer saw the little clouds, she felt all her happiness with him trembling inside her, and she loved him so much that she could have died in his arms.

XXXII

U RANIA'S LETTER was very sweet. She wrote that they were leading a very quiet life at San Stefano with the old prince, that they had no guests because the castle was too gloomy, too run down, too isolated, but that they would be delighted if Cornélie could spend some time with them. And, she added, she would also send Mr Van der Staal an invitation. The letter was addressed to Via dei Serpenti and was forwarded to Cornélie from her previous residence. So she realised that Gilio had not mentioned her living in Duco's studio, and also realised that Urania accepted their liaison, without criticism …

The *Banner* watercolour had been sent to London and in the studio, still cool while the city was sweltering, there was a slight air of idleness and boredom, now that Duco was no longer working. And Cornélie replied to Urania that that she would be delighted to accept and promised to come in a week. She was glad that she would not find any other guests at the castle, since she had no outfits for a *vie-de-château*. But with her usual flair she rejigged her wardrobe without spending much money. It took up all her time for days and she sewed while Duco lay on the sofa smoking cigarettes. He had accepted the invitation too, for Cornélie's sake, and because the area around the lake of San Stefano appealed to him. Smiling, he promised Cornélie not to be so stiff. He would do his best to be friendly. He rather looked down on the prince. He thought him a rogue, if no longer a blackguard. He thought him a child, if not ignoble and base.

Cornélie left; he took her to the station. In the carriage she kissed him fervently and told him how much she would miss him for those few days … Would he come soon? In a week? She would be longing for him: she could not do without him. She looked deep into his eyes, which she loved. He too said how bored he would be without her. Couldn't he come any sooner, she asked. No, Urania had fixed the date …

As he helped her into the second-class carriage, she was sad to be going without him. The compartment was full, and she got the last seat. She sat between a fat farmer and an old farmer's wife: the farmer kindly helped her put her valise in the net, and asked her if she would mind if he smoked his pipe. She told him in a friendly tone that she would not. Opposite them sat two priests in worn cassocks and between their feet they had an unobtrusive brown wooden box: it was the Last Sacrament that they were taking to a dying soul.

The farmer made conversation with Cornélie and asked if she were a foreigner, English probably? The old farmer's wife offered her a mandarine.

The rest of the compartment was occupied by a bourgeois family of father, mother, a little boy and two little sisters. The slow train shook, rattled and swayed, and kept stopping. The sisters hummed. At one station a lady got off with a little girl of five, in a white dress and white ostrich feathers on her hat.

"*Oh, che belleza!*" cried the little boy. "Mama, mama,

look! Isn't she beautiful? Isn't she wonderful? *Divinamente!* Oh, mama … !"

He closed his black eyes, in love, dazzled by the five-year-old-girl in white. The parents laughed, the priests laughed, everyone smiled. But the little boy was not embarrassed.

"Era una belleza!" he repeated with conviction and looked around.

It was very hot on the train. Outside the mountains glowed white on the horizon and shimmered like a fire-reflecting opal. Close to the railway rose a line of eucalyptus trees, their leaves sickle-shaped, exuding a pungent smell. On the plain, dry and scorched, wild buffalo were grazing, lifting their black curly heads indifferently towards the train. The slow train shook, rattled and swayed and kept stopping. In the stifling heat people's heads nodded up and down, while an odour of sweat, tobacco smoke and orange peel mixed with the scent of the eucalyptus outside. The train rounded a corner, rattling like a toy train with tin carriages almost tumbling over each other. And a smooth strip of azure without a ripple: a mirror of metal, crystal, sapphire became visible and spread into an oval dish among the rolling mountain country, like a vase placed very low in which a sacred liquid was preserved, very blue and pure and still, and protected by a wall of rocky hills, which climbed higher until as the train rattled and careered around the clear dish a castle rose up high on a peak, rock-coloured, broad, massive and monastery-like, with arcades running down the slope. It rose nobly and with a gloomy melancholy and from the train it was hard to make out what was rock and what masonry, as if

it were a single bleakness, as if the castle had grown naturally from the rock and in its growth had assumed something of the form of human habitation in distant times.
And as if the oval dish with its sacred blue water was a
divine sacrificial bowl, the mountain closed off the lake of
San Stefano and the castle arose like its gloomy guardian.

The train wound along the water in a sinuous swirl for
a moment, described an arc and came to a halt: San
Stefano. It was a small, silent town, sleepy in the sun, without any life or traffic, and only visited every day in winter
by tourists who came from Rome to see the cathedral and
the castle, and taste the local wine in the *osteria*. When
Cornélie got out she saw the prince at once.

"How sweet of you to visit us in our eyrie!" he said
excitedly, squeezing her hands.

He led her through the station to his carriage, a kind of
gig with two little horses and a small groom. A porter
would bring her case to the castle.

"It's wonderful that you've come!" he repeated again.
"Have you never been to San Stefano? You know that
the cathedral is famous. I'll drive right through the town,
the road to the castle is round behind it … "

He was beaming with pleasure. He geed up the horse
by clicking his tongue, with a repeated shaking of the
reins, like a child. They flew down the road, among the
low, sleepy houses, across the square where the splendid
cathedral rose in the sun's glow, Lombard Romanesque
in style, begun in the eleventh century and added to century
after century since, with the campanile on the left, the
baptistery on the right: architectural wonders in marble,
red, black and white, a single structure of angels, saints

and prophets covered as it were in a thick dust of antiquity that had long ago tempered the colours of the marble into pink, grey and yellow and which hung mistily among the group as if it were the only thing that had remained of all those centuries as if they had crumbled to dust and vanished into every joint. The prince rode across a long bridge, whose arches were the remains of an ancient aqueduct, and now stood in the riverbed, which was completely dried up and had children playing in it. Then he let the horses climb at a walking pace; the road climbed steeply upwards, winding up dry and stony from the sunken valleys of olives to the castle, and looking out wider and wider over the ever expanding panorama of bluish white mountains dissolved in the glow of the sun and opal horizons, with a sudden glimpse of the lake: the oval dish, set deeper and deeper, now as if in a circle of channelled hills, gleaming blue, deeper and more fathomless, and absorbing in its mystical blue all the blue of the sky, until the air shimmered, as if in long spirals of light that swirled before one's eyes. Until suddenly an overpowering scent of orange blossom wafted towards one, a breath heavy and sensual as that of a panting lover, as if thousands of mouths were exhaling scented breath that hung stiflingly in the becalmed atmosphere between sky and lake.

The prince, happy and hectic, talked a lot, pointed here, pointed there with his whip, smacked his lips at the horses, asked Cornélie things, whether she liked the area … The horses, flexing their muscular hind legs, slowly made headway. The castle, massive and monumental, extended in front of them. The lake dropped from sight.

The horizons became wider, like a world; the hint of a breeze blew away something of the scent of orange blossom. The road became wide, easily negotiable, level. The castle extended like a fort, like a town, behind its turreted walls with gate after gate. They drove in, across a courtyard, under an arch into a second courtyard, and through a second arch into a third. Cornélie was enveloped by a sense of awe, a vision of columns, arches, statues, arcades and fountains. They alighted.

Urania came to meet her, embraced her, welcomed her warmly and led her up the stairs and down the corridor to her room. The windows were open; she looked out at the lake, the town and the cathedral. Again Urania kissed her and sat her down. And it struck Cornélie that Urania had become thin and no longer had her former dazzling young American girlish beauty, with that unconscious element of coquettishness in her eyes, her smile, her clothing. She had changed. She had lost a little weight, and was not as striking as before, as if her beauty had been a short-lived manifestation, more to do with freshness than with line. But if she had lost her sheen she had gained a certain distinction, a certain style: something that surprised Cornélie. Her gestures were calmer, her voice softer, her mouth seemed smaller and was not constantly opening to reveal white teeth; her outfit was the essence of simplicity: a blue skirt and a white blouse. Cornélie found it difficult to comprehend that the young Princess di Forte-Braccio, Duchess of San Stefano, was Miss Urania Hope from Chicago. A melancholy had descended on her that was very flattering, even though she was less beautiful. And Cornélie felt that there was some unhappiness that tempered her and gave her more depth, but that she also fitted tactfully into her new surroundings. She asked Urania if she was happy. Urania said yes, with her melancholy smile that was so new and surprising. And she talked about herself. They had had a pleasant winter in Nice. But with a cosmopolitan group of friends, because although her new family was very kind, they were very condescending and Virgilio's friends— especially the women—excluded her almost insultingly. She had realised even at her wedding that the aristocracy would tolerate her, but that people would never forget that she was the daughter of Hope, the stocking-manufacturer from Chicago. She had seen that she was not the only one who even though she was now a princess was tolerated and tolerated only for her millions: there were others like her. She had not made friends. People had come to her at homes and balls: everyone was the best of friends and thick as thieves with Gilio; the ladies called him by his first name, laughed with him, flirted with him and seemed to think it a very good idea that he had married several millions … With Urania they were barely, brusquely polite. The women particularly, the gentlemen were easier-going. But it hurt her, particularly when those high-ranking aristocratic women—all the famous names in Italy— treated her with condescension, and always managed to exclude her from all intimacy, every intimate gathering, every intimate collaboration on parties for charity. Once everything had been discussed, they would ask the Princess di Forte-Braccio to join in, and offered her the place she deserved, with scrupulous exactness indeed. They treated her clearly as a princess and equal in the eyes of the world, the public. But in their own coterie she remained Urania Hope. And the few other bourgeois millionaire elements came to call, of course, but *she* kept them at bay and Gilio approved. And what had Gilio said when she had complained of her plight to him? That with tact she would certainly win a position for herself, but with great patience and after many, many years. Now she cried, with her head on Cornélie's shoulder: oh, she thought, she would never win, with all those proud women! And anyway what was she, a Hope, compared to all those famous families who together created Italy's ancient glory and who, like the Massimos, claimed a pedigree that went back to the Romans?

Was Gilio good to her? Certainly, but he had immediately treated her as "his wife". All his charm, all his jollity was for others: he never talked much to her. And the young princess wept: she felt lonely, and was sometimes homesick for America. She had invited her brother to stay with her, a nice lad of seventeen, who had come over for her wedding and had travelled through Europe, before leaving for his farm out West. He was her favourite, and he consoled her, but he would be going in a few weeks' time. What would she have left then? Oh, how glad she was that Cornélie had come! And how well she looked, more beautiful than she had ever seen her! Van der Staal had accepted: he would be coming in a week. She asked in a whisper whether they were considering getting married. Cornélie was adamant that they would not; she would not marry, she would never marry again. And suddenly, with complete honesty, not being able to dissemble with Urania, she announced that she was no longer living at Via dei Serpenti, but in Duco's studio. Urania was shocked by that break with convention, but she regarded her friend as a woman who could do things that others could not. So just their happiness and love, she whispered as if afraid, without social sanction? Urania remembered Cornélie's imprecations against marriage and before that, against the prince. But surely she liked Gilio a little now? Oh, she, Urania, would no longer be jealous. She thought it was marvellous that Cornélie had come, and Gilio too, who was bored, had also greatly looked forward to seeing her. Oh no, Urania was no longer jealous …

And with her head on Cornélie's shoulder, and her eyes still full of tears, she seemed to be asking only for a little friendship, a little kindness, a few words of affection and cherishing, the rich American child, who now bore the name of an ancient Italian dynasty. And Cornélie felt for her, because she was suffering, because she was only a small human being whose lifeline happened to cross her's. She wrapped her arms round her, she comforted her—the weeping princess—as if with a new friendship: she took her into her life as a friend, no longer as a little person. And when Urania, with a wide stare, recalled Cornélie's warning, Cornélie interrupted her, and said that she, Urania, must have more courage. She had tact, innate tact. But she must be brave, must face up to life …

They got up, and at the open window, arms round each other, they looked out. The bells of the cathedral pealed through the air; the cathedral rose noble and proud above the low writhing mass of roofs, a gigantic cathedral for such a little town: an immense symbol of the power of spiritual authorities over the reverently kneeling town of roofs. And the awe that had filled Cornélie in the courtyard, among the arcades, statues and fountains, filled her again, because a fame and grandeur, dying, yet not dead, in decay but not yet consumed, seemed to rise in dusky shadows from the blue of the lake, from the centuries-old structure of the cathedral, along the orange-covered hills to the castle, where a foreign young woman stood and felt disheartened, but whose millions were required by this shadow of greatness in order to survive for a few more generations ...

It is beautiful and exalted, so much past, thought Cornélie. It is great ... But it is something more. It is a ghost. Because it has gone, it has all gone, it is all just a memory of proud nobles, of narrow-minded souls, who do not look to the future ... And the future, with a tangle of social conundrums, with the waving of new banners and streamers, then swirled in the long spirals of light, which, like blue question marks, shimmered before her eyes between the lake and the sky.

XXXIII

Cornélie had changed and left her room. She walked down the corridor and saw no one. She did not know the way, but kept on walking; suddenly, in front of her, a wide staircase led downwards, between two rows of giant marble candelabras, and Cornélie found herself in an atrium that opened on to the lake: the wall panels with frescos by Mantegna—depicting the deeds of the San Stefanos—arched up to a cupola painted with sky and clouds so that it appeared to be open, and where cherubs and nymphs gathered around a balustrade to look down.

She went outside and saw Gilio. He was sitting on the balustrade of the terrace, smoking a cigarette and looking out at the lake. Now he came towards her.

"I was almost certain you would come this way. Aren't you tired? Can I show you around? Have you seen our Mantegnas? They have suffered greatly. They were restored at the beginning of this century. Yes, they're in a sorry state, aren't they? Do you see the little mythological scene above, by Giulio Romano? Come here, through this gate. But it's locked. Wait … "

He called outside to someone down below. After a while an old servant brought a heavy bunch of keys and handed it to the prince.

"Off you go, Egisto! I know the keys."

The man went. The prince opened a heavy bronze door. He pointed out the reliefs to her.

"Giovanni da Bologna," he said.

They went on, through a room with *arazzi*, tapestries on the walls; the prince pointed out the ceiling by Ghirlandaio: the apotheosis of the only pope in the San Stefano family. Then through a room with mirrors, painted by Mario de' Fiori. The dusty dankness of a poorly maintained museum, shrouded in a haze of neglect and indifference, made it hard to breathe; the white silk drapes were yellow with age and fouled by flies; the red top curtains of Venetian damask were threadbare and moth-eaten; the painted mirrors were weathered and dulled; the arms of the glass Venetian chandeliers were broken. Carelessly pushed aside the most precious cabinets, inlaid with bronze, mother-of-pearl and ivory panels, mosaic tables of lapis lazuli, malachite and green, yellow, black and pink marbles, stood as if in an attic like lumber; the *arazzi* of Saul and David, Esther, Holofernes, Solomon, were no longer alive with the emotion of the figures, smothered as they were under the thick grey layer of dust that covered their perished fabric and neutralised all colour.

Through the immense rooms, in their curtained semi-darkness, there wafted something like a sadness, a melancholy of bitterness, hopeless, vanquished, a slow extinction of greatness and grandeur; among the masterpieces of the most famous painters there were sad gaps, pointing to an acute shortage of money, to paintings, despite everything, sold off for a fortune ... Cornélie remembered an incident of a few years ago involving a court case, an attempt to send Raphaels out of the country illegally and sell them in Berlin ... And Gilio guided her through the spectral rooms, as cheerful as a young boy, light-hearted as a child, happy to have a diversion, mentioning names to her hurriedly, without love or interest, which he had heard in his childhood, but still making mistakes, correcting himself, and finally admitting with a laugh that he had forgotten.

"And here is the *camera degli sposi* ... "

He searched through the bunch of keys, reading the copper tags, and when he had opened the creaking door, they went inside.

There was a suddenly intense, exquisite, glorious feeling of intimacy: a large bedroom, all in gold, all matt gold, tarnished and perished and softened gold thread; on the walls gold-coloured *arazzi*: the birth of Venus from the golden foam of a golden ocean, Venus with Mars, Venus with Adonis, Venus with Cupid: the pale pink nakedness of mythology flowering for a moment in nothing but a golden atmosphere and ambience, in gold bunches among gold flowers; and cupids and swans and wild boar in gold; gold peacocks at gold fountains; water and clouds of elemental gold, and all the gold with a patina and perished and softened into a single languorous sunset of dying rays: the four-poster bed, gold under a canopy of gold brocade on which the family coats-of-arms were embroidered in heavy relief: the gold bedspread, but all the gold lifeless, all the gold reduced to a melancholy of an almost greying glimmer, erased, swept away, jaded, as if the dusty centuries had cast a shadow, spread a cobweb over it.

"How beautiful!" said Cornélie.

"Our famous bridal chamber," laughed the prince. "Strange idea those ancestors of ours had, to sleep in such a remarkable room on their first night. If they married into our family, they slept here on their first night. It was a kind of superstition. The young woman would only stay faithful if she had spent the first night here with her husband. Poor Urania! We did not sleep here, *signora mia*, among all those indecent goddesses of love. We no longer observe the family tradition. Urania is destined by fate to be unfaithful to me. Unless I take that fate upon myself … "

"I expect no mention was made in the family tradition of the faithfulness of the men?"

"No, not much importance was attached to it—then or now."

"It is wonderful," repeated Cornélie, looking round. "How marvellous Duco will find this. Oh prince, I have never seen a room like this! Look at Venus there with the wounded Adonis, his head in her lap, the nymphs lamenting … It's a fairy tale … "

"There's too much gold for me … "

"Perhaps that's what it used to be like, too much gold … "

"Lots of gold stood for riches and the power of love. The riches have gone now … "

"But the gold has softened now, become so grey … "

"The power of love has remained: the San Stefanos have always been great lovers."

He went on joking and pointed to the lewdness of the scenes and ventured an allusion.

She pretended not to hear, and looked at the *arazzi*. In the side panels golden peacocks drank from golden fountains and cupids played with doves.

"I love you so much!" he whispered in her ear and put his arms round her waist. "Angel, angel!"

She warded him off.

"Prince … "

"Call me Gilio … !"

"Why can't we be just good friends … "

"Because I want more than friendship."

She now freed herself completely.

"I don't," she replied coolly.

"So you have only one love?"

"Yes … "

"That's impossible."

"Why … "

"Because in that case you would marry him. If you loved no one but him, Van der Staal, you would marry him."

"I am against marriage."

"Hot air. You're not marrying him, in order to be free. And if you want to be free, I also have a right to ask, for my moment of love."

She looked at him strangely and he could feel her contempt.

"You don't … understand me at all," she said slowly and pityingly.

"You understand me though."

"Oh yes. You are so very simple."

"Why don't you want to?"

"Because I don't want to."

"Why not?"

"Because I have no feelings for you."

"Why not!?" he persisted, and his hands clenched.

"Why not?" she repeated. "Because I find you jolly and charming to play around with, but apart from that your temperament and mine are not compatible."

"What do you know about my temperament?"

"I see you."

"You're not a doctor."

"I'm a woman."

"And I am a man."

"But not for me."

Furiously and with a curse he embraced her with trembling arms. Before she could stop him he had kissed her wildly. She struggled free and struck him straight in the face. He cursed again, grabbed wildly at her, but she drew herself up higher.

"Prince!" she said, bursting out laughing. "Surely you don't think you can force me?"

"Of course I do."

She laughed mockingly.

"You can't," she said loudly. "Because I don't want to and I won't be forced."

This was a red rag to a bull: he was furious. He had never been defied and resisted like this, he had always been triumphant. She saw him charging toward her, but calmly threw open the door of the room.

The long galleries and rooms stretched into the distance, apparently endlessly. There was something about that perspective of ancestral space that restrained him. He was more beside himself than a calculating violator. She walked on very slowly looking intently left and right.

He joined her and walked beside her.

"You struck me," he panted, furious. "I shall never forgive you for that. Never!"

"I ask your forgiveness," she said with her sweetest voice and smile. "But I had to defend myself, didn't I?"

"Why?"

"Prince," she said persuasively. "Why all that anger and passion and violence. You can be so sweet; a little while ago in Rome you were so charming. We were such good friends. I loved your conversation and your wit and kind heart. Now everything's spoiled."

"No," he begged her.

"Oh yes. You refuse to understand me. Your temperament and mine are not compatible. Can't you understand that? You force me to put things crudely by being crude yourself."

"I ... ?"

"Yes; you do not believe in the integrity of my independence."

"No!"

"Is that a courteous way to behave to a woman?"

"I am only courteous up to a certain point."

"We've passed that point. So please be courteous again as you were."

"You're playing with me. I shan't forget. I'll have my revenge."

"So, a life and death battle?"

"No, a victory, for me."

They had almost reached the atrium.

"Thank you for the guided tour," she said, a little mockingly. "The *camera degli sposi* in particular was magnificent. Don't let us be so angry any more."

She proffered her hand.

"No," he said. "You struck me in the face, here. My cheek is still glowing. I won't take your hand."

"Poor cheek," she teased. "Poor prince! Did I hit you hard?"

"Yes … "

"How can I cool your glowing cheek?"

He looked at her, still panting, angry and red, with his eyes like sparkling carbuncles.

"You are more of a flirt than any Italian woman I know." She laughed.

"With a kiss?" she asked.

"Demon!" he hissed through his teeth.

"With a kiss?" she repeated.

"Yes," he said. "There, in our *camera degli sposi*."

"No, here."

"Demon!" he said, more softly and with more of a hiss.

She give him a fleeting kiss. Then she offered him her hand.

"And now this is over. The incident is closed."

"Angel, devil," he hissed after her.

She looked over the balustrade at the lake. Night had fallen and the lake was shrouded in mist. She was no longer thinking of him, although he was still standing behind her. She thought of him as a young boy, who sometimes amused her and now had misbehaved. She thought no more of him; she thought of Duco.

"How beautiful he will find it here," she thought. "Oh, I miss him so! … "

From behind them came the rustle of women's clothes. It was Urania and the Marchesa Belloni.

XXXIV

URANIA ASKED CORNÉLIE to come in, as it was not healthy outside, with the mist rising from the lake after sunset. The *marchesa*'s greeting was cool, stiff and she narrowed her eyes as if she could not quite remember Cornélie.

"I can quite imagine that," said Cornélie, with an acerbic smile. "You see lodgers in your *pensione* every day, and I stayed for a much shorter time, than you'd counted on. I hope that my rooms were quickly relet and that you did not suffer any loss as a result of my departure, *marchesa?*"

The *marchesa* looked at her dumbfounded. Here, at San Stefano, she was in her element as a marchioness; she, the sister-in-law of the old prince, never spoke about her *pensione* for foreigners here; she never met guests from Rome, who only visited the castle occasionally as tourists at certain times, while she, the marchioness spent several weeks here for her summer vacation. Here she had left behind her dexterity in extolling chilly rooms, her business acumen in charging as much for them as she dared. Here she carried her coiffeured mane with great dignity and though she still wore her glass jewellery in her ears, a shiny new spencer covered her ample bosom. She could not help it if she, born a countess, she the Marchesa Belloni—the marquess had been a brother of the late princess—lacked distinction, in spite of all the quarters on her coat-of-arms, she still felt what she was, an aristocrat. Her acquaintances,

195

the *monsignori*, whom she sometimes met at San Stefano, glossed over the Pensione Belloni, and called it Palazzo Belloni.

"Oh yes," she said finally, with a distinguished blinking of the eyes, very coolly. "Now I remember you … although I have forgotten your name … A friend of Princess Urania's, are you not? Pleased to meet you again … very pleased."

"And what do you say to your friend's marriage?" she asked as she walked up the stairs side by side with Cornélie for a moment, between the marble candelabras of Mino de Fiesole. Gilio, still angry and flushed, and not calmed by the kiss, had withdrawn and Urania had quickly gone on ahead.

The *marchesa* knew of Cornélie's initial opposition, of her previous advice to Urania, and she was certain that Cornélie had acted in this way because she had fancied Gilio for herself. There was irony and triumph in her question.

"That it was made in heaven," replied Cornélie, equally ironically. "I believe this marriage is truly blessed."

"By His Holiness," said the *marchesa* naively, not understanding.

"Of course; the blessing of His Holiness … and the blessing of Heaven … "

"I did not think you were religious?"

"Sometimes … When I think of their marriage, I become religious again. What a comfort for the soul of Princess Urania that she should have become a Catholic. What a joy in her life that she should have married *caro* Gilio. There is still happiness and peace in life."

The *marchesa* had a vague inkling of her mockery, and thought her a dangerous woman.

"And you, does our religion have no attraction for you?"

"A great deal! I have a great feeling for beautiful churches and paintings. But that is an artistic view. You probably won't understand that, because I don't believe you are artistic, are you, *marchesa*? And marriage too has an attraction for me, a marriage like Urania's. Couldn't you help me, *marchesa*? I could stay a whole winter at your *pensione*, and who knows, I might become a Catholic myself ... You could try Rudyard for me, or if that fails, the two *monsignori* ... Then I would be bound to convert ... And it would certainly be profitable."

The *marchesa* looked at her haughtily, white with rage.

"Profitable ... "

"If you arrange an Italian title for me, with money that is, it would definitely be profitable."

"How do you mean?"

"Just ask the old prince and the *monsignori*, *marchesa* ... "

"What do you know? What are you thinking?"

"I? Nothing!" replied Cornélie coolly. "But I have second sight. Sometimes I suddenly see things ... So stay on the good side of me, and don't pretend to forget your old lodgers any more ... Is this Princess Urania's room? After you, *marchesa* ... "

The *marchesa* went in shivering: witchcraft crossed her mind. How did that woman know *anything* about her negotiations with the old prince and the *monsignori*? How did she suspect that Urania's marriage and her conversion had brought her some tens of thousands of lire?

She had not only been taught a lesson: she was trembling, she was afraid. Was the woman the devil then? Did she have the evil eye? And in the folds of her dress the *marchesa* made the sign of the *gettatura* with her little finger and index finger, and murmured, "Get thee behind me, Satan … "

Urania poured tea in her own drawing-room. The room looked out through three-pointed arch windows on the town and the ancient cathedral, which in an orange reflection of the last rays of sunlight emerged for a moment from its grey dust of ages with the indistinct swirl of its saints, prophets and angels. The room, hung with beautiful *arazzi*, an allegory of abundance—nymphs with gushing cornucopias—was half antique, half modern, not in uniformly good taste or pure in tone, with some ghastly banal modern ornaments, a few jarring examples of modern convenience, but still comfortable, lived-in, and Urania's home. A young man rose from his chair and Urania introduced him as her brother. Young Hope was a sturdy, fresh-faced young man of eighteen; he was still wearing his cycling suit: she would let him, said his sister, just to have a cup of tea. She stroked his short-haired round head, and with the permission of the ladies gave him his cup first: then he would go and change. He looked so odd sitting there, so new, and so healthy, with his fresh pink complexion, his broad chest, his strong hands and firm calves, the youthfulness of a young Yankee farmer who, despite the millions of Hope Senior, was working on his farm way out West, to make his own fortune; he looked so odd there in old San Stefano, with a view of that severely symbolic cathedral, against that background of antique *arazzi*, and suddenly Cornélie found the new young princess even stranger … Her name, her American name of Urania, sounded good: Princess Urania suddenly a acquired a very nice ring … But the young woman, a little pale, a little melancholy, with her Yankee English between her teeth, suddenly did not look so at home amid this tarnished glory of the San Stefanos … Cornélie kept forgetting that she was the Princess di Forte-Braccio: she still saw her as Miss Hope. And yet Urania had tact, ease of manner and the ability to assimilate; a very considerable ability. Gilio had come in, and the few words that she addressed to her husband, natural, dignified almost, and yet to Cornélie's ear with a tone of resigned disillusion, made her pity the princess. From the outset she had felt a vague sympathy for Urania. Gilio was cool with her in an offhand way, the *marchesa* condescending and protective. And then the terrible loneliness around her of all that dilapidated grandeur. She stroked her young brother's head. She spoiled him, asked if the tea were nice and stuffed him full of sandwiches, as he was hungry after his cycle trip. In him she had something of home, something of Chicago: she almost clung to him … But apart from that she was surrounded by the oppressive melancholy of the huge castle, the neglected glory of its classical artistic splendour, the superciliousness of aristocratic pride, which had no need of her, though it did need her millions. And for Cornélie she lost all her ridiculousness as an American parvenue; and on the contrary acquired something tragic as a youthful victim. How strange they looked sitting there, she, the young princess and her brother, with his muscular calves!

Urania showed them her portfolio of pictures and drawings: ideas of a young architect from Rome for the restoration of the castle. And Urania became excited, colour came into her cheeks when Cornélie asked whether so much restoration would be aesthetically pleasing. She defended her architect. Gilio smoked cigarettes without showing any interest and was out of humour. The *marchesa* sat there like an idol, with her lion's mane, in which the crystal earrings glittered. She was afraid of Cornélie and resolved to be on her guard. A steward came to tell the princess that dinner was ready. And Cornélie recognised him as old Guiseppe from Pensione Belloni, the old arch-ducal steward, who had dropped a spoon, as Rudyard had told her. She looked at Urania with a smile and Urania blushed.

"Poor man!" she said when Giuseppe had left. "Yes, I took him over from Auntie. He was so busy at the Pensione Belloni. He has very little to do here, and he has a young steward under him. We needed more staff anyway. He is enjoying his old age here: poor dear old Giuseppe … Bob, you haven't changed!"

"What a kind heart!" thought Cornélie, as they all got up and Urania very gently reproached her brother for being a spoiled brat and coming to table with bare thighs.

XXXV

THEY WERE IN THE large gloomy dining-room, with the almost black *arazzi*, with the almost black waffle ceiling, with all the almost black statuary; with the black monumental fireplace, and above it, in black marble, the family coat-of-arms. The candlelight of two large silver candelabras gave only a faint glow on the damask and glass. But apart from that the over-large room was plunged into shadowy darkness, in the corners intensified with masses of deep shadow, thinner shadow wafting from the ceiling, like an evaporation of dark velvet that floated above the candlelight in atoms. The timeless antiquity of Stefano weighed oppresively here as a feeling of reverence, together with a melancholy of black silence and black pride. Words sounded muffled here. This had remained exactly as it had always been, this was like a shrine to their distinguished tradition, in which Urania would not dare to change anything, as if she scarcely dared speak or eat. They waited for a moment, until a double door was opened. And a tall, grey old man came in like a ghost, his arm through the arm of the clergyman next to him. Old Prince Ercole approached slowly and with dignity, while the chaplain adjusted his step to that slow dignified pace. He wore a long black coat, with an ample old-fashioned cut, which hung in folds about him, with something of the air of a tabard, and on his gleaming grey hair, slightly wavy at the neck, a black velvet skull cap. He was treated with great respect. First the *marchesa*, then Urania, whom he kissed very slowly on the forehead—as if consecrating her; then Gilio approached him and subserviently kissed his father's hand. The old man nodded at young Hope, who bowed and turned to look at Cornélie. Urania introduced her. And as if giving an audience, the old prince said a few friendly words to her and asked whether she liked Italy. When Cornélie had answered, Prince Ercole sat down and gave his cap to Giuseppe, who received it with a deep bow. Then they all sat down: the *marchesa* with the chaplain opposite Prince Ercole, who sat between Cornélie and Urania, Robert Hope next to his sister.

"No one can see my calves," he whispered to his sister.

"Sh!" said Urania.

Giuseppe, reviving now that he had been restored to his former dignity, filled the plates ceremoniously with soup at an old dresser. He was obviously back in his element here; he was visibly grateful to Urania; he had an expression of deep contentment and in his tailcoat looked like an old diplomat. He amused Cornélie, who thought back to Belloni, when he became impatient when guests did not arrive, when he exploded at the green young waiters, whom the *marchesa* employed because of their cheapness. When two lackeys had brought round the soup, the chaplain stood up and said the *benedicite*. Still not a word was said. The soup was eaten in silence, while the three servants stood motionless. The spoons tapped against the plates and the *marchesa* smacked her lips. The candelabra occasionally trembled and the shadow fell more oppressively from the ceiling, like an evaporation of velvet. Then the prince turned to the *marchesa*. And he addressed everyone in turn, with a friendly, condescending dignity, in French, in Italian. The conversation became slightly more general, but the prince continued to take the lead. And he was very friendly towards Urania, Cornélie noticed ... But Cornélie remembered Gilio's words: papa almost had a stroke because Hope Senior haggled about Urania's dowry. Ten million? Five million? Less than three million! Dollars? Lire!! And the old prince suddenly appeared to her as the grizzled, selfish embodiment of San Stefano's glory and aristocratic pride, seemed to her the living ghost of that shadowy past, that she had felt that afternoon, gazing with Urania into the deep, blue lake: the demanding ghost; the ghost that demanded millions, the ghost that demanded new viability; a spectral parasite, who had sold his depreciated symbols to the vanity of a new commercial company, but for all his distinction could not cope with the cunning of a businessman. Their princess's and duchess's title for less than three million lire! Papa had almost had a stroke ... Gilio had said. And Cornélie, in the measured, affable stiffness of the conversation led by Prince Ercole, looked from the old prince-duke—of seventy—to the young, fresh-faced Westerner—of eighteen—and looked from him to Prince Gilio: the hope of the old family, their only hope. Here in the gloom of this dining-room, where he was bored, and in addition still out of humour, she saw him as small, insignificant, insubstantial, a scrawny, distinguished *bon viveur*, his carbuncle eyes, which could twinkle merrily with perverse wit, were focused beneath the drooping eyelids on his plate, at which he picked listlessly.

She felt sorry for him, and she thought of the gold

bridal chamber … She despised him a little. She did not regard him as a man, he could not achieve what he wanted: she regarded him more as a naughty boy. And he must be jealous of Robert, she thought: of his fresh blood that tingled in his cheeks, of his broad shoulders and broad chest. But he still amused her. He could be charming, jolly and witty, quick-witted and sharp, when in a bright mood: quick-tongued and quick-witted. She liked him well enough. And he was good-hearted. The bracelet and particularly the thousand lire. She still thought of them with affection; how moved she had been, during that walk, back and forth past the post office; moved by his letter and his generous help. There was no substance in him, to her he was not a man: but he was witty and he had a very good heart. She liked him, as a friend and a pleasant companion. How dejected and out of humour he was. But then why did he venture on those crazy assaults … ?

She spoke to him now and then, but she was unable to cheer him up. For that matter the conversation dragged on, stiffly and affably, still led by Prince Ercole. Dinner was coming to an end and Prince Ercole rose up. He received his cap from the hands of Giuseppe, all of them said goodbye to him, the doors were opened, and on the chaplain's arm Prince Ercole withdrew. Gilio disappeared angrily. The *marchesa*, still shuddering at the thought of Cornélie, disappeared and under her dress pointed the *gettatura* at her. And Urania took Cornélie and Robert back to her drawing-room. All three breathed more easily. They spoke freely, in English now: the young man said despairingly that he was not eating enough, that he did not dare eat until his hunger was assuaged, and Cornélie laughed, finding his healthy appetite appealing, while Urania hunted for rusks for him and a piece of cake, left from tea, and promised him bread and meat before they went to bed. And they relaxed their minds after the solemn dinner. Urania said that they never saw the old prince except at dinner, but she always visited him in the mornings, stayed and talked to him for an hour or so or played chess with him. Otherwise he played chess with the chaplain. She had a busy life, Urania. The reorganisation of the household, formerly left to a poor blood relation, now living in a *pensione* in Rome, took up a lot of her time: in the mornings she discussed the details with Prince Ercole, who despite his seclusion, was completely *au courant*. Then she had the consultations with her Roman architect on the restoration of the castle: these sometimes took place in the old prince's study. Then she was commissioning the building of a large institution in the town, an *albergo dei poveri*, a home for elderly men and women, for which Hope Senior was giving her separate funds: when she first came to San Stefano, she had been struck by the run-down, collapsing houses and cottages in the poor districts, leprous and scrofulous with dirt, eaten up by their own destitution, where a whole population vegetated like mushrooms. She was now having a home built for the elderly, and on the estate she provided work for the young and able-bodied, she concerned herself with neglected children and had founded a new school. She talked about all this quite simply, cutting the cake for her brother Robert, who was tucking in with relish after the etiquette of dinner. She invited Cornélie to accompany her the following day to see the work on the *albergo*, the new school, run by two clergymen from Rome, recommended to her by the *monsignori*.

Through the pointed arch windows one could see the dim shape of the town below, and in the sultry summer night, strewn with stars, the silhouette of the cathedral rose up. And Cornélie thought: it is not only for ghosts and shadows that she has come here, the rich American girl, who was so mad about the aristocracy—'so nice'—the child, who collected samples of the queen's ball gowns—an album that she now kept hidden as a 'black' princess, the girl who tripped across the Forum in her light linen tailored jacket, and understood neither ancient Rome nor the new future that was dawning …

And now that Cornélie was returning to her own room through the silent brooding night of the castle of San Stefano, she thought: I write, but she does things. I dream and think, but she teaches the children, even though it is with a priest: she feeds and houses old men and women.

Then, in her room, looking out over the lake in the summer night sprinkled with stars, she reflected that she would like to be rich too and to have a wide scope of action. Because as it was she had no scope, no money and … she longed only for Duco, and he must not leave her alone for too long, in this castle, amid all this gloomy grandeur, which oppressed her with the weight of centuries.

XXXVI

THE FOLLOWING MORNING Urania's chambermaid was leading Cornélie outside through a warren of galleries to where they were to have breakfast, when she met Gilio on the stairs. The maid turned back.

"I still need guidance to find my way around," laughed Cornélie.

He grunted something.

"How did you sleep, prince?"

He grunted again.

"Really, prince, that bad temper has to change. Do you hear? It *has to*. I insist, I don't want to see any more sulking today, and hope you will resume as soon as possible your merry, witty tone of conversation, which I appreciate in you."

He muttered.

"Goodbye, prince," said Cornélie abruptly.

And she retraced her steps.

"Where are you going?" he asked

"To my room. I shall take breakfast in my room."

"But why?"

"Because I don't like you as a host."

"You don't?"

"No I don't. Yesterday you insult me, I defend myself, you persist in being coarse, I am immediately as agreeable as usual, give you my hand and even a kiss. At dinner you sulk with me in the rudest possible way. You go to your room without wishing me good night. This morning you meet me without saying hello. You grunt and sulk like a naughty child. There is an angry look in your eyes, you look bilious. Indeed, you look awful. It's very unflattering. You are most unpleasant, rough, impolite, and small-minded. I have no wish to breakfast with you in such a mood … And I'm going to my room."

"No," he begged.

"Oh yes,"

"No, no."

"Well then, change your attitude. Force yourself, stop thinking about your defeat, and be nice to me. You are acting like the injured party, whereas I'm the injured party. But I can't sulk and I'm not petty. I can't act in a petty way. I forgive you, forgive me too. Say something affectionate, say something nice."

"I'm mad about you."

"I haven't noticed. If you are mad about me, be friendly, polite, cheerful and witty. I demand it from you as my host."

"I shan't sulk any more … but I love you so much! And you hit me."

"Can you never forgive that act of self-defence?"

"No, never!"

"Farewell, then."

She turned on her heel.

"No, no, don't go back. Come with me to the pergola, where we are having breakfast. I ask your forgiveness. I shall no longer be rude or petty. You, you are not petty. You are the most remarkable woman I know. I worship you."

"Worship me in silence then, and amuse me."

His eyes, his black carbuncle eyes, began to revive, to fill with laughter; his face lost its wrinkles and brightened.

"I am too unhappy to be amusing."

"I don't believe a word of it."

"Really, I'm unhappy, I'm suffering … "

"Poor prince!"

"You won't believe me. You never take me seriously. I simply have to be your clown, your jester. And I love you, and must not hope? Tell me, must I never hope?"

"Not much."

"You are merciless, and so severe."

"I have to be severe with you, you're just like a naughty boy … Oh, I see the pergola. So you promise me you will mend your ways?"

"I'll be good."

"And amusing."

He sighed.

"*Povero* Gilio! " he sighed. "Poor clown!"

She laughed. Urania and Robert Hope were in the pergola. The pergola, overgrown with a grapevine and a pink baby's breath with pendant bunches of pink flowers, was supported by a line of caryatids and hermes—nymphs, satyrs and fauns—whose upper bodies ended in a slim sculptured pedestal and who with raised hands supported the flat canopy of leaves and flowers; while in the middle there was an open rotunda like an outdoor temple, the circular balustrade of which was also borne by caryatids and where an ancient sarcophagus had been converted into a cistern. In the pergola a table had been laid for breakfast; they were having breakfast without old Prince Ercole and the *marchesa* was breakfasting in her room. It was eight o'clock, a morning freshness was still wafting up from the lake, a haze of blue velvet was still covering the hills like down, among which the lake sank as if in gently curving channels like an oval dish.

"Oh, how beautiful it is here!" cried Cornélie delightedly.

Breakfast was a sunny and cheerful meal, after yesterday's black and gloomy dinner. Urania was very excited about her *albergo*, which she was shortly to visit with Cornélie. Gilio was his old amiable self and Bob ate heartily. And afterwards when Bob went cycling, Gilio actually came to town with the ladies. They drove down the road from the castle in a landau at walking pace. The sun grew hotter and the old town loomed up white, creamy white and grey white with houses like stone mirrors in which the sun was reflected; the squares like wells into which the sun poured its glowing heat. The coachman stopped at the works for the *albergo*, they got out and the builder approached dutifully, while the sweating masons looked at the prince and princess. It was sweltering hot. Gilio constantly wiped his forehead, and took refuge behind Cornélie's parasol. But Urania was a bundle of vitality and interest, quick and energetic in her white piqué suit, with her white matelot hat under her white parasol, she tripped across beams past piles of bricks and cement with her builder, listened to explanations and gave advice, did not always agree, pulled a knowing face; said that she did not like such and such dimensions, did not believe what the builder was assuring her, that as the building progressed she would come to terms with the dimensions, shook her head, impressed this and impressed that on him, all in rapid, not entirely correct and staccato

Italian, which she chewed between her teeth. But Cornélie found her adorable, charming; Cornélie found her the Princess di Forte-Braccio. There was no doubt about it. While Gilio, frightened of dirtying his light flannel suit and yellow shoes on the plaster, stayed under the shade of the parasol, puffing with the warmth, uninterested, his wife was indefatigable, did not worry about her white skirt acquiring a dirty hem, and she talked to the builder with such sureness of touch, lively but dignified that it commanded respect. Where had the child learned this? From where had she got her ability to assimilate? And from where did she get that love for San Stefano, that love for the poor? How had this American girl acquired the talent to fulfil her exalted new position so well? *Ammirabile*! was Gilio's verdict and he whispered it to Cornélie. He was not blind to her qualities. He thought Urania was wonderful, outstanding; she never ceased to surprise him. No Italian woman from his circles would have behaved in that way. And they loved her. The servants at the castle loved her, Giuseppe would go through fire for her, the builder admired her, the masons watched her go with respect, because she was so clever and knew so much and was so good to them in their misery. *Ammirabile!* said Gilio. But he was puffing. He knew nothing about stones, beams and dimensions and did not know from where Urania had got her technical eye. She was tireless. She went right round the site, while he looked up imploringly at Cornélie. And finally, in English, he asked his wife in heaven's name to call it a day. They got in, the builder said goodbye, and the workmen followed suit with a show of gratitude and affection.

And they drove to the cathedral, which Cornélie wanted to see, and where Gilio, while Urania kindly showed her round, asked his ladies for mercy, and sat down on the altar steps, arms hanging over his knees, in order to cool off.

XXXVII

SEVEN DAYS HAD GONE BY and Duco had arrived. It was after the formal dinner in the gloomy dining-room, where Duco had been introduced by Cornélie to Prince Ercole, and it was a dreamlike summer evening, when Cornélie and Duco went outside. The castle was already sound asleep, but Cornélie had asked Gilio to get her a key. And they went outside, to the pergola. The stars were sprinkled across the night sky like a blond light, and the moon crowned the summits of the hills and was briefly quiveringly reflected in the mystical depths of the lake. An odour of sleeping roses wafted from the flower garden on the other side of the pergola, and below, amid the roofscapes of the town, the cathedral in its moonlit square pitted its giant silhouette against the stars. And everywhere was cloaked in sleep, the lake, the town and the windows of the castle; in their sleep the caryatids and her-mes—the satyrs and nymphs—bore the leafy canopy of the pergola, as if in an attitude of enchantment of servants of the goddess of Sleep. A cricket chirped, but stopped as soon as Duco and Cornélie approached. They sat down on an antique bench, and she put her arms round him and pressed against him.

"A week!" she whispered. "A whole week since I've seen you, Duco, my darling! I can't do without you for so long. With everything I thought and did, and admired, I thought of you and of how beautiful you would find it

here. You've been here before, as a tourist. Oh, but this
is different. What makes it so nice is staying, not passing
through, but staying. That lake, that cathedral, those hills!
Those rooms inside. Neglected but so beautiful. The three
courtyards are run-down, the fountains are crumbling …
But the style of the atrium, the gloominess of the dining-
room, the poetry of this pergola … Duco, isn't this pergola like a classical ode? We've sometimes read Horace
together, you translated those poems for me so beautifully, you improvised so wonderfully! How handsome
you are, you know so much, you have such a beautiful
sensibility. I love your eyes, your voice, and all of you,
everything that is you … I can't tell you, Duco. I have
gradually surrendered to your every word, to your love of
Rome, your love of museums, to the way you see the skies
that you wash on to your watercolours. You're so wonderfully calm, almost like this lake. Oh, don't laugh, don't
push me away: I haven't seen you for a week, I need to
speak to you like this. Am I exaggerating? I don't feel
ordinary here, there's something in that air, that sky, that
light that makes me speak like this. It's so beautiful that I
can't believe it's ordinary life, ordinary reality … Do you
remember in Sorrento on the terrace of that hotel, when
we looked out over the sea, over the pearly sea, with
Naples so white in the distance, I felt the same way then
too, but did not dare put it into words: it was in the morning, there were people around us, who though we could
not see them could see us and whom I was aware of
around us: but now we're alone, and now I want to say it
to you, in your arms, at your breast: I'm so happy! I love
you so much! I feel that my soul, everything that is best in

me is you! You're laughing, but you don't believe me. Do you? Do you believe me?"

"Yes, I believe you, I'm not laughing at you, I'm just laughing. I'm so happy about you and about my art. You've taught me to work, you've roused me from my dreams! I'm so happy about *Banners*: I have letters from London, which I can let you read tomorrow. I owe everything to you. It's scarcely believable that this is ordinary life. Life was so quiet in Rome. I didn't see anyone, I worked a bit—but not much; and I ate alone in the *osteria*. The two Italians, you know, were sorry for me, I think. Oh, it was a terrible week. I can no longer do without you. Do you remember our first walks and conversations in Borghese, and on the Palatine? What strangers we still were to each other, not fitting together. But I felt at once, I think, that something beautiful would grow between us … "

She said nothing, and remained against his chest. The cricket chirped again in a kind of long vibrato. But apart from that everything slept …

"Between us … " she repeated as if in a fever, and she surrendered completely.

The whole night slept, and while they breathed their lives in each other's arms, above their heads the enchanted caryatids—fauns and nymphs—bore in their sleep the leafy canopy of the pergola, between them and the star-strewn sky.

XXXVIII

GILIO FOUND THE VACATION in San Stefano dreadful. Every morning at six o'clock he had to be ready to attend mass with Prince Ercole, Urania and the *marchesa* in the castle chapel. Afterwards he had too much time on his hands. He had gone cycling a few times with Robert Hope, but the young Westerner was too energetic for him, as was his sister, Urania. He flirted and argued with Cornélie a little, but secretly he was still insulted, and angry with himself and her. He remembered when she first arrived that evening at Palazzo Ruspoli; when she had interrupted his rendezvous with Urania. And in the golden *camera degli sposi* she had again proved too strong for him! He seethed when he thought of it, and he hated her and swore to the great gods that he would be avenged. He cursed his own indecision. He was too weak to force her with the strength of his passion and he should never have had to force her: he was used to people giving in. And he was forced to hear from her, the Dutch woman, that his temperament was not compatible with hers! What was it with that woman? What did she mean by that? He was so unused to thinking, such a thoughtless child with an easy-going Italian nature, so used to letting himself be swayed by his whim and impulse, that he scarcely understood her—although he suspected the sense of her words—scarcely understood her diffidence. Why was she like this with him, the foreign woman with her new devilish ideas, who did not bother about the world, who was not interested in marriage, who lived with a painter, as his mistress! She had no religion, and no morals—*he* knew all about religion and morals—she was a devil; she was demonic: didn't she know all about the manoeuvres of Lucia Belloni, and hadn't Aunt Lucia warned him the other day that she was dangerous, demonic, a devil? She was a witch! Why did she refuse him? Hadn't he seen her silhouette crossing the court-yard last night in the moonlight, clearly next to the figure of Van der Staal, and hadn't he seen them opening the door to the terrace with the pergola on it? And had he not watched sleeplessly for an hour, two hours, until he had seen them return, closing the door behind them? And why did she love only him, that painter? Oh, he hated him with all the burning hatred of his jealousy, he hated her, because of her exclusivity, her contempt, all her joking and flirting, as if he were a jester, a clown! What was he asking? The favour of her love such as she granted her lover! He was not asking for anything serious; no oaths, no lifelong bonds; he was asking for so little: the occasional hour of love. It didn't matter: he had never attached much importance to it. And she refused him it. No, he didn't understand her, but he did understand that she despised him, and he, he hated both her and him. And he was in love with her with all the violence of his thwarted passion. In the boredom of the vacation, which was forced upon him by his wife in her new-found love for their dilapidated eyrie, his hatred and the thought of revenge was something for his empty mind to occupy itself with. Outwardly he was his old self again, and he flirted with

Cornélie, and indeed more than before, in order to tease Van der Staal. And when his cousin, the Countess di Rosavilla, his 'white' cousin—lady-in-waiting to the queen —came to visit them for a few days, he flirted with her too, and tried to awaken Cornélie's jealousy, which he failed to do, and he consoled himself with the countess. She compensated him for his disappointment. She was no longer a young woman, but had the cold, sculptural, slightly stupid looks of a Juno: she had bulging Juno eyes: she was one of the leaders of fashion at the Quirinal and in the 'white' world, and her romantic reputation was common knowledge. She had never had a liaison with Gilio lasting more than an hour. She had simple ideas about love, fairly black and white. Her cheerful perversity amused Gilio. And as they flirted in corners, touching toes under her gown, Gilio told her about Cornélie, Duco and the adventure in the *camera degli sposi*, and he asked his cousin if *she* understood? No, the Countess di Rosavilla didn't really understand either. Temperament? Well, perhaps she—*questa Cornelia*—preferred blond or brown: there were women who were choosy … And Gilio laughed. It was so simple, *l'amore*, there wasn't much to talk about.

Cornélie was glad that Gilio had the countess. With Duco she took an interest in Urania's plans; he had conversations with the architect. And Duco was indignant and advised against refurbishing in that unstylish restoration manner—it cost a fortune, and ruined everything.

Urania was taken aback, but Duco continued, rubbished the architect, advised her to restore only what was really collapsing, but to prop up, support and preserve as much as possible. And one morning Prince Ercole deigned to walk through the long rooms with Duco, Urania and Cornélie. One could do so much—argued Duco—by simply regularly maintaining and artistically arranging what was at present piled up unthinkingly. The curtains? Asked Urania. Leave them, said Duco: at most new net curtains, but the old red Venetian damask ... Oh, leave it, leave it: it was so beautiful: here and there, with great care, it could be repaired! And the old prince was delighted, because the restoration of San Stefano, done in this way, would cost thousands less and be more artistic: he regarded his daughter-in-law's money as his own and he loved it even more than he loved her. He was delighted: he took Duco with him to the library: he showed him the old missals; the old family books and documents, charters and gifts; he showed him his coins and medals. It was all a mess, neglected, disregarded at first because of lack of money and then out of indifference, but now Urania wanted to reorganise the family museum with scholars from Rome, Florence and Bologna. The old prince was in favour, now that there was money again. And the scholars came and stayed at the castle, and Duco was tied up with them for whole mornings. He was in his element. He lived in an enchantment with the past, no longer the Classical past, but the Middle Ages and the Renaissance. The days were too short. And his love for San Stefano was so great that once an archivist took him for the young prince: Prince Virgilio. At dinner Prince Ercole told the anecdote. Everyone laughed, but Gilio found the joke simply priceless, while the archivist, who was at the table, did not know how to make himself small enough to atone.

XXXIX

GILIO HAD TAKEN THE ADVICE of his cousin, the Countess di Rosavilla. Immediately after dinner he crept outside, and walked through the pergola as far as the rotunda, through which moonlight fell as if into a white dish. But there was shadow behind some caryatids and there he hid. He waited for an hour. But the night slept, the caryatids slept, standing motionless and supporting the canopy of leaves. He cursed and crept inside. He walked down the corridors on tiptoe and listened at Van der Staal's door. There was no sound, but perhaps he was asleep ... ?

But Gilio crept down another corridor, and listened at Cornélie's door. He held his breath ... Yes, there was the sound of voices. They were together! Together!! He clenched his fists and went back, But why was he getting excited! He knew about their affair, didn't he? Why should they not be together here? And he knocked at the countess's door ...

The following evening he again waited at the rotunda. But they did not come. After a few evenings, as he sat waiting, fighting down his irritation, he saw them approaching. He saw Duco closing the terrace gate behind him: the lock creaked rustily in the distance. He saw them approaching slowly in the light, then fading in the shadow and emerging again into the moonlight. She sat on a marble bench ... How happy they seemed! He was jealous of their happiness; mainly jealous of him. And

how soft and tender she was, she who thought him, Gilio,
fit only for amusement, for flirting with: a clown; she, the
demonic woman, was angelic with the man she loved!
She leaned towards her lover with a smiling caress, with
a curving of her arm, and an approach of her lips, with a
fervently enfolding motion, with such a velvety languor of
love, that he would never have suspected in her, with her
cold, joking flirting with him, Gilio. Now she was leaning
on Duco's arm, on his chest, her face against his … Oh
her kiss, how it set Gilio aflame and enraged him! This
was no longer her icy sensual indifference to him, Gilio,
in the *camera degli sposi!* And he could no longer contain
himself: he would at least disrupt this moment of love.
And trembling with nervousness, he emerged from behind
the caryatid, and went towards them through the rotunda.
They did not see him immediately, lost as they were in
each other's eyes … But suddenly they started, both at
once; their arms dropped to their sides, and they stood up
on a single movement and saw him approaching, obviously
not recognising him at once. Only when he was very
close did they recognise him and they looked at him
silently in alarm, waiting to hear what he had to say. He
made an ironic bow.

"A lovely evening, isn't it? The view is so lovely from the
pergola at night. You're right to come and enjoy it. I hope
I'm not disturbing you with my unexpected presence!"

His trembling voice was so malevolently quarrelsome
that they could be in no doubt about his intense displeasure.

"Of course not, prince!" replied Cornélie, regaining
her composure. "Although I'm puzzled as to what you're
doing here at this hour."

"And what are you doing here at this hour?"

"What am I doing here? I'm sitting here with Van der Staal … "

"At this hour?"

"At this hour! What do you mean, prince, what are you getting at?"

"What am I getting at? That the pergola is closed at night."

"Prince," said Duco, "I don't like your tone."

"And I don't like you at all … "

"If you were not my host, I'd give you a slap in the face … " Cornélie held Duco's arm back: the prince cursed and clenched his fists.

"Prince," she said. "It's obvious that you want to provoke a scene with us. Why? What objection do you have to my meeting Van der Staal here at night? Firstly, our affair is no secret to you. And secondly, I consider it unworthy of you to come and spy on us here."

"Unworthy? Unworthy?" He was incapable of controlling himself any longer. "I'm unworthy, petty, coarse, and not a real man, I don't have the kind of temperament that suits you? His temperament suits you all right, doesn't it? I heard the sound of your kiss. Devil! Devil! Demon! No one has ever insulted me like you. I have never put up with as much from anybody. I won't any longer! You struck me, demon, devil! He, he threatens to hit me. My patience is at an end. I can't bear your refusing me, in my own house, what you grant to him … He is not your husband! He is not your husband! I have just as much right as he has, and if he reckons that he has more right than I do, then I hate him! … "

And he flew at Duco in blind fury, attacking his throat. The assault was so unexpected that Duco stumbled. They wrestled together, both furious. All their suppressed antipathy exploded into rage. They did not hear Cornélie's entreaties, they punched each other, encircled each other's arms and legs, chest pressed against chest. Then Cornélie saw something flash. In the light she saw the prince draw a knife. But the very movement gave Duco the advantage; he seized the prince's wrist in a grip of iron and forced him to the ground, pressed his knee firmly against Gilio's chest and with the other hand grasped his throat.

"Let go," screamed the prince.

"Let go of that knife!" screamed Duco.

The prince refused and hung on to it.

"Let go," he screamed again.

"Let go of that knife … "

The knife fell from his grasp. Duco grabbed it and stood up.

"Get up!" he said. "If you want we can continue this fight tomorrow in a less primitive way. Not with a knife but with swords or pistols."

The prince had got up. He was panting, blue in the face … He came to his senses.

"No," he said slowly. "I don't want to fight a duel. Unless you do. But I don't want to. I'm beaten … There's a demonic force in her, which would always ensure that you won, whatever game we played. We have already duelled. This fight means more to me than an ordinary duel. Only if you wish, then I have no objection. But now I know for sure that you would kill me. *She* is protecting you … "

"I don't want a duel," said Duco.

"Then let us regard this fight as a duel, and let us shake hands … "

Duco put out his hand , and Gilio shook it.

"Forgive me," he said condescendingly to Cornélie, "I have insulted you … "

"No," she said. "I won't forgive you."

"We must forgive each other. I forgive you your slap."

"I'm not forgiving you anything. I will never forgive you this evening, not your spying, not your lack of self control, not your rights that you seem to think you can exert over me as an unmarried woman, although I concede you no rights: neither your attack, nor your knife."

"So we are enemies for ever?"

"Yes, forever. I shall leave your house tomorrow … "

"I acted wrongly," he admitted humbly. "Forgive me. My blood is hot."

"Up to now I have known you as a gentleman … "

"I am also an Italian."

"I won't forgive you."

"I have proved to you in the past that I could be a good friend."

"This is not the moment to remind me."

"I'm reminding you of everything that might make you better disposed towards me."

"That is all to no avail."

"Enemies then?"

"Yes. Let us go in. I shall leave your house tomorrow … "

"I will perform any penance you impose on me."

"I am not imposing anything on you. I want to end this conversation and I want to go home."

"I shall lead the way … "

He did so. They walked through the pergola. He opened the terrace gate himself and let them through first.

They went to their rooms in silence.

The castle was asleep and in darkness. The prince lit the way with a match. Duco reached his room first.

"I shall light your way a little further," said the prince humbly.

He accompanied Cornélie to her door with a second match. There he fell on his knees.

"Forgive me," he whispered with a catch in his throat.

"No," she said.

And without further ado she closed the door behind her. He stayed kneeling for a moment. The he slowly got up. His neck was hurting. His shoulder felt as if he had dislocated it.

"It's over," he muttered. "I am beaten. She is stronger than me now, but not because she is a devil. I saw them together … I saw their embrace. She is stronger, he is stronger than I am … because of their happiness … I feel that, because of their happiness, they will always be stronger than me … "

He went to his room, which adjoined Urania's bedroom. Sobs welled up in his chest. He threw himself, fully clothed on his bed, swallowing his sobs in the slumbering night, which wrapped the castle in its downy folds. Then he got up, and looked out of the window. He saw the lake. He saw the pergola where they had fought a moment ago. The night was asleep, the caryatids rose gleaming from the shadow. And he tried to pinpoint the place of their fight and his defeat. And thinking superstitiously of their happiness he felt that it would never be possible to fight against it, never. Then he shrugged his shoulders, as if throwing off a burden.

"*Non fa niente!*" he said, consoling himself. "*Domani meglio …* "

By that he meant that tomorrow he would win, if not *this* victory, then another. And with his eyes still wet, he fell asleep like a child.

XL

URANIA SOBBED NERVOUSLY in Cornélie's arms when Cornélie told the young princess that she was leaving the next day. They were alone with Duco in Urania's private drawing-room.

"What happened?" she asked, sobbing.

Cornélie told her about the previous evening.

"Urania," she said seriously, "I know I'm a flirt. I loved talking to Gilio; call it flirting if you like. I have never made a secret of it, either with Duco or with you. I regarded it as amusement and nothing more. Perhaps I was wrong; I have irritated you by it in the past. I promised you never to do it again, but it seems to be stronger than I am. It's in my nature, and I won't try to defend myself ... I regarded it as something so trifling, a piece of fun and amusement. But perhaps it is bad. Will you forgive me? I've grown so fond of you: it would pain me if you did not forgive me ... "

"Make it up with Gilio and stay ... "

"Impossible, dearest girl. Gilio has insulted me, Gilio drew his knife against Duco, and I shall never forgive him that double insult. So it is impossible to stay any longer."

"I shall be left so alone!" she sobbed. "I am very fond of you too, of both of you. Is there no way ... ? Robert is leaving me tomorrow too. I shall be all alone here. What do I have here? No one who loves me ... "

"You have a lot, Urania. You have a goal to live for;

227

you can do much good for those around you … You are interested in this castle, which is now yours."

"It's all so hollow!" she sobbed. "It gives me nothing. I need sympathy. Who cares for me? I have tried to love Gilio, and I do love him, but he, he cares nothing for me. No one here cares for me … "

"I believe your poor folk care about you. You have a noble cause."

"I am glad of that, but I'm too young to live just for a cause. I have nothing else. No one cares for me here."

"What about Prince Ercole … "

"No, he despises me. Shall I tell you something? I told you before that Gilio had told me there were no family jewels, that everything had been sold? Do you remember? Well, there *are* family jewels. I realised that from something the Countess di Rosavilla said. There are family jewels. But Prince Ercole keeps them in the Banca di Roma. They despise me and I am unworthy to wear them. And with me they act as if there is nothing left. And the worst thing! … is that all their friends, their whole coterie know that they are kept in the bank and they all approve of what Prince Ercole has done. My money is good enough for them, but I'm not good enough for their old jewels, their grandmothers' jewels!"

"It's scandalous," said Cornélie.

"It's the truth!" she sobbed. "Oh, make it up; stay here with me … "

"Judge for yourself, Urania: we really can't."

"It's true," she admitted with a sigh.

"It's all my fault."

"No, no. Gilio is sometimes so hot-headed … "

"But his hothcadedness, his passion and his jealousy are my fault. I am very sorry about it, Urania, for your sake. Forgive me. Come and see me in Rome, if you go there. Don't forget me, and write to me, won't you? Now I must pack. What time is the train?"

"Ten twenty-five," said Duco. "We'll go together."

"Can I say goodbye to Prince Ercole? Have me announced."

"What will you say to him?"

"The first thing that comes into my head: that a friend in Rome is ill, that I am going and Van der Staal is accompanying me, because I am nervous. I really don't care what Prince Ercole thinks."

"Cornélie … "

"Darling, I really have no more time. Give me a hug. Forgive me. And don't forget me. Adieu, we had a precious time together: I've grown very fond of you … "

She struggled free of Urania, and Duco also said good-bye. They left the princess alone, sobbing. In the corridor they met Gilio.

"Where are you going?" he asked humbly.

"We're leaving on the ten twenty-five train … "

"I am deeply sorry … "

But they went on and left him standing there, while Urania sobbed in the drawing-room.

XLI

IN THE TRAIN, in the scorching morning heat, they were silent, and they found the houses of Rome almost bursting out of their walls in the blazing sun. But in the studio it was cool, solitary and peaceful.

"Cornélie," said Duco. "Tell me what happened between you and the prince. Why did you hit him?"

She pulled him on to the sofa, threw her arms round his neck and told him about the incident in the bridal chamber. She told him about the *camera degli sposi.* She told him about the thousand lire and the bracelet. She explained that she had kept quiet about this, so as not to bring up money worries, while he was finishing his water-colour for the exhibition in London.

"Duco," she went on, "I had such a scare yesterday when I saw Gilio draw that knife. I felt as if I was going to faint, but I didn't. I had never seen him like that, so passionate, capable of anything … Only then did I realise how much I loved you … I would have killed him if he had hurt you … "

"You shouldn't have played with him," he said severely. "He loves you … "

But despite his severe tone, he pulled her more firmly to him. She nuzzled against him as if in token of her sense of guilt.

"He's just a little infatuated … " she said, defending herself weakly.

"He is passionately in love … You shouldn't have played with him … "

She did not reply, caressing his face with her hand. She thought it was very sweet of him to reproach her like this: she liked the severe, serious tone, which he scarcely ever took with her. She knew she had that need to flirt in her, had done since she was a very young girl: for her it didn't count, it was innocent amusement. She did not agree with Duco, but she considered it unnecessary to go on discussing it: it was as it was, she did not think about it, she did not argue about it: it was a difference of opinion, almost of taste, that did not matter. She was lying too comfortably against him, after the agitation of last night, after a sleepless night, after a hasty departure, a three-hour rail journey in the blistering heat, to make too many objections. She loved the quiet coolness of the studio, being alone together after the three weeks at San Stefano. There was such peace here, such a sense of repose, that it was wonderful. The high window was pulled full up and the warm air rushed balmily into the natural chilliness of the north-facing room. Duco's easel, empty, stood waiting. It was their home, among all that colour and those artistic forms around her. Now she understood that colour and form: she was learning about Rome. She learned it all in the dream of her happiness. She thought little about the women's question and scarcely glanced at the reviews of her pamphlet; they interested her very little. She thought Lippo's angel was beautiful and the triptych panel by Gentile da Fabriano and the flickering colours of the old chasubles. It was very little after the treasures of San Stefano, but it was theirs and their home. She said nothing else, she felt content, resting on Duco's chest, and her fingers stroked his face.

"*Banners* is are virtually sold," he said, "for ninety pounds. I'll send a telegram to London this afternoon … And then we can quickly give the prince back his money."

"It's Urania's money," she said faintly.

"But I don't want the debt any longer … "

She sensed that he was a little angry, but she wasn't in the mood to talk about money matters, and a heavenly languor flew through as she lay on his chest …

"Are you angry, Duco?"

"No … but you shouldn't have done it … "

He held her closer, to show her he did not want to scold her, even though he felt she had acted wrongly. She felt that she had been wise not to mention the thousand lire to him, but she did not defend herself. They would be point-less words and she felt too content to talk about money.

"Cornélie," he said. "Let's get married … "

She looked at him in alarm, startled out of her happiness. "Why?"

"Not for us. We're just as happy without being married. But for the world, other people. Yes; we'll start to feel more and more isolated. I've talked to Urania about it a few times. She was very sad, but she tolerated us … She thought it was an impossible relationship. Maybe she's right. We can't go anywhere. At San Stefano people acted as if they didn't know that we lived together. That's over now … "

"What do you care about the opinion of 'little indifferent people, who cross your path by chance', as you say? … "

"That is no longer the case: we owe the prince money and Urania is the only friend you have … "

"I have you: I don't need anyone."

He kissed her.

"Cornélie, it would be better if we got married. Then no one will be able to insult us as the prince dared to do."

"He had narrow-minded ideas: how can you want to get married for the sake of a world and people like San Stefano and the prince?"

"The whole world is like that and we are in the world. We live among other people. It's impossible to isolate yourself completely and isolation always takes its toll later. We have to conform with other people: it's impossible existing by yourself the whole time, without any sense of community."

"Duco, I don't recognise you: such social ideas."

"I've been thinking more recently."

"I on the other hand am forgetting how to think … My darling, how serious you are this morning. While I am resting against you so beautifully after all that emotion, and that hot journey."

"Really Cornélie, let's get married … "

She rubbed up against him rather nervously, upset that he was persisting and violently shattering her happy mood …

"You are an unpleasant fellow. Why must we get married. It would make no difference to our situation. We wouldn't worry about other people. We have such a wonderful life here, with your art. We don't need anything except each other, your art and Rome. I love Rome so much now: I've changed completely. You've got to find another motif—

to get down to work. When you're doing nothing, you start thinking … in a social direction … and that's not you at all … I don't recognise you like that. And so narrow-mindedly social too. In order to get married! For God's sake why, Duco? You know my ideas about marriage. I know from experience: it's better not to … " She had got up and was searching mechanically in a portfolio among half-finished sketches.

"Your experience … " he repeated. "We know each other too well to be frightened of anything."

She took the sketches out of the portfolio: they were the ideas that had emerged and which he had noted down while he was working on *Banners*. She looked through them and spread them out.

"Frightened?" she repeated vaguely.

"No," he suddenly continued more firmly. "A person never knows another person. I don't know you, I don't know myself."

Something deep inside herself warned her: don't get married, don't give in to him. It's better not, it's better not to … It was scarcely a whispering hint of a warning presentiment, it was not thought out, but unconscious and in her secret self. Because she was not aware of it, she did not think it, she scarcely heard it in herself. It went through her and it was not a feeling and it left only a recalcitrant resistance in her, very clearly … Only years later was she to understand that resistance …

"No, Duco, it's better if we don't … "

"Think about it, Cornélie."

"It's better if we don't," she repeated stubbornly. "Come on, let's stop talking about it. It's better if we don't, but I hate saying no to you, because you want to. I never refuse you anything else. Apart from that I'd do anything in the world for you. But I have the feeling about this: it's … better … if we don't!"

She came over to him and embraced him, filled with the desire to caress.

"Don't ask me again. What a cloud across your face! I can see that you'll go on thinking about it."

She stroked his forehead as if to wipe his frown away.

"Don't think about it any more. I love you! I love you! I want nothing else but you … I am happy as we are, why aren't you? Because Gilio was coarse and Urania prim? Come and look at your sketches. Are you going to get straight back to work? I love it when you're working. Then I shall write something else: a piece about an old Italian castle. My memories of San Stefano. Perhaps a novella with the pergola as the background. Oh, that beautiful pergola … But yesterday, that knife! Duco, are you going to get back to work? Let's have a look together. What a lot of ideas you had then! But don't get too symbolical: I mean, don't acquire those tics, those repetitions of yourself … That woman here, she's beautiful … She is walking unconsciously on a downward path and those pushing hands around her, and those red flowers in the abyss … Duco, what did you mean by that?"

"I don't know. I wasn't clear about it myself … "

"I like it, but I didn't like that sketch. I don't know why. There's something unpleasant about it I find. I find the woman stupid. I don't like those downward sloping lines: I like ascending lines, like in *Banners*. That flowed completely upwards out of the night, to the sun! How beautiful that was! What a pity we no longer have it, that it is being sold. If I were a painter I could never sell anything. I shall keep the sketches for it, as a souvenir. Don't you think it's awful that we no longer have it … He agreed: he also missed his *Banners*, which he loved. And together with her he searched through the other studies and sketches. But except for the unconscious woman there was nothing among them that was clear enough to be developed. And Cornélie did not want him to finish the unconscious woman: no, she did not like those downward sloping lines … But then he found sketches of landscape studies, of clouds and skies above the Campagna, Venice and Naples … And he set to work.

XLII

THEY WERE VERY THRIFTY, they had a little money and the months flowed past as if in a dream, through the scorching Rome summer. They continued their happy, isolated existence, seeing no one but Urania, who occasionally came to Rome, visited them, lunched with them in the studio and left again in the evening. Then Urania wrote to say that Gilio could no longer stand it at San Stefano and that they were going on a trip, first to Switzerland and later to Ostend. She came once more to say goodbye, and after that they saw no one else.

In the past Duco had known one artist, a painter and compatriot in Rome: now he knew no one, and saw no one. Their life in the cool studio was a lonely oasis existence in the sun-baked desert of Rome in August. To save money, they did not go into the mountains to somewhere cooler. They spent only what was absolutely necessary and their bohemian poverty with its backdrop of triptych and chasuble colours was still full of happiness.

But money remained tight. Duco sold the occasional watercolour, but sometimes they had to resort to selling a knick-knack. And it was always very painful for Duco to part with something he had collected. Their needs were few, but the rent for the studio occasionally had to be paid. Cornélie wrote the odd letter or sketch, which paid for what clothes she needed. She had a certain chic way of wearing clothes, a talent for looking elegant in a worn old blouse. She took great care of her hair, her skin, her teeth and her nails. She would wear an old hat with a new veil; and a pair of fresh gloves with an old walking dress, and she wore everything with style. At home, in her pink *peignoir*, now completely faded, she made such a charming picture that Duco was forever sketching her. They scarcely ever went out to eat any more. Cornélie would cook up something at home, dreaming up easy recipes, would buy a flask of wine from the first wine and oil shop she passed, with coachmen drinking outside at tables, and they would eat better and cheaper at home than in the *osteria*. And Duco, now he no longer frequented the antique dealers down by the Tiber, spent nothing. But money remained tight. Once, after they had sold a silver crucifix for far too little, Cornélie was so discouraged that she sobbed against Duco's chest. He comforted her, stroked her hair and maintained that he did not care that much for the crucifix. But she knew that it was a very beautiful anonymous sixteenth-century piece, and it pained him greatly to have lost it. And she told him seriously that things could not go on like this, that she could not be a burden on him, and that they must separate: that she would look for something, would go back to Holland … He was startled by her despair, and said that there was no need, that he would look after her, as a wife, but that he was an impractical fellow who could do nothing but daub a little, and not even enough to make a living. But she said that he must not talk like that, that he was a great artist, who did not have a facile, profitable productivity, but he was all the greater for that. She said that she did not want to live on his money, but wanted to fend for herself.

And she gathered up the scattered remnants of her feminist ideas. Again he asked her to consent to a marriage: they would make things up with his mother and Mrs Van der Staal would restore the allowance she had given him when he had lived with her at Belloni. But in the first place she refused to contemplate marriage and in the second place to accept any support from his mother, just as he did not want money from Urania. How often Urania had offered to help! He had never wanted to accept: he had even been angry when Urania had given Cornélie a blouse, which she had accepted with a kiss.

No, things could not go on like this: they must separate: she would go back to Holland, look for something. It was easier in Holland than abroad … But the sight of their happiness tottering before his eyes filled him with such despair that he hugged her to him and she too sobbed, her arms round his neck. "Why separate?" he asked. They would be stronger together. He could no longer do without her: life without her would be no life at all. In the past he had lived in his dream, now he lived in the reality of their happiness.

And that was as far as they got: unable to change anything, they were as miserly as possible, in order to stay together. He finished his landscapes, which always sold, but he sold them at once, so as not to have to wait. But then penury threatened once more and she thought of writing to Holland. At that very moment she received a letter from her mother, followed by one from one of her sisters. In those letters they asked if it was true what they were saying in The Hague, that she was living with Van der Staal. She had always seen herself as so far away from

The Hague and Hague society that she had never suspected that her life could become public knowledge. She spoke to no one, she knew no one with Dutch connections … But whatever the case, her independence was now out in the open. She answered the letters in a feminist vein: confessed her antipathy to marriage, and admitted that she was living with Van der Staal. She wrote in a cool, businesslike tone, in order to impress people in The Hague with her liberated state. They knew her brochure of course. But she realised now that she could no longer think of Holland. She wrote off her family. She did feel a slight wrench, an unconscious sense of family ties. But the ties were already loosened by lack of sympathy, especially at the time of her divorce. She felt completely alone: all she had was her happiness, her love, her Duco. Oh, it was enough, enough for a whole lifetime. If only she could earn some money! But how? She went to the Dutch consul and asked his advice: to no avail. She was not cut out to be a sister of mercy: she wanted to start earning at once and she could not study. She could serve in a shop. And she offered her services, without telling Duco, but despite her worn-out coat everyone thought her too much of a lady, and she considered the wages too low for a full day's work. And when she felt that it was not in her blood to work for a living, despite all her ideas, all her logic, despite her pamphlet and her liberated lifestyle, she felt helpless to the point of despair, and as she went home, tired, worn out by climbing stairs and useless job interviews, the old lament rose to her lips:

"Oh God, tell me what I'm to do … !!"

XLIII

SHE WROTE REGULARLY to Urania, in Switzerland, to Ostend, and Urania always wrote back so sweetly and offered her help. But Cornélie invariably rejected it, frightened as she was of hurting Duco. She herself felt easier about it, especially now she realised that she was incapable of working. But she understood Duco's attitude and respected it. Personally, though, she would have accepted, now her pride was wavering anyway, now her ideas were crumbling, too weak for the unremitting pressure of the daily grind. It was like a great finger brushing against a house of cards: every thing that had been built with care and pride, collapsed at the slightest touch. All that remained standing were her love and happiness, unshakeable amid the ruins, Oh, how she loved him, how simple and true their love was! How precious he was to her, for his softness, his even temper, as if his nervous tension served only to experience art with greater delicacy. She had a wonderful feeling that his calm was imperturbable, had been found for all time. Without that happiness they would never have been able to drag themselves through their difficult existence from day to day. As it was they did not feel the daily weight, as if they were pulling the load forward together, from one day to the next. As it was they felt the weight only occasionally, when the following day was completely dark and they did not know where they were dragging their burden of existence into the darkness of that future. But over and over again they won through: they loved each other too much to collapse under the load. Again and again they took heart: with a smile they supported each other's strength.

September came, and October, and Urania wrote to say that they were returning to San Stefano and would stay for a month or two, before going to Nice for the winter. And one morning, unexpectedly, Urania came into the studio. She found Cornélie alone: Duco had gone to see an art dealer. They greeted each other warmly.

"I'm so happy to see you again!" chattered Urania cheerfully. "I'm happy to be back in Italy and to stay a little longer at San Stefano. And is everything as it was in your cosy studio? Are you happy? Oh, I needn't ask … !"

And exuberant as a child she embraced Cornélie, never finding it in her heart to disapprove of her friend's over-free lifestyle, especially not now, after her own summer in Ostend … They sat side by side on the sofa, Cornélie in her old *peignoir*, which she wore with her own unique grace, and the young princess in her light-grey tailored suit that clung fashionably to her shape, its heavy silk lining rustling, with her silver sequined hat with black feathers, her jewelled fingers, playing with a very long watch chain that she wore round her neck: the very latest fashion. Cornélie was able to admire without jealousy and she made Urania stand up and twirl round in front of her, and loved the cut of her skirt; she said that her hat looked absolutely charming on her and studied the chain closely. And she became absorbed in talk of chiffons; Urania described the outfits worn in Ostend … and Urania admired Cornélie's old *peignoir*. Cornélie laughed.

"Particularly after Ostend, I suppose?" she joked. But Urania was serious and meant it: Cornélie wore it with such style! And, changing the subject, she said she wished to speak very seriously. That she knew of something that might suit Cornélie, since Cornélie never wanted to accept her help. In Ostend she had met an elderly American lady, Mrs Uxeley, quite a character. She was ninety and spent her winters in Nice. She was wealthy: a petrol empire fortune. She was ninety, but still acted as if she were forty-five. She went out, appeared in society, flirted. People laughed at her, but accepted her, for the sake of her money and her magnificent parties. In Nice the whole cosmopolitan colony came to her place. Urania took out an Ostend casino magazine and read out a news item about a ball in Ostend in which Mrs Uxeley was called *'la femme la plus élégante d'Ostende'*. The journalist had received a certain sum for this, the whole world laughed and enjoyed itself. Mrs Uxeley was a caricature, but with enough tact to be taken seriously. Well, Mrs Uxeley was looking for someone. She always had a companion with her, a young woman, and there had been an endless succession of such ladies. She had had cousins with her, distant cousins, very distant cousins and total strangers. She was difficult, capricious, impossible: it was common knowledge. Would Cornélie like to try? Urania had already raised it with Mrs Uxeley and recommended her friend. Cornélie did not find the prospect very appealing, but it was worth thinking about. Mrs Uxeley's companion was staying on till November, when 'the old thing' returned to Nice via Paris. And in Nice they, Cornélie and Urania, would see a lot of each other. But Cornélie was appalled

by the thought of leaving Duco. She thought it would
never be possible, they were so accustomed to each other.
Financially it would be an ideal solution—an easy life that
appealed to her after the blow to her moral pride—but
she could not think of leaving Duco. And what would
Duco do in Nice! No, she simply couldn't: she would stay
with him … She felt a reluctance to go, as if a hand were
restraining her. She told Urania to put off the old lady,
tell her to look for someone else. She couldn't do it. What
good was such a life—dependent but financially independent, without Duco! And when Urania had gone—
she was continuing on to San Stefano—Cornélie was glad
that she had immediately refused this stupid, easy, dependent life of lady's companion to a rich old battleaxe. She
looked round the studio. She loved its beautiful colours,
its noble old objects, and behind that curtain her bed and
behind that screen her paraffin stove, which served as a
kitchen. With its bohemian mix of precious knick-knacks
and very primitive comforts, it had become indispensable
to her, her home. And when Duco came home, and she
put her arms round him, she told him about Urania and
Mrs Uxeley, happy to nestle against him. He had sold
some watercolours. There was absolutely no reason to
leave him. He did not want her too either, he would never
want it. And they held each other tight, as if they could
feel something that might separate them, an inexorable
necessity, as if hands were floating around them, pushing,
guiding, restraining and defending, a battle of hands, like
a cloud around the two of them; hands trying to sunder
violently their glistening lifeline, their merged lifeline,
though too narrow for both their feet, and the hands

would wrest them apart, making the single great line spiral apart into two. They said nothing: in each other's arms they looked at life, shuddered at the hands, felt the approach of that pressure, already piling up more densely around them. But they felt each other's warmth: in their close embrace they hugged their little happiness, hid it between them, so that the hands could not point to it, touch it, push it …

And under their fixed gaze life receded gently, the cloud dissolved, the hands disappeared and a sigh of relief rose from their chests, as she lay silently against him, and closed her eyes, as if to sleep …

XLIV

BUT THE PRESSURE of life returned, the floating hands reappeared, as a gentle, mysterious force. Cornélie wept bitterly, and admitted it to herself and to Duco: they could not go on like this. At one point they did not have enough for the rent of the studio and had to appeal to Urania. Gaps had appeared in the studio, colours had thinned, because things had been sold that Duco had collected with tenderness and sacrifice. But the angel of Lippo Memmi, which he refused to sell, with its gesture of proffering lilies, was as radiant as ever in its robe of gold brocade. Around them there were sad spaces on the walls where nails had been exposed. At first they tried rearranging things, but they lost heart. And as they sat together, in each other's arms, feeling their little happiness, but also the pressure of life with its pushing hands, they closed their eyes, so as not to see the studio that seemed to be crumbling around them, where in the first cooler days a sunless chill descended from the ceiling that looked higher and more distant and where the easel awaited, empty. They both closed their eyes and kept them closed, feeling, despite the strength of their happiness and love, gradually defeated by life, which was remorseless in its pressure and robbed them of something every day. Once when they were sitting like this their hands fell limply apart, their embrace disengaged, as if hands were pulling them away from each other. For a long time they remained sitting there, side by side, without touching. Then she broke into a loud sob and threw herself face down on his knees. There was nothing more for it: life had proved stronger, silent life, the remorseless pressure of life that surrounded them with so many hands. And it was as if their little happiness was lost to them like an angelic child that had died and slipped from their embrace.

She said that she would write to Urania: the Forte-Braccios were in Nice. Unenthusiastically, he agreed. And as soon as she received a reply, she took out her suitcase and, like an automaton, packed her old clothes. Urania wrote telling her to come and saying that Mrs Uxeley wanted to see her. Mrs Uxeley sent her the fare. She was at her wits' end, nervous and constantly breaking into sobs, and felt as if she were tearing herself away from him, from the home she loved that was crumbling around them, through her fault alone. When she received the registered letter containing the fare, she had a fit of hysteria, nestling against him like a child, crying plaintively that she could not do it, that she did not want to do it, that she could not live without him, that she would love him forever, that she would die so far from him. She lay on the sofa, her legs stiff, her arms stiff, and screamed with her mouth contorted as if in physical pain. He rocked her in his arms, dabbed her forehead, gave her ether to sniff, comforted her, said that it would all come right later … Later … She looked blankly at him, almost crazed with the pain. She threw everything out of her case again, across the room, underwear, blouses, and laughed and laughed … He begged her to control herself. When she saw the dismay on his face and when he too sobbed in her arms, she hugged him tightly to her, kissed him, comforted him in turn … And everything in her subsided, dull and limp … They repacked the case together. Then she looked round and in a burst of energy arranged the studio for *him*, got him to remove her bed, fixed his own sketches to the wall, tried to rebuild something of what had crumbled around them, rearranged everything and did her best. She cooked their final meal, banked up the fire … But a desperate threat of loneliness and desolation was all-pervading. They could not do it, they could not do it … They fell asleep sobbing, in each others' arms, close together. The next morning he took her to the station. And once she had boarded the train and was in her compartment, both of them lost control. They embraced sobbing, as the conductor tried to close the door. She saw him walking away like a madman, barging his way through the thronging crowd, and broken with sorrow threw herself back in her seat. She was so overcome and so close to fainting that a lady next to her came to her assistance and washed her face with eau-de-Cologne …

   She thanked the lady, apologised and seeing the other passengers looking at her with sympathy, she controlled herself and fell into a dull stupor, staring blankly out of the window. She travelled on and on, stopping nowhere, getting out only to change trains. Though hungry, she had no energy to order anything at the stations. She ate nothing and drank nothing. She travelled for a day and a night and arrived late the next evening in Nice. Urania was at the station and was alarmed at Cornélie's grey pallor, utter exhaustion and hollow-eyed expression. She was very sweet to her; she took Cornélie home with her, nursed her for a few days, made her stay in bed, and went personally to Mrs Uxeley to tell her that her friend was too unwell to report. Gilio briefly paid his respects to Cornélie, and she could only thank him for the days of hospitality and care under his roof. The young princess was like a sister, a mother, building up Cornélie's strength with milk, eggs, and fortifying tonics. Obediently she submitted to Urania's ministrations, dull and indifferent, and ate in order to please Urania. After a few days Urania said that Mrs Uxeley, curious to see her new companion, was going to visit that afternoon. Mrs Uxeley was now alone, but could wait until Cornélie was better. Dressed as smartly as she could she sat with Urania and awaited the old lady's arrival. She made an exuberant entrance, talking non-stop, and in the dim light of Urania's drawing-room Cornélie could not believe that she was ninety. Urania winked at her, but she could only smile feebly: she was dreading this first interview. But Mrs Uxeley, probably because Cornélie was the friend of the Princess di Forte-Braccio, was very unstuffy, very pleasant, not at all condescending towards her future lady's companion; she inquired after Cornélie's health in an exhaustingly expansive stream of exclamations and phrases and helpful hints. In the subdued light of the lace-shaded standard lamps, Cornélie surveyed her and saw a woman of fifty, with her wrinkles carefully powdered, in a mauve velvet outfit embroidered with old gold and sequins and beads, her brown wavy chignon topped by a hat with white feathers. She was very mobile and hectic, so that her jewels were constantly sparkling. She now took Cornélie's hand

and began talking intimately … So Cornélie would be coming the day after tomorrow? Good. She usually paid a hundred dollars a month, or five hundred francs: never less, but never more. But she realised that Cornélie needed something at once, for new outfits: so would she order what she needed from this address, on Mrs Uxeley's account? A couple of ball gowns, a couple of less dressy evening outfits, everything in fact. Princess Urania would no doubt tell her and go with her. And she got up, doing her best to behave like a young woman, fluttering about with her lorgnette, but all the while leaning on her parasol, while a sudden twinge of rheumatism revealed all kinds of wrinkles. Urania accompanied her to the corridor and came back shrieking with laughter; Cornélie joined in very feebly. It mattered nothing to her: she was more astonished than amused by Mrs Uxeley. Ninety! Ninety!! What energy, worthy of a better goal than trying to remain elegant: *'la femme la plus élégante d'Ostende!!'*

Ninety! How that woman must suffer, the hours of time-consuming toilet, in order to turn herself into this caricature. Urania said that everything was false, her hair and her neckline! And Cornélie felt revulsion at the prospect of living from now on with that woman, as if with something unworthy. Much of her energy had been drained by her happy love life, as if their twin happiness—Duco's and hers—had made her less fit for further existential struggle and had softened her in its splendour, but it had refined and purified something in her soul and she was revolted by so much pretence for so petty and vain a purpose. And it was only pure necessity—the gradualness of life that impelled her and pushed her gently

with its guiding finger along a lifeline that was now winding away into loneliness—necessity that gave her the
strength to hide away her sorrow, her longing, her homesickness for all she had left behind, deep within her. She
decided to say no more about it to Urania. Urania was so
happy to see her, regarded her as a good friend, in the
loneliness of her exalted life, in her isolation amid her
aristocratic acquaintances. Urania had enthusiastically
accompanied her to seamstresses and shops and helped
her choose her new trousseau. It left her cold. She, the
elegant woman, innately elegant, who in her appearance
had always defended herself against poverty, who with a
fresh ribbon was able to wear an old blouse gracefully, in
the days of her happiness, was totally indifferent to everything she was now buying at Mrs Uxeley's expense. It was
as if it were not for her. She let Urania ask and choose,
and went along with everything. She tried things on like
an automaton. She was so upset to have to spend so
much at a stranger's expense. She felt demeaned, humil-
iated: all her haughty pride in herself had gone. She was
afraid of what might be thought of her in Mrs Uxeley's
circle of acquaintances, unsure whether they would know
of her liberal ideas, her relationship with Duco, and she
was afraid of Mrs Uxeley's opinion. Because Urania had
had to be honest and tell her everything. It was only
because of Urania's warm recommendation that Mrs
Uxeley was still prepared to employ her. She felt out of
place, now she had to join in with all those people again,
and she was afraid of showing her true colours. She
would have to play-act, disguise her ideas, weigh her
words, and she was no longer used to that. And all that

for money. All because she did not have the strength to earn her living alongside Duco, and happily and independent, encourage him in his work, his art. Oh, if only she had been able and had found some way, how happy she would have been. If only she had not allowed to fester in her the wretched languor of her blood, her upbringing, her brilliant drawing-room education languor, which rendered her unfit for anything! In her blood she was both a woman of love and a woman of luxury, but more love than luxury: she could be happy with the simplest thing if only she could love. And now life had torn her from him, slowly but surely. And now she had luxury, dependent luxury, and it no longer satisfied her blood, because she could no longer satisfy her deepest need. Fatal discontent ran riot in that lonely soul. The only happiness she possessed were his letters, his long letters, letters of longing, but also letters of comfort. He wrote to her of his longing, but also wrote to give her courage and hope. He wrote to her every day. He was in Florence now and sought consolation in the Uffizi and the Pitti Palace. He had not been able to stay in Rome, and the studio was now closed up. In Florence he was slightly closer to her. And his letters were like a book of love to her, the only novel she read, and it was as if she saw his landscapes in his style, the same haziness of intensely felt colour, the pearly white and dreamily hazy light distance: the horizon of his longing, as if his eyes were always straying to the horizon, where the night of their parting had disappeared as if into a peacock-grey sunset; a whiff of the sad Campagna. In those letters they were still living together. But she could not write to him in the same way. Although she wrote to him every day, she wrote concisely, always the same thing in different words: her longing, her dull indifference. She told him, though, how she loved his letters, which were like her daily bread.

She was now with Mrs Uxeley and occupied two charming rooms of the huge twelve-roomed villa, with a view of the sea and of the Promenade des Anglais. Urania had helped her arrange them. And she lived in an unreal dream of alienation, non-existence, of soulless being, of unfelt actions and gestures, in accordance with the will of others. In the mornings she would visit Mrs Uxeley in her boudoir and read to her: American and French newspapers, and sometimes an extract from a French novelette. Humbly, she did her best. Mrs Uxeley thought she read well, but simply said she should cheer up now, that her sad days were over. No mention was made of Duco and Mrs Uxeley acted as if he did not exist. The great boudoir, with its balcony doors open, looked out over the sea where the morning promenade was already beginning, with the colourful and patchy shapes of parasols, delicately garish against the deep-blue sea, a sea of luxury, water of wealth, wavelets that had an expensive look before charmingly consenting to break into foam. The old lady, already made up, with her wig on and a white lace cap over it against the draught lay on her chaise-longue piled with cushions in the black and white lace of her white silk *peignoir*. With her lorgnette, initialled in diamonds, in her wrinkled hand, she liked to peer at the brash patches of the parasols outside. Now and then a rheumatic twinge would suddenly make her wince so that her face became a single crumpled surface of wrinkles, beneath which the even sheen of her make-up almost cracked, like craquelé china. In daylight she seemed scarcely alive, she seemed an automaton assembled from desiccated limbs, which still spoke and gesticulated. She was always a little tired in the mornings, at night she never slept; after eleven she took a nap. She lived according to a strict regime, and her doctor, who called every day, seemed to breathe new life into her every time, enabling her to hold out till evening. In the afternoons she drove around, got out at the Jetée and made her calls. But in the evenings she revived, with a hint of real animation, dressed, put on her jewels, recovered her exuberance, her exclamations, and her poses … Then it was balls, parties, the theatre. Then she was not a day over fifty.

But those were the good days. Sometimes, after a night of unbearable pain, she stayed in her bedroom, the previous day's make-up not retouched, a black lace shawl over her bald head, in a black satin morning coat, which hung round her like a comfortable sack, and she groaned, screamed, shouted and seemed to be begging for mercy from her torment. This went on for a few days and occurred at regular three-week intervals: then she gradually revived again.

Her hectic conversation was limited to a regularly recurring discussion of all kinds of family matters. She explained to Cornélie all the family relations of her acquaintances, American and European, but was particularly fond of expanding on the great European families that she included among her acquaintances. Cornélie could never bear to listen and immediately forgot the acquaintances. It was sometimes intolerable to listen for so long, and for no other reason, as if compelled, Cornélie found the strength to talk a little herself, tell an anecdote or a story. When she saw that the old woman was very partial to anecdotes, riddles, puns, especially with a slightly risqué edge, she collected as many as she could from the *Vie Parisienne* and the *Journal pour Rire*, and always had them to hand. And Mrs Uxeley found her amusing. Once, noticing Duco's daily letter, she made an allusion, and Cornélie suddenly realised that she was dying with curiosity. So she calmly told the truth: her marriage, her divorce, her liberal ideas, her meeting and relationship with Duco. The old woman was a little disappointed that Cornélie should talk about this with such simplicity. Her only advice was that the proprieties should now be observed. What friends said about the past was less important. But there must be no offence given now. Cornélie meekly gave her word. And Mrs Uxeley showed her albums, her own portraits from when she was a young woman, and the portraits of all kinds of men. And she talked of this friend and that, and in her vanity hinted at a very turbulent past. But she had always observed the proprieties … That was her pride. What Cornélie had done was not good …

The time between eleven and twelve-thirty brought relief. The old woman regularly had a siesta at that time—her only sleep—and Urania would come to collect Cornélie. They drove round a little or walked along the Promenade or sat in the Jardin Public. It was the only moment when Cornélie appreciated some of her new-found luxury and to some extent flattered her vanity. Walkers looked round at the two beautiful young women in their immaculate linen outfits, whose fashionably hatted heads withdrew under the twilight of their parasols and they admired the gleaming victoria, the impeccable livery and the grey horses of the Princess di Forte-Braccio.

Gilio was diffident and modest in his dealings with Cornélie. He was polite, but at a courteous distance, if he joined the two ladies for a moment in the garden or on the Jetée. Since the night in the pergola, after the sudden flash of his angry dagger, she was afraid of him, partly because she had lost much of her courage and her pride. But she could not be any cooler to him in her replies than she already was, since she was grateful to him, as she was to Urania, for looking after her for the first few days, and for the tact with which they had not left her immediately to the mercy of Mrs Uxeley, but had kept her at their place where she had regained some strength.

On those mornings off, when she felt released from the caricature of her life, from the old woman—vain, selfish, insignificant, ridiculous—she felt herself, with Urania's friendship, regaining her old self, became aware of being in Nice, saw the colourful bustle around her with clearer eyes and lost the sense of unreality of the first few days. And it was as if she were seeing herself again for the first time, in her light linen walking suit, sitting in the Garden, her gloved fingers playing with the tassels of her parasol. She could still scarcely believe in herself, but she could see herself. She kept her longing, her homesickness, her oppressive discontent, deep inside, hidden even from Urania. Sometimes she felt she would choke. But she listened to Urania and talked and joined in the laughter and looked up at Gilio with a laugh, as he stood in front of her posing on the toes of his shoes, his walking stick dangling in his hands, behind his back. Sometimes— as in a vision swirling through the crowd—she would suddenly see Duco, the studio, her past happiness fading away for a brief moment. And then placing her fingertips between the lace strips curling in front of her bolero she would feel his letter of that morning and crumpled the stiff envelope against her breast like something of his that caressed her.

There was no escaping it: she saw herself, and Nice around her, and she felt her new life: it was not unreality, although for her soul it was not real: it was sad play-acting in which, dull, tired, weak and listless—she played a part.

XLV

EVERYTHING WAS ARRANGED as if according to a strict regime, which excluded even the slightest variation: everything was fixed as if by law. The reading of the newspaper, her one and a half hours off; then lunch, after lunch the drive, the Jetée, the visits; every day the calls, afternoon teas; occasionally a dinner, in the evenings generally a ball, a soirée, a play. She made scores of new acquaintances and immediately forgot about them, and when she saw them again could never remember whether she knew them or not. In general she was quite well treated in those cosmopolitan circles, as it was known that she was a close friend of Princess Urania. But like Urania herself, on the female side of the old Italian names and titles, who sometimes made their dazzling appearance in those circles, she experienced devastating haughtiness and contempt. The gentlemen were always introduced to her, but whenever she was occasionally introduced to their ladies, a vague, astonished nod of the head was the only response. It mattered little to her personally, but she felt sorry for Urania, For she saw clearly, at Urania's own soirées, how they scarcely regarded her as the hostess, how they surrounded and fêted Gilio, but gave his wife only a minimum of politeness due to her as Princess di Forte-Braccio, without forgetting for a moment that she was Miss Hope. And such lack of respect was harder for Urania to endure than for her. She assumed her role of lady's companion. She kept a constant watch on Mrs Uxeley, repeatedly joining her for a moment, fetching a fan that Mrs Uxeley had left behind from another drawing-room, constantly performing some small service or other. Then, alone in the hectic hubbub of the room, she sat down against the wall, looking indifferently ahead of her. She sat there, still elegant, in an attitude of graceful indifference and dull boredom. Tapping her foot, or opening her fan. She paid no attention to anyone. Sometimes a few gentlemen would come over to her, and she would talk to them or dance a little, indifferently as if she were bestowing a favour. Once, when Gilio was talking to her, she seated and he standing, and the Duchess di Luca and Countess Costi came up together and, still standing, began bantering exuberantly with him without giving her so much as a look or a word, she first sat and looked the ladies up and down with mocking irony, then slowly rose and taking Gilio's arm said, giving them a piercing needle-like look from narrowed eyes:

"I'm sorry … you'll have to excuse me if I steal the Prince di Forte-Braccio away from you; I need to speak to him privately for a moment … "

And with the pressure of her arm she forced Gilio two steps further, immediately sat down again, made him sit next to her and began whispering to him in a familiar tone, leaving the duchess and the countess standing two metres away open-mouthed at her impudence, and moreover spread her train wide between herself and the ladies and waved her fan as if to keep a distance. She was able to do this with such calm, such tact and hauteur, that Gilio was tickled to death, and giggled with her in delight.

"Urania should be able to act like that occasionally," he said, grateful as a child for the amusement she had accorded him.

"Urania is too sweet to be so spiteful," she replied.

She did not make herself popular, but people became afraid of her, afraid of her calm spitefulness, and henceforth were wary of offending her. In addition, the gentlemen found her beautiful and attractive, partly attracted by her indifferent hauteur. And without really wanting to, she gained a position, apparently with the greatest diplomacy and in reality, of course, a step at a time. While Mrs Uxeley's egoism was flattered by her little attentions, which she remembered religiously and performed with a charming youthful maternal air, in contrast to which Mrs Uxeley delighted in posing as a young girl, she gradually gathered an entourage of gentlemen around her, and the ladies became cloyingly polite. Urania often told her how clever she thought her, what tact she had. Cornélie shrugged her shoulders: it all went of its own accord, and she did not really care. Still, slowly, she regained something of her cheerfulness. When she saw herself standing in the mirror opposite, she could not help but admit that she was more beautiful than she had ever been, as a young girl, as a newly married woman. Her tall slim figure had a line of pride and languor, which gave her a special grace; her neck was noble, her bosom fuller, her waist slimmer in these new outfits, her hips were heavier, her arms had become plumper and though she no longer had that sheen, that happiness across her face that she had had in Rome, her mocking laugh, the indifferent irony gave her a special attraction to those strange men, something that enticed and provoked more than the most outrageous flirting would have done. And Cornélie had not wanted this, but now it came of its own accord, she accepted it. It was not in her blood to refuse. And apart from that Mrs Uxeley was satisfied with her. Cornélie could whisper so sweetly to her, "Ma'am, you were in such pain yesterday. Shouldn't you go home a little earlier tonight?" Whereupon Mrs Uxeley postured like a girl being warned by her mother not to dance too much that evening. She loved these niceties, and Cornélie, indifferent, gave her what she wanted. And they amused her more on those evenings but the amusement was mixed with self-reproach the moment she thought of Duco, of their parting, of Rome, of the studio, of past happiness that she had lost through her weakness.

XLVI

A ND SO SEVERAL MONTHS had passed; it was
January and these were busy days for Cornélie,
since Mrs Uxeley was soon to give one of her famous
parties, and Cornélie's morning breaks were now taken
up with running all kinds of errands. Urania usually drove
with her and was very supportive. They had to go to wall-
paperers, *patissiers*, florists and jewellers, where Cornélie
and Urania chose presents for the *cotillon*. Mrs Uxeley
did not go out shopping, but at home concerned herself
with every detail and there were endless discussions,
followed by further drives to the shops, since the old lady
was far from easy, conceited about the reputation of her
parties, and frightened of that reputation being lost
through the slightest slip.

On one of those drives, as the victoria turned into the
Avenue de la Gare, Cornélie started so violently that she
grabbed Urania by the arm and could not suppress a cry.
Urania asked her what she had seen, but she could not
speak and Urania made her get out at a confectioner's to
drink a glass of water. She was on the point of fainting
and was white as a ghost. She was not able to finish the
shopping, and they drove back to the villa. The old lady
was not happy about the fainting fit and made such a fuss
that Urania went off to do the rest of the shopping herself.
By the afternoon Cornélie had recovered, made her apolo-
gies and accompanied Mrs Uxeley to an afternoon tea.

The following day, sitting on the Jetée with Mrs Uxeley and some acquaintances, she appeared to see the same thing again. She went as white as a sheet, but kept her composure and laughed and chatted cheerfully. These were the days of preparation. The date of the party approached; finally the evening arrived. Mrs Uxeley was a-tremble with excitement like a young girl, and found the strength to inspect the whole house, which was ablaze with lights and flowers. And with a sigh of contentment she sat down for a moment. She was dressed. Her face was as smooth as porcelain, her hair, waved, glittered with diamond pins. She was dressed in a low-cut gown of light-blue brocade, and she sparkled like a saint's shrine. A constantly winding necklace of fabulous pearls came to below her stomach. In her hand—she was not yet wearing gloves—she held a gold-topped walking stick, indispensable for standing up. And only when she got up was she aware of her age, when she worked her way upright like a gymnast, with the pain on her face, with the twinge of rheumatism that shot through her. Cornélie, as yet undressed, after a final inspection of the villa, blazing with light, swooning with flowers, went to her room, and sank wearily into the chair in front of her dressing table to have her hair quickly done. She was nervous and hurried the chambermaid along. She was ready just as the first guests arrived, and was able to join Mrs Uxeley. The carriages rolled up; Cornélie, at the top of the monumental staircase, looked down into the hall-cum-vestibule, into which guests were pouring, the ladies still in their long cloaks—almost even more sumptuous than their gowns—which they then carefully deposited in the busily buzzing *vestiaire*. And the first guests came up the stairs, being careful not to be the first, to be smiled at by Mrs Uxeley. The drawing-rooms soon filled. Besides the reception rooms the hostess's own rooms were open and there was a continuous suite of twelve rooms. While the corridors and staircases were decorated with arrangements of just red and white camellias, in the rooms the floral decorations where in hundreds of vases and bowls, which were placed everywhere and, together with the naked candle flames, gave an intimate atmosphere to the party. This was the special feature of Mrs Uxeley's decoration of the reception rooms: no electric light, but candles in protective holders everywhere, the dishes and glasses full of flowers on all sides, making it like a fairy garden. If it lacked an overall unity of line, it gained a charming cosiness, allowing groups to form at will, behind a screen, in a loggia, everywhere there were intimate spots; and perhaps this was the reason for the rage for Mrs Uxeley's parties. The villa, fit to host a court ball, gave only parties of luxurious intimacy to hundreds of people who were total strangers to each other. The coteries found their own niches, and were immediately at home. A tiny boudoir, all in Japanese lacquer and Japanese silk, was intended for general use but was immediately commandeered by Gilio, the Countess di Rosavilla, the Duchess di Luca and the Countess Costi. They did not even venture into the music-room, where a concert was the first item on the programme. Paderewski was on the bill and Sigrid Arnoldson was to sing. The music-room was lit in the same way and it was generally whispered that in this delicate light Mrs Uxeley looked forty. In the interval she fluttered around two very young journalists, who were to write a piece on her party. Urania, sitting next to Cornélie, was addressed by a Frenchman, whom she introduced to her friend as the Chevalier de Breuil. Cornélie knew that Urania knew him from Ostend, and that his name had been mentioned in connection with the Princess di Forte-Braccio. Urania had never talked to her about De Breuil, but Cornélie now saw from her smile, her blushes and the sparkle in her eyes that people were right. She left the two of them alone, feeling sad for Urania. She understood that the young princess was consoling herself for the indifference of her husband—and found this whole life of appearances disgusting. She longed for Rome, for the studio, for Duco, for independence, love, happiness. She had had everything, but had not been allowed to stay. She had been forced back into pretence, convention, the disgusting comedy of life. It surrounded her like a great lie, more glittering than in The Hague, but even falser, more impudent, more perverse. People no longer even pretended to believe the lie: there was an impudent honesty in this. The lie was held in honour, but no one believed it, no one imposed the lie as truth; the lie was nothing but a form. Cornélie walked through the rooms alone, joined Mrs Uxeley for moment—as usual—asked whether she wanted anything, whether everything was in order—and continued on alone through the rooms. She was standing by a vase, arranging some orchids, when a woman in black velvet, blond, with a low neckline, spoke to her in English.

"I'm Mrs Holt: you may not know my name, but I know yours. I've been dying to meet you. I've been to Holland a lot and read a bit of Dutch. I read your pamphlet on the

Social Position of Divorced Women, and I was interested in much that you wrote."

"You're very kind; shall we sit down for a moment … I remember your name too … Weren't you on the committee of the Womens' Conference in London?"

"Yes … I spoke about the upbringing of children … Weren't you able to come to London?"

"No, I did think about it, but I was in Rome at the time, and I couldn't."

"What a shame. The conference was a great step forward. If your pamphlet had been translated for it, and become known, you would have had great success."

"I'm not really striving for success of that kind … "

"Of course, I quite understand. But the success of your book surely also benefits the great cause."

"Do you really mean that? Is there something valuable in my pamphlet?"

"Do you doubt it?"

"Very often … "

"Unbelievable… Yet it is written with such assurance."

"Perhaps for that very reason … "

"I don't understand you. There is sometimes a vagueness about the Dutch that we English find hard to understand. Something like the reflection of your beautiful skies in your characters."

"Do you never doubt? Are you sure about your ideas on the upbringing of children?"

"I have studied children in schools, crèches, at home, and I've developed very clear ideas. And following those ideas I am working for the people of the future. I'll send you my pamphlet, the quintessence of my speeches at the conference. Are you working on a new brochure at present?"

"No, unfortunately not … "

"Why not? We must all close ranks in order to triumph."

"I think I've said all I have to say … I wrote on impulse, from my own experience. And then … "

"Then … "

"Then everything changed … All women are different, and I never liked generalising. And do you believe that *many* women can work for a worldwide goal with the perseverance of a man, if they have found a small goal for themselves, a small happiness, for example, a love for their own self, in which they are happy? Do you not think that in every woman there is a latent egoism for her own love, happiness, and that when she has found that … she loses interest in the world and the future?"

"Perhaps … But how few women find that."

"I don't think many do … But that is a different question. And I believe that for most women interest in world affairs is a second best."

"You have lost the faith. You speak quite differently than you wrote a year ago … "

"Yes. I've become very humble, because I am more honest. Of course I believe in a few women, in a few great spirits. But I wonder if the majority are not stuck with their female frailty … "

"No, not with a sensible upbringing."

"Yes, I think it's the upbringing … "

"Of the infant, of the young girl … "

"I don't think I was ever brought up properly, and I expect that's my weakness."

"Our girls must be told very young about life's struggles."

"You're right. We, my girlfriends, my sisters and I, were steered as soon as possible towards the safe haven of marriage … Do you know who I feel most sorry for? Our parents! Didn't they think that they were teaching us everything we needed to know? And now at this point they have to realise that they could not look into the future, and that their upbringing wasn't an upbringing, since they did not point out to their children the struggle that was being fought out before their very eyes. They are our parents and they deserve our pity. They cannot put anything right at this stage. They see us, girls, young women from twenty to thirty, overwhelmed by life, and they did not give us the strength to deal with it. They kept us safe for as long as possible in the parental niche, and then they thought about marrying us off. In no way in order to get rid of us, but for our happiness, our safety and our future. We may be unhappy, we girls and women, who did not, like our younger sisters, have the struggle close to home pointed out to us, but I believe that we still have the hope of our own youth, and I feel that our poor parents are unhappier and more pitiable than we are, because they have nothing left to hope for, because secretly they *must* admit to themselves that they went astray in their love for their children. They brought us up by the rules of the past, when the future was already so close at hand. I feel sorry for our parents and it almost makes me love them more than I ever did … "

XLVII

SHE HAD SUDDENLY GONE PALE as if seized by a powerful emotion. She covered her face with her waving fan and her fingers trembled violently; her whole body shuddered.

"That is a beautiful thought," said Mrs Holt. "It was a pleasure to meet you. I always find a particular charm in Dutch people. There is that vagueness that we find so elusive, and then a sudden light that flashes as if from a cloud … I hope to meet you again. I am at home every Tuesday at five o'clock. Would you drop in sometime with Mrs Uxeley?"

"Certainly, with great pleasure … "

Mrs Holt proffered a hand, which she shook, and disappeared among the other guests. Cornélie had got up, her knees unsteady. She stood there, half turned towards the room, looking in the mirror. Her fingers played with the orchids in a Venetian glass on the console. She was still a little pale, but she controlled herself, though her heart was pounding and her chest heaving. She looked in the mirror and saw first her own figure, her slender beautiful shape in her black and white chantilly outfit, with its white lace train, foaming with flounces; the black lace tunic over it was scalloped and strewn with steel sequins and blue stones with a spray of orchids on her completely sleeveless corsage, which left her neck, arms and shoulders bare. Her hair was held in place by three Greek pearl bands, and her white feather fan—a present from Urania —was as light as foam against her neck. In the mirror she saw first herself and then *him*. He approached her. She did not move, only her fingers played with the flowers in the glass. She had an impulse to flee, but her knees were shaking and her feet seemed paralysed. She seemed rooted to the spot, as if hypnotised. She could not move. And she saw him coming closer and closer, while her back was half turned to the room. He approached and in so doing seemed to emit a web in which she was trapped. Mechanically she looked up and her eyes met his in the mirror. She thought she would faint. She felt wedged between him and the glass. In the mirror the room revolved, the candles whirled giddily, like a dancing firmament. He still said nothing. Then in the unbearably narrow space between him and the mirror, which did not even protect her as a wall might have done, but reflected him so that he seemed to have caught her twice over, from two directions at one—she slowly turned and looked him in the eye, but did not speak either. They surveyed each other in silence.

"You never thought … you'd ever see me here," he said at last.

It was over a year since she had heard his voice. But she felt it inside her.

"No," she said at last, haughty, cold and distant. "Although I saw you a few times, in town, on the Jetée."

"Yes," he said. "Should I have said hello, do you think?"

She shrugged her bare shoulders, and he looked at them. She felt for the first time that she was half-naked that evening.

"No," she replied, still cold and distant. "Just as you needn't have spoken to me just now."

He smiled at her. He stood before her like a wall. Like a man. His head, his shoulders, his chest, his legs, his whole figure loomed in front of her in their intense masculinity.

"Naturally I didn't need to," he replied, and she felt his voice inside her, and she felt the sound of him pouring into her like molten bronze into a vase. "And if I'd met you somewhere in Holland, I would have simply taken off my hat, but not talked to you. But we're in a foreign country here … "

"What has that got to do with it?"

"I felt like talking to you … I wanted a talk with you. Can we do that as strangers?"

"Strangers … " she repeated.

"Well, all right, we're not strangers. In fact, we are surprisingly intimately acquainted, aren't we? Come and sit next to me and tell me how you've been getting on. Did you like Rome … "

"Yes," she said.

As if by willpower he had guided her towards a chaise-longue behind a Louis XV screen, half damask, half glass—and she sank down into a rosy twilight of candles, surrounded by bouquets of pink roses in all kinds of Venetian glasses. He sat down on a pouf, leaning slightly towards her, arms across his knees, hands folded.

"There was quite a lot of talk about you in The Hague. First about your pamphlet. And then about your painter."

Her eyes bored into him like needles. He laughed.

"You can look just as angry as you used to. Tell me, do you still hear from your family? They're in a bad way."

"Now and then. I was able to send them some money recently."

"That's damned nice of you. They don't deserve it. They said that you'd ceased to exist for them."

"Mama wrote to say they had such terrible money worries. So I sent a hundred guilders. I couldn't afford any more."

"Oh, now they see you send money, I expect you'll exist for them again."

She shrugged her shoulders.

"I don't care about that. I felt sorry for them. I was sorry I couldn't send more."

"No, not if you look so extraordinarily chic … "

"I don't pay for this … "

"I just mention it in passing. I'm not venturing to criticise. I think it's damned nice of you to send money. But you're still extraordinarily chic. Listen, shall I tell you something. You've grown into a damned beautiful woman."

He looked at her with that smile of his, which she had to look at. Then she answered very calmly, waving her fan lightly over her bare neck, concealed in the froth of her fan:

"I'm damned pleased you think so."

He guffawed loudly.

"Right, I like that, you're still good at witty repartee. Always on the ball. Damned good show!"

She got up, nervous, her face contorted.

"I must leave you, I have to go to Mrs Uxeley."

He spread his arms a little.

"Stay and sit for a bit. It's a tonic talking to you."

"Restrain yourself a bit then and don't 'damn' so much. I'm not used to it any more."

"I'll do my best, if you stay."

She flopped down and hid behind her fan.

"Let me say then that you really have become a very, very beautiful woman. Is that what you call a compliment?"

"It's more like it."

"Well, I can't do any better than that, you know. You'll have to make do with that. So tell me something about Rome. What was your life like there?"

"Why should I tell you?"

"Because I'm interested."

"You've no business to be interested in me … "

"No, but I just am. I've never forgotten you completely. And I'd be amazed if you'd forgotten me."

"Completely," she said coolly.

He looked at her with that smile of his. He did not reply, but she sensed that he knew better. She was afraid to go on trying to persuade him.

"Is it true what they say in The Hague? About Van der Staal?"

She looked at him loftily.

"Well, tell me … "

"Yes … "

"My, you're a shameless one. Don't you care about anything any more?"

"No … "

"And how are you getting on here, with the old woman?"

"How do you mean?"

"Do they accept that just like that here in Nice?"

"I don't flaunt my independence and my behaviour here is beyond reproach."

"Where is Van der Staal?"

"In Florence."

"Why isn't he here?. . ."

"I don't feel like giving any more answers. You're being indiscreet. It's no business of yours and I won't be interrogated."

She became very agitated and got up again. He stretched out his arms.

"Really, Rudolf, let me go," she begged him. "I must see Mrs Uxeley. They're dancing a *pavane* in the ballroom and I have to receive and give some orders. Let me go."

"I'll take you then. May I offer you my arm."

"Rudolf, please go away. Can't you see how nervous you're making me? It was so unexpected meeting you again here. Please go away, leave me alone, otherwise I won't be able to keep up appearances. I'll start crying. Why did you speak to me, why did you come here, where you knew you would meet me?"

"Because I wanted to see one of Mrs Uxeley's parties, *and* because I wanted to meet you."

"Surely you realise that seeing you again makes me nervous. What good does that do you? We're dead for each other ... What's the point of taunting me like this ... "

"That's precisely what I'd like to know. Whether we're dead for each other."

"Dead, dead, completely dead!" she cried violently.

He laughed.

"Come on, stop being so theatrical. Surely you can understand that I was curious to see you again and talk to you. I saw you in the streets, in your carriage, on the Jetée, and I liked seeing you looking so good, so chic, so happy, and so lovely. You know that I simply have a great weakness for beautiful women. You're much lovelier than you were when you were my wife. If you had been as you are now back then, I would never have divorced you … Come on, don't be childish. No one knows us here. I think it's damn wonderful to meet you here, to chat to you and give you my arm. Take my arm. Stop nagging and I'll take you where you have to go. Where will we find Mrs Uxeley?… Introduce me … as an acquaintance from Holland … "

"Rudolf … "

"Come on, I want to, stop nagging. What harm will it do? It amuses me, and it's fun walking around with your ex-wife at a ball in Nice. Wonderful town, isn't it? I go to Monte Carlo every day, and I've been damn lucky. Won three thousand francs yesterday. Do you fancy coming with me … ?"

"You're out of your mind!"

"I'm not out of my mind. I want to enjoy myself. And I'm proud to have you on my arm."

She pulled her arm free.

"There's nothing for you to be proud about … "

"Now don't get spiteful, I'm just joking; let's enjoy ourselves. There's the old woman … She's looking for you."

She had gone through a number of rooms on his arm and at a tombola, where people were jostling to win gifts and trinkets, they saw Mrs Uxeley, Gilio and the ladies Rosavilla, Costi and Luca. They were very cheerful, acting like children round the pyramid of baubles, when the roulette wheel had come up with their number.

"Mrs Uxeley," Cornélie began, her voice trembling. "May I introduce a compatriot of mine, Baron Brox … "

Mrs Uxeley fluttered, and said a few friendly words, and asked if he would like to draw a number … The roulette wheel spun …

"A countryman of yours, Cornélie?"

"Yes, Mrs Uxeley."

"How do you … say his name?"

"Baron Brox … "

"A splendid fellow! A handsome man! An amazingly handsome specimen. What is he, what does he do?"

"He's an officer, a first lieutenant … "

"What regiment?"

"Hussars … "

"In The Hague?"

"In The Hague."

"An amazingly handsome fellow. I like big, strong men like that … "

"Mrs Uxeley, is everything going as planned?'

"Yes, darling."

"Are you feeling well?"

"I'm having a few twinges, but it's all right."

"Shouldn't they be dancing the *pavane* soon?"

"Yes, make sure the girls go and change. The hairdresser has brought the wigs for the young people, hasn't he?"

"Yes … "

"Gather the youngsters together then and tell them to hurry. They must begin in the next half hour … "

Rudolf Brox came back from the tombola, where he had won a silver matchbox. He thanked Mrs Uxeley, who fluttered, and when he saw Cornélie moving away, he followed her.

"Cornélie … "

"Please, Rudolf, leave me; I have to collect the girls and young people for the *pavane*. I'm very busy … "

"I'll help you … "

She beckoned a pair of girls, told a couple of servants to find the young people in the various rooms and tell them to make their way to the dressing-rooms. He could see that she was pale and trembling all over.

"What's wrong?"

"I'm tired."

"Let's go and have a drink then."

She was beside herself with nervousness. The music of the invisible orchestra pounded ferociously in her brain. And the countless candles sometimes spun before her eyes like a dancing firmament. The rooms were crammed full. People bustled, laughed loudly, showed each other their gifts, trod on ladies' trains. An intoxicating oppressive atmosphere of flowers and festivities and tepid perfumed femininity hung like a cloud. Cornélie went hither and thither, looking, and had finally collected the girls. The master of ceremonies came to ask her something. A steward came to ask her something. And Brox did not budge from her side.

"Let's go and have a drink now … " he repeated.

She took his arm mechanically and her hand trembled on his black sleeve. He pushed through the throng with her and they passed Urania and De Breuil. Urania said a few words that Cornélie did not catch. The buffet-room was also crowded, buzzing with high-pitched laughing voices. The steward stood behind the long tables like a minister. He controlled the whole process of serving. There was no pushing and shoving, no fighting for a glass of wine or a roll. People waited until a lackey presented what they had ordered.

"Everything is well organised," said Brox. "Is it all your work … ?"

"No it's been like this for years … "

She slumped into a chair, looking pale.

"What do you want?"

"A glass of champagne."

"I'm hungry. It was a poor dinner in my hotel. I want something to eat."

He ordered the champagne for her. First he had a pie, then another, and then a châteaubriand steak with petits pois. He drank a couple of glasses of red wine, and then a glass of champagne. The lackey brought him everything one at a time on a silver salver. His handsome virile face had a brick red hue and an animal strength. The tough hair on his massive round head was cut short all over. His large grey eyes were smiling, with a clear, direct, impudent look. A heavy, well-tended moustache, full and luxuriant, sat above a mouth full of sparkling white teeth. He stood with his feet slightly apart, with a military solidity about his tailcoat, which he wore with simple correctness. He ate slowly and with relish, savouring his good glass of fine wine.

Involuntarily she watched him from her chair. She had drunk a glass of champagne and asked for a second, and this stimulus revived her. Her cheeks regained some of their colour, her eyes sparkled.

"It's damned nice here," he said, approaching her with his glass in his hand. He emptied it.

"It's almost time for the *pavane*," she murmured.

And they went through the busy rooms to a long corridor outside, decorated with an avenue of camellia bushes. They were alone for a moment.

"This is where the dancers must assemble ... "

"Let's wait for them here then. It's nice and cool here."

They sat down on the bench.

"Are you feeling better?" he asked. "You were acting so oddly in the room."

"Yes ... I'm better ... "

"Don't you think it's fun meeting your ex-husband again?"

"Rudolf ... I don't understand how you can talk like that, pursue me, tease me ... After everything that's happened ... "

"Well that's over and done with ... "

"Do you think it's a discreet ... and tactful way to behave?"

"No. Neither discreet nor tactful. You know that those are simply the kind of charming things I never am; you've thrown that in my face often enough in the past. But if it's not tactful, it's certainly amusing. Have you lost your sense of humour? There's a damned funny side to our meeting here ... And listen to me a moment. We're divorced, fine. In the eyes of the law that's the situation. But a legal divorce is only for the benefit of the law, good form and society. For money matters and such like. The two of us were too much husband and wife not to feel something for each other when we meet later, like here. Oh yes, I know what you're trying to say. It's simply not true. You were too much in love with me, and I with you, for everything

279

to be dead. I still remember everything. And you must remember everything too. Do you remember that time when we ... " He laughed, slid closer to her and whispered into her ear. She felt his breath trembling over her skin like a warm breeze. She blushed deeply and became nervous. And she felt with her whole body that he had been her husband, that she had him in her blood. His voice rang like molten bronze through the nerves of her ear, deep inside her. Her flesh shivered under the breeze of his breath. She knew him completely. She knew his eyes, his mouth, she knew his chest and his thighs. She knew his hands, broad, well manicured, with the large round nails and the dark signet ring—as they rested on his knees, tensing squarely in the curve of his black trouser leg. And she felt in a sudden wave of despair that she knew and felt him in the whole of her body. However rough he had been with her in the past, however he had abused her, punched her with his clenched fist, slammed her against a wall ... she had been his wife. She had become his wife as a virgin, and he had made her a woman. And she felt as if he had left his imprint on her and made her his, she felt it in her very blood and marrow. She admitted to herself that she had never forgotten him. In her first loneliness in Rome she had longed for his kiss, had thought of him, called up his manly image, convinced herself that with tact and patience she might have remained his wife ...

Then the great happiness had come, the gentle happiness of complete harmony ...

It all flashed through her in a second.

Oh, in her great, gentle happiness she had been able to

forget everything, she had not felt the past in her. But now she felt that the past is always there, inexorable, ineradicable. She had been his wife and kept him in her blood. *Now* she felt it with every breath. She was indignant that he dared to whisper about the past, in her ear, but it had been as he said. Inexorable, ineradicable.

"Rudolf!" she implored him, folding her hands. "Have pity!!"

She almost screamed it, in a cry of fear and despair. But he laughed and with one hand took hold of both her hands folded in supplication.

"If you act like that, if you look at me so imploringly with those beautiful eyes, I won't even have pity on you here and I'll kiss you till … "

His words wafted over her like a hot wind. But laughing voices approached, and a pair of young girls, a pair of young people, already dressed as Henri IV and Marguérite de Valois for the *pavane*, came down the stairs.

"Where have the others got to?" they cried, looking back up the stairs. And they came cheerfully up to Cornélie, dancing. The dancing master also approached. She did not understand what he was saying.

"Where have the others got to?" she repeated after the girls automatically, in a hoarse voice.

"There they come … Now we're all here … "

There was chatter, laughter and a buzz of voices around her. She summoned all her feeble strength, and gave some orders. The guests poured into the large ballroom, sat down on chairs at the front, jostled in the corners. The *pavane* was danced in the middle of the room, to the slow rhythm of an old melody: a gently winding

281

arabesque with elegant steps, deep bows and satin shining like porcelain … the wave of a cape … the long gleaming shape of a sword …

XLVIII

"Urania, I beg you, help me!"

"What is it?"

"Come with me … "

She had dragged Urania away from De Breuil by the hand and pulled her into one of the deserted rooms. The suite of rooms had been almost completely abandoned, the throng of people were packed along the sides of the large ballroom to see the *pavane* being danced.

"What is it, Cornélie?"

Cornélie was trembling all over and was clinging to Urania's arm. She pulled her to the furthest corner of the drawing-room. It was empty.

"Urania," she begged, in a paroxysm of nervousness. "Help me! What am I to do? I've met him unexpectedly. Don't you know who? My husband. My ex-husband. I had already seen him a few times, in the street and on the Jetée. That time when I gave such a start, you remember, when I almost fainted … it was because of him. Now, here, just now he spoke to me. And I'm afraid of him. I don't know what it is, but I'm afraid of him. He was very friendly, he needed to talk to me. It was so strange. Everything was over between us. We were divorced. And suddenly I meet him, and he talks to me, he asks how I've been in the meantime; he tells me I look good, that I've become beautiful. Tell me what I'm to do, Urania. I'm afraid. I'm feverish with fear. I want to get away. I'd like to leave at once, and go to Florence, to Duco. I'm so afraid, Urania. I want to go to my room. Tell Mrs Uxeley that I want to go to my room."

She scarcely knew what she was saying. The words tumbled out in a delirious stream. Male voices approached. It was Gilio, De Breuil, the Duke di Luca and the young journalists, who were busy making a name for themselves.

"Where has Signora de Retz got to? She's needed everywhere," said the duke, and the journalists, in the shadow of these grand gentlemen, agreed: she was needed everywhere …

"Call Mrs Uxeley and ask her to come here," Urania whispered to Gilio. "Cornélie is ill, I think … I can't leave her alone. She wants to go to her room. It's better if Mrs Uxeley knows, otherwise she might get angry."

Cornélie joked nervously, feverishly merry, with the duke, De Breuil and the journalists.

"Would you prefer me to take you straight to Mrs Uxeley?" whispered Gilio.

"I want to go to my room!" she whispered imploringly in reply from behind her fan.

The *pavane* seemed to be over. A hubbub of voices approached, as if the guests were spreading back through the rooms.

"There's Mrs Uxeley," said Gilio.

He went over to her, and talked to her. First she fluttered, leaning on the gold knob of her walking stick. Then she frowned angrily. She came closer. Cornélie went on joking with the duke: the journalists found everything equally amusing.

"Aren't you well?" whispered Mrs Uxeley who had

come closer and was put out. "And what about the *cotillon*?"

"I'll look after everything, Mrs Uxeley," said Urania.

"Impossible, my dear princess: and I wouldn't dare accept."

"Introduce me to your friend, Cornélie!" boomed a deep voice behind her.

She felt the voice inside her like bronze. She turned round automatically. It was him. She seemed not to be able to get away from him. And beneath his gaze, strangely enough, she seemed to regain her strength. He seemed not to want her to be ill … She murmured.

"Urania, may I … introduce … a countryman of mine … Baron Brox … the Princess di Forte-Braccio."

Urania knew his name and knew who he was.

"Dearest," she whispered to Cornélie. "Let me take you to your room. I'll look after everything."

"It's no longer necessary," she said. "I'm much better. I'd just like some champagne. I'm much better, Mrs Uxeley."

"Why did you run away from me?" asked Rudolf Brox with that smile of his and his eyes in Cornélie's eyes.

She smiled and had no idea what she said.

"The ball has begun," said Mrs Uxeley. "But who is going to lead my *cotillon*?"

"If I can be of service, Mrs Uxeley," said Brox. "I have a modest talent for leading *cotillons* … "

Mrs Uxeley was delighted. It was agreed that De Breuil and Urania, Gilio and Countess Costi, and Brox and Cornélie would lead the figures in turn.

"Poor darling," said Urania in Cornélie's ear, "can you manage it?"

Cornélie smiled.

"Yes, of course, I'm better," she whispered.

And she went off to the ballroom on Brox's arm, watched by a flabbergasted Urania.

XLIX

IT WAS TWELVE O'CLOCK when Cornélie woke next morning. With its swirling particles the sun pierced the gold slit of the slightly parted curtains. She felt exhausted. She remembered that after such a party Mrs Uxeley gave her a morning off to rest: the old woman also stayed in bed, although did not sleep. And Cornélie lacked the strength to get up, and stayed in bed, weighed down with fatigue. Her eyes wandered about the messy room; her beautiful ball gown was draped helplessly over a chair, limply and immediately reminding her of yesterday. For that matter, all her thoughts were focused on yesterday, on her husband, with a fixed hypnotic concentration. She felt as if emerging from a nightmare, a hangover, a fainting fit. Only by drinking a glass of champagne had she been able to keep up appearances, to dance, with Brox, take their turn in leading a figure. But not only with champagne. His eyes too had kept her on her feet, prevented her from fainting, from bursting into sobs, from starting to scream and waving her arms like a madwoman. When he had said goodnight, when everyone had gone, she had collapsed, and had been taken to bed. The moment she was no longer under his gaze, she had felt her wretchedness and her weakness and the champagne seemed to befuddle her instantly.

Now she thought of him in the bruised languor of her devastating morning fatigue. And it seemed to her that her whole Italian year had been a dream intermezzo. She saw herself back in The Hague; the young girl who went out a lot, with her nice face and flirtatious manners and her ever-ready quips. She saw their first meetings and the way she had immediately bent to his will and had not been able to flirt with him, because he laughed at her womanly defences. He had been too strong from the first. Then their engagement. He laid down the law to her and she rebelled, angrily, with violent scenes, not wanting to be controlled, offended as a pampered, fêted and spoiled young girl. And as if by the brute force of his fist—and always with that smile on his lips—he kept her down. Until they were married, until she made a scandal and ran away. At first he had not wanted a divorce, but had later given in, because of the scandal. She had freed herself, she had run away!

The women's movement, Italy, Duco … Was it a dream? Was the great happiness, the precious harmony a dream and was she now awaking from a year's dreaming? Was she divorced or not? She had to force herself to remember the formalities: yes, they were legally divorced. But *was* she divorced, was everything over between them? And was she really no longer his wife?

What had been the point of his searching for her once he had seen her in Nice? Oh, he had told her, during the *cotillon*. That endless *cotillon*! He had become proud of her when he saw how beautiful and chic and happy she seemed in the victoria of Mrs Uxeley or the princess— and he had grown jealous. She, that beautiful woman, had been his wife! He had felt he had a right to her, despite the law! What was the law? Did the law make her a wife, or had he made her a wife? And he had made her feel that right, together with the irredeemability of the past. It had been irredeemable, ineradicable …

She looked around her, at her wit's end. And she began to cry, sob … Then she felt something in her strengthen, resistance cry out in her like a spring that finally tensed again now she was resting and was no longer under his gaze. She didn't want this. She didn't want it. She didn't want to feel him in her blood. If she met him again, she would speak to him more calmly, curtly, and order him to leave her, she would show him the door, have him thrown out … Her fists clenched in fury. She hated him. She thought of Duco … And she thought of writing to him, telling him everything. And she thought of returning to him as soon as possible. He wasn't a dream: he existed, though he lived far away, in Florence. She had saved some money; they could find happiness again in the studio in Rome. She would write to him and she wanted to leave as soon as possible. With Duco she would be safe. Oh, she longed for him, to lie so softly and luxuriantly in his arms, against his chest, as if in the embrace of a single wondrous happiness. Had it been true, their happiness, their love and harmony? Yes, it had existed, it wasn't a dream. There was his portrait; there on the wall a couple of his watercolours: the sea at Sorrento and the skies above Amalfi, produced in those days that had been like poetry. She would be safe with him. With Duco she would not feel Rudolf, her husband, in her blood … She felt Duco in her soul, and her soul would be stronger! She would feel Duco in her soul, in her heart in the whole of her deepest being and from him would gather her supreme strength, like a bundle of gleaming swords! Even now, when she thought of him with such longing, she could feel herself growing stronger. She could have talked to Brox now. Yesterday he had taken her by surprise, wedged her between himself and the mirror, till she had seen him double and had no longer known what to do and was lost. That would never happen again. It had simply been the surprise. If she talked to him again, *she* would triumph with what she had learned and as a woman who had stood on her own feet. And she got up, and opened the windows and put on a *peignoir*. She looked at the blue sea, at the colourful movement on the Promenade. And she sat down and wrote to Duco. She wrote everything, the first startled encounters, her surprise and defeat at the ball … Her pen raced across the paper. She did not hear a knock at the door or Urania cautiously entering, expecting to find her still asleep and anxious to know how she felt. She read a portion of her letter excitedly and said she was ashamed of her weakness of yesterday. How could she have behaved like that: she did not understand herself.

No, she didn't understand herself. Now she felt somewhat rested, was talking to Urania, who reminded her of Rome, with a long letter to Duco in her hand … now she did not understand it all herself and asked what was a dream: her Italian year of happiness or yesterday's nightmare?

L

SHE STAYED AT HOME for a day, tired, and deep
inside, almost unconsciously, nevertheless frightened
of meeting him. But Mrs Uxeley, who would not hear of
sickness or exhaustion, was so upset that the following
day Cornélie accompanied her to the Promenade des
Anglais. Acquaintances came up and talked to them and
thronged about their chairs; and among them was Rudolf
Brox. But Cornélie avoided all familiarity. A week later,
though, he appeared at Mrs Uxeley's at home day, and
in the round of the formalities—these were courtesy calls
after the party—he was able to speak to her alone for a
minute. He approached her with that smile of his, as if his
eyes, as if his moustache, were smiling. And she collected
her thoughts, so as to be strong with him.

"Rudolf," she said in an aloof tone. "It's simply ridiculous. If you don't find it tactless, then at least try to find it
ridiculous. It tickles your sense of humour, but just think
what people would say about this in Holland … The
other day at the party you took me by surprise and—I
don't know how—I found myself giving in to your
strange desire to dance with me and lead the *cotillon* figures. I freely admit I was confused. Now I can see everything plainly and clearly and I'm telling you: I don't want
to see you again. I don't want to talk to you. I don't want
to turn the high seriousness of our divorce into farce."

"You know from before that that lofty tone gets you

nowhere with me these airs and graces and that grand manner, and on the contrary it prompts me to do exactly what you don't want … "

"If that's the case, I'll simply tell Mrs Uxeley about my relationship with you and ask her to deny you access to her house … "

He laughed. She got angry.

"Do you intend to act like a gentleman? Or like a blackguard?"

He went red and his fists clenched.

"Damn!" he hissed into his moustache.

"Would you like to strike me and abuse me perhaps?" she went on contemptuously.

He controlled himself.

"We're in a full drawing-room at the moment," she continued, taunting him. "What if we were alone? Your fist is already clenching! You'd beat me as you did once before. Brute! Brute!!!"

"And you're brave in that full drawing-room!" he laughed, with that laugh of his that drove her into a fury, if she was not held in check by it. "No, I wouldn't beat you," he went on. "I'd kiss you … "

"This is the last time you'll ever talk to me!" she hissed in fury. "Go away! Go away! I don't know what I'll do, I'll make a scene!"

He sat down calmly.

"Go ahead," he said quietly.

She stood in front of him trembling, powerless. People talked to her, the servant brought round tea. She was in a circle of gentlemen, and controlling herself she joked with a shrill, nervous kind of jollity and flirted more provocatively than ever. There was a small court around her, with the Duke di Luca the most forward of all. Rudolf Brox sat close by drinking his tea, ostensibly calm, as if biding his time. But his powerful, domineering blood was seething wildly. He could have killed her and was apoplectic with jealousy. That woman was his, whatever the law said. He would no longer shrink from any scandal. She was beautiful, she was as he wanted her and he wanted her, his wife. He knew how he would win her back and once he had he did not want to lose her again: then she would be his, for as long as he chose. As soon as it was possible to speak to her alone, he turned to her again. She was about to go over to Urania, whom she saw sitting with Mrs Uxeley, when he spoke in her ear, severe, brusque, gruff, "Cornélie … "

She turned round involuntarily, but with her haughty look. She would have preferred to walk on past, but she could not: something prevented her, a mysterious power and superiority, which sounded in his voice and sank into her with a bronze weight that drained and paralysed her energy.

"What is it?"

"I want to speak to you alone for a moment."

"No."

"Oh yes. Listen to me calmly for a moment if you can. I'm calm too, you can see, There's no need to be afraid of me. I assure you I won't mistreat you, or even swear. But I must speak to you, alone. After our meeting, and after the ball last week, we can't part just like that. You don't even have the right to throw me out any more after talking to me and dancing with me the other day. There's no reason or logic in that. You got worked up ... But don't let either of us get worked up any more. I'd like to talk to you ... "

"I can't: Mrs Uxeley doesn't like me to leave the drawing-room, when people are here. I'm dependent on her."

He laughed.

"You're even more dependent on her than you once were on me. But you can allow me a moment, in the next room."

"No."

"Yes."

"What do you want to talk to me about?"

"I can't say that here."

"I can't talk to you alone."

"Shall I tell you something? You're afraid."

"No."

"Oh, yes you are, you're afraid of me. For all your airs and graces and snootiness you're simply afraid to be alone with me for a moment."

"I'm not afraid."

"Yes you are. You're not sure of yourself. You received me with a nice speech that you rehearsed in advance. Now you've said your piece ... it's over and you're frightened."

"I'm not afraid ... "

"Come with me for a moment then, brave writer of the Social Position ... how did it go again? Come on, come with me for a moment. I promise you, I swear to you that I'll be calm, will say calmly what I have to say to you and you have my word of honour that I won't strike you ... What room can we go into ... ? Don't you want to? Listen:

if you don't come with me for a moment, it won't be the end of it. Otherwise it might be … and you'll never see me again."

"What can you have to say to me."

"Come with me … "

It was because of his voice, not what he said.

"But no more than three minutes."

"No more than three minutes."

She took him into the corridor and into an empty drawing-room.

"What is it?" she asked, afraid.

"Don't be afraid," he said, with his smiling moustache. "Don't be afraid. I simply wanted to say to you … *that you're my wife.* Do you understand? Don't try to contradict me. I felt it the other day at the ball, when I had you in my arms, waltzing with you. Don't try to deny that you pressed yourself against me for a moment. *You're my wife.* I felt it then and I feel it now. And you feel it too, though you're trying to deny it. But it won't do you any good. You can't change what has been and what has been … is still inside you. Try and tell me that I'm not speaking politely and tactfully now. You won't hear a single curse or a word out of place from my lips. Because I don't want to upset you. I just want to get you to admit … that what I'm saying is true: and *that you're still my wife.* That law means nothing. There's another law that governs us. There's a law that governs you in particular. A law that brings us back together, without our ever having imagined it, even if it is by a strange roundabout route that you, you especially, took. That law governs you in particular. I am convinced you're still in love with me. I feel it, I'm sure of it: don't try to deny it. None of it will do you *any* good, Cornélie. And shall I tell you something else? I'm still in love with you too and more than before. When you flirt with those fellows, I feel it. I could strangle you and give those fellows a good hiding … Don't worry, I shan't do it: I'm not in a rage. On the contrary, I wanted to talk calmly to you and show you the truth. Can you see it in front of you … so ir…re…vo…cably? You see, you've nothing to say against it. It is as it is. Are you going to throw me out? Are you going to speak to Mrs Uxeley? I wouldn't if I were you. Your friend, the princess, knows who I am: let that suffice. Had the old girl never heard my name, or had she forgotten it? Must have forgotten it. Don't prod her old memory now. Let it be. It's better if you say nothing. No, the situation is not ridiculous and it's not funny. It's become very serious: the simple truth is always serious. It's strange, though, I would never have thought it. It's a revelation for me too … And now I have said all I wanted to you. Less than five minutes by my watch. They will scarcely have missed you in the drawing-room. And now I'm going, but first give your husband a kiss, because I'll always be your husband."

She stood before him trembling. It was his voice, pouring into her soul, into her body like molten bronze, draining her strength and paralysing her. It was his persuasive voice, his persuasive, seductive voice, the voice that she remembered from the past that forced her to bow to his will. Beneath that voice she was like an object, a thing that belonged to him, after he had first left his imprint on her as his wife. She was helpless to expel him from within her, to shake him off, to erase the brand of possession from her. She was his, and everything that was hers had deserted her. There was no more memory or thought in her brain.

She saw him approaching and putting his arms around her. He hugged her slowly but so firmly that it was as if he were taking complete possession of her. She felt herself melting away in his arms as if in a warmth-giving flame. She felt his mouth on her lips, his moustache pressing, pressing, pressing, till she closed her eyes, half fainting. He went on speaking softly into her ear with that voice, beneath which she counted for nothing, as if she were nothing, as if she existed only through him. When he let go of her, she swayed.

"Come on, pull yourself together," she heard him saying, omnipotent and sure of himself. "And accept things as they are. That is just how it is. There's nothing to be done. Thank you for letting me say my piece. Everything's right between us now, I'm sure of it. And now good bye for now. *Au revoir* … "

He kissed her again.

"Give me a kiss in return," he asked, with that voice of his …

She threw her arms round him and kissed him on the mouth.

"*Au revoir*," he said again.

She saw him smiling, that smiling moustache, and his eyes smiled at her with a golden flame, and he went. She heard his steps descending the stairs, then ringing on the marble of the hall, with the power of his firm tread … She stood there, her mind a blank. In the drawing-room, next to the room she was in, there was a loud buzz of laughing

voices. She saw Rome before her, Duco, in a short lightning flash … It had gone … And sinking on to a chair,
she let out a stifled cry of despair, covered her face with her
hands and gave a muffled sob—keeping her helplessness
hidden from all those people—as if she were suffocating.

LI

S HE HAD ONLY ONE THOUGHT: to flee. To flee from his mastery, to flee the emanation of his dominance, which mysteriously but inexorably erased every trace of will, energy, self, with his embrace. She remembered she had felt the same before: rebellion and anger when he became angry and coarse, but an annihilation of herself when he embraced her, an inability to think when he laid his hand on her head, a swooning into a single great nothingness, when he took her in his arms and kissed her. She had felt it from the first time she had seen him, that he stood in front of her and looked down at her with that hint of irony in his voice and his moustache, as if he were enjoying her resistance—then still in the form of flirtatiousness, later irritability, later passion and rage—as if he were enjoying her vain woman's attempts to escape his domination. He had seen at once that he dominated this woman. And she had found in him her master, her sole master. No other man oppressed her like this with this majesty that stemmed from blood and flesh. On the contrary, she was usually the superior one. She had a cool indifference about her, which always prompted her to destructive criticism. She had a need for jokes, for a merry conversation, for coquettishness and flirting, and being never lost for an answer she created openings for ripostes, but apart from that she did not have a high opinion of men, and saw the ridiculous side of everyone:

this one was too small, that one too tall, this one gauche, the other stupid; in everyone she found something that provoked her laughter and criticism. She would never be a woman who gave herself to many men. She had met Duco and given him her love totally and unconditionally, as a great, indivisible, golden gift, and after him she would never love again. But before Duco she had met Rudolf Brox. Perhaps if she had met him after Duco, his mastery would not have dominated her … She did not know. And what was the good of puzzling about that? It was as it was as it was. In her blood she was not a woman for many: in her blood she was all wife, spouse, mate. In her flesh, in her blood she was the wife of the man who had been her husband, she was his wife, even without love. Because she could not call this love; love was only that exalted, tender feeling, that deep perfection of harmonious existence, that progression together along a golden line, merged from two glistening lines … But as if in a cloud the hands had loomed up around them, and mysteriously, fatefully forced their golden line apart, and hers, a winding arabesque, had sprung back like a trembling coil and had crossed a dark line from her past, a gloomy path from the past, a dark avenue of unconsciousness and fateful slavery. Oh, how strange, how infinitely mysterious and strange those lifelines were: they could be curled back, forced back to their starting point! Why had it all been necessary?

She had only one thought: to flee. She did not see the gradualness of things, and the fatefulness of those paths, and she did not want to feel the force of the ghostly hands. She wanted to flee, to turn back along the dark path, back to the point of division, back to Duco, and fight with him, wrestle those two paths that had gone astray back into a single pure direction, back into a single line of happiness …

To flee, to flee. She told Urania that she was going. She begged Urania to forgive her, since Urania had recommended her to an old woman whom she was now suddenly deserting.

And she told Mrs Uxeley, without worrying about her anger, her fury and her abuse. She admitted that she appeared ungrateful. But there was a matter of life and death that obliged her to leave Nice suddenly. She swore that it was true. She swore that she feared disaster and doom if she stayed. She explained to Urania in a few words. But she did not explain it to the old woman, and left her in a state of helpless fury that contorted her body with rheumatic pains. She left behind everything that she had received from Mrs Uxeley, her sumptuous wardrobe of dependency. She put on an old dress. She made her way furtively to the station, trembling at the possibility of meeting him. But she knew that at this time of day he was always in Monte Carlo. Still, she went in a closed cab, and bought a second-class ticket to Florence. She sent a telegram to Duco. And she fled. She had nothing but him. She could no longer count on Mrs Uxeley, and Urania too had been cool, unable to understand this sudden flight, because she did not understand the simple truth: Rudolf Brox's dominance. She thought Cornélie was making life difficult for herself. In the circles in which Urania moved, her sense of social morality had been wavering since her liaison with the Chevalier de Breuil.

Surrounded by the whispered Italian law of love according to which love is as simple as a rose that opens, she could not understand Cornélie's struggle. She no longer blamed Gilio for anything and on his side, he left her free. What was Cornélie thinking of? It was so simple, if she still loved her ex-husband! Why was she running away to Duco, and making herself ridiculous in the eyes of all their friends! And she had said goodbye coolly, but still missed her friend. She was the Princess di Forte-Braccio and recently, for her birthday, Prince Ercole had sent her a large emerald from the carefully preserved family jewels, as if she were slowly becoming worthy of them, stone by stone! But she missed Cornélie, and she felt alone, dreadfully alone, despite her emerald and her lover …

Cornélie fled: she had nothing but Duco. But in him she would have everything. And when she saw him in Florence, at Santa Maria Novella station, she threw herself into his arms, as if he were a cross of salvation, a Saviour and a sanctuary. He took her sobbing to a cab and they drove to his room. Once there she looked round nervously, exhausted with the strain after her long journey, constantly thinking that Rudolf would pursue her. She told Duco everything, she opened herself completely to him, as if he were her conscience, her soul, her god. She nestled against him like a child, she stroked him, she caressed him; she said he had to help her. It was as if she were praying to him; her fear rose up to him like a prayer. He kissed her, and she knew that way of comforting, she knew that soft caressing. She suddenly collapsed against him inertly, and stayed there and closed her eyes. It was as if she were sinking into a lake, a blue sacred lake, mystical as the lake of San Stefano at night when the world was asleep, powdered with stars. And she heard him say that he would help her. That her fear meant nothing. That the man had no power over her. That he would never have power over her if she became his, Duco's wife. She looked at him and did not understand. She looked at him feverishly, as if he were suddenly waking her, while she was sleeping blissfully in the blue calm of the mystical lake. She did not understand, but exhausted hid in his arms and fell asleep.

She was worn out. For several hours she slept on his chest, motionless, breathing deeply. When he shifted his arm she stirred for a moment like a flower on a limp stalk, but went on sleeping, with her hand in his. She slept as she had not slept for days, weeks.

LII

"THERE'S NO REASON to be afraid, Cornélie," he said persuasively. "The man has no hold over you, if you don't want him to, and your will is strong. I can't imagine what he could do. You're completely free, complete independent of him. The fact that you left in haste was certainly not sensible of you: he will think you ran away. Why didn't you tell him calmly that he has no claim on you? Why didn't you say you loved me? If need be you could have said we were engaged. How could you be so weak, and so afraid? That's not the Cornélie I remember. But now you're here, now it's all right. We're together now. Shall we go back to Rome tomorrow, or shall we stay here for bit? I've always longed to show you Florence. Look, there's the river Arno in front of us, there's the Ponte Vecchio, there is the Uffizi. You've already been here but you didn't know Italy then. You'll get more from it now. Oh, it's so beautiful here. We'll stay here for a few weeks first. I've got a little money, so you needn't be afraid. It's cheaper here than in Rome. Here in this room we'll spend almost nothing. By this window I have enough light to sketch now and then. Or I'll go and work in San Lorenzo or San Marco, or above the city around San Miniato. It's wonderfully calm in the cloisters—there are occasionally a few tourists, but that doesn't disturb me. And you'll come with me, with a book, a book on Florence: and I'll tell you what to read.

You must get to know Donatello, Brunelleschi and Ghiberti too, but mainly Donatello. We'll see him in the Bargello museum. And the *Annunciation* of Lippo, the golden *Annunciation*! You'll see how much it looks like our beautiful lucky angel that you gave me! There's such wealth here; we shan't feel poor. We need so little. Or have you been spoiled by the luxury you lived in Nice? But I know you, you'll forget it all at once, and we'll fight our way through together. And later we'll go back to Rome. But when we do … we'll be man and wife, my darling, and you'll be mine completely, before the law too. We must, you can't refuse me any longer. We'll go to the consul tomorrow and ask what papers we need from Holland and how we can get married as soon as possible. And in the meantime I shall regard you as my wife. True, up to now we've been very happy … but you weren't my wife. And I *feel* you are my wife—even though we have to wait a few more weeks for those papers before we can sign on the dotted line—then you'll feel safe and calm. No one and nothing will have a hold over you. You must be ill to think so. And I'm convinced that when we're married, mama will make it up with us. It will all come right, my darling, my angel … But you mustn't say no, we *must* get married as soon as possible."

She sat next to him on a sofa, staring outside, where in the square frame of the tall window, the slender bell tower rose like a marble lily among the harmonious interplay of the domes of the Duomo and the Baptistery, while to the side the Palazzo Vecchio, a crenellated fortress sat massively among a swirl of streets and roofs, raising its tower spire that suddenly spread out at a high level. Beyond it the hills of Fiesole hazy in evening violet. The noble, graceful city glowed dull golden bronze in the last rays of sunshine.

"We *must* get married as soon as possible?' she repeated hesitantly, questioningly."

"Yes, as soon as possible, my darling … "

"But Duco, my dear Duco, it's less possible now than ever. Can't you see that it's impossible, impossible … It might have been possible, before, months ago, a year ago … Perhaps … perhaps not even then, perhaps it could never have been possible. It's so difficult to say this. But it's really not possible now … "

"Don't you love me enough?"

"How can you ask … How can you ask, my darling? But it's not that … It's … It's … it's impossible, because I'm not free … "

"Not free … "

"I'm *not* free … Perhaps I'll feel free later … Perhaps not, perhaps never … My dear Duco, I can't. I wrote to you about it, didn't I, that first meeting at the ball … It was so strange … Despite everything I felt that … "

"That what … "

She took his hand and stroked it, her eyes vague, her words vague.

"You see … despite everything he was my husband."

"But you are separated, completely, divorced!"

"Divorced, yes. But that's not the point … "

"But what is it then, my love … ?"

She shook her head and buried her face in his chest.

"I can't say, Duco … "

"Why not?"

"I'm ashamed … "

"Tell me, are you still in love with him?"

"No, it's not love. I love you."

"But what is it then, my love! Why are you ashamed?"

She began crying as she held him.

"I feel … "

"What … "

"That I'm not free, even though … I'm divorced. Despite everything I feel like his wife."

She whispered almost inaudibly.

"But then you love him, and more than me."

"No, I swear to you I don't!"

"But how is that possible then, my love!"

"It's possible."

"No, it's not possible! It's impossible!"

"It's possible. It's a fact. And he told me … and I felt it … "

"He's hypnotising you!"

"No, it's not hypnosis. It's not intoxication … it's a reality, deep inside me. You see … you know me: you know what I'm like … I love only you. That's the only love. I've never loved anyone else. I'm not a woman who's susceptible to … who's hysterical. But with him … Not one man, no one I have ever met provokes that feeling in me, the feeling that I'm not myself. That I belong to him. That I'm his property, his chattel."

She threw her arms round him, and hid like a child in his arms.

"It's so strange … You know me, don't you … I can be brave, can't I? And I'm independent, and I'm never lost for words. With him I know nothing, I am nothing anymore. And I do as he says … "

"That's hypnosis: you can break free of that if you truly want to. I'll help you … "

"It's not hypnosis. It's a truth, deep inside me. It lives deep within me. I know that that's how it is, that it cannot be otherwise … Duco, it's impossible. I can't be your wife. I have no right to be your wife. Now less than ever. Perhaps … "

"Perhaps?"

" … I've always felt this, unconsciously. That I did not have the right. Not for you … or for myself … or for him … Perhaps that was what I felt unconsciously while I was spouting my slogans: my antipathy to marriage."

"But surely that antipathy stemmed from your marriage … to him!"

"Yes. That's the strange thing. I don't like him … and yet … "

"And yet you're in love with him!!"

"And yet I belong to him … "

"And you say you love me!!"

She took his head in her hands.

"Try to understand. It'll make me so tired if you don't understand. I love you … But I'm his wife … "

"Are you forgetting what you were for me, in Rome?"

"Your everything, love, happiness, deep happiness … Such deep harmony: I shall never forget it … But I wasn't your wife."

"Not my wife!!"

"I was your mistress … I was unfaithful to him … Don't push me away! Have pity!"

Without realising, he had made a gesture that alarmed her.

"Let me stay like this, close to you like this … May I
… ? I'm so tired, and I feel calm lying against you like
this, my darling. My darling, my darling … it will never
be like it was. What are we to do!"

"I don't know," he said despairingly. "I wanted to
marry you, as soon as possible. You don't want to."

"I can't. I haven't the right."

"Then I don't know."

"Don't be angry. Don't leave me alone! Help me,
please! I love you, I love you, I love you!"

She suddenly gave herself fully as if in helplessness and
despair. And he returned her kisses passionately …

"Oh God, tell me what I'm to do!" she prayed helplessly in his embrace.

LIII

THE FOLLOWING DAY as Cornélie walked through Florence with Duco and they entered the courtyard of the Palazzo Vecchio, viewed the Loggia dei Lanzi and stopped by the Uffizi to see Memmi's *Annunciation*, at his side she seemed to feel the perceptions of the past bursting irresistibly into flower. It was as though their lifelines, which had sprung apart, had through human force bent back together into a single path, and along that path the white poppies and white lilies sprang up with a tender, gently mystical recognition, almost like a dream. And yet it was slightly different from what had been. The pressure of a grey cloud seemed to hang between her and the deep blue sky that stretched like strips of ether, swathes of lofty trembling air above the narrow streets, above the domes and towers and spires. She had lost her former fretfulness; she was filled with a sense of remembrance, a heavy brooding in her head, and anxiety about what was to happen. She had a kind of sultry, stormy premonition, and after they had had a bite to eat after their walk, she dragged herself up the steps, wearier than she had ever felt in Rome, to Duco's room. And she suddenly saw a letter lying on the table, addressed to her! But what an address! It was such a violent shock that she began to tremble all over, and stuffed the letter into her pocket even before Duco had entered the room behind her ... She took off her hat and told Duco that she needed something

310

from her suitcase, which was out in the hall. He asked if she needed his help. But she refused and went out of the room into the narrow hall. By the small window that looked out over the Arno, she took out the letter ... It was the only place where she could read undisturbed for a moment. And again she read that address, in his handwriting, which she knew, big, broad, heavy characters ... The name that she used abroad was her maiden name, and she called herself Madame De Retz van Loo. But on this letter she was abruptly addressed as: Baronne Brox, 37 Lung'Arno Torrignani, Florence. She blushed deeply. She had borne that name for a year ... But why did he call her that now? What was the logic of that title, which in law she no longer bore? What did he mean, what did he want ... ? And at the small window she read his short but imperious letter. He wrote to say that he took great exception to her flight, particularly since their last conversation. He wrote that in that last conversation she had ceded all rights over herself to him, that she had not contradicted him and she had shown with her kiss and her embrace that she considered herself his wife, in the same way as he considered her his wife. He wrote to say that he would not hold the independent life that she had lived for a year in Rome against her, as at that time she had still been free. But that he was insulted that she still considered herself free now, and that he would not accept the insult of her flight. That he commanded her to return. That he had no right in law to do so, but that he was doing so because he did nonetheless have a right, a right she could not deny and had not denied, but on the contrary had acknowledged with her kiss. He had been given her

311

address by the concierge of the Villa Uxeley, with whom she had left it. And he ended by telling her again that she must return to Nice, to him, at the Hotel Continental. That if she did not he would come to Florence and she would be responsible for the consequences of her refusal.

Her knees were knocking: she was on the verge of collapse. Should she show the letter to Duco, or hush it up … ? But she had to decide. He called out from the room, to ask what was taking her so long, in the hall. And she went in and was too weak not to throw herself into his arms. She showed him the letter. Leaning against him sobbing, she felt his rage and fury rising, she saw the swelling of the veins in his temples, his fists clenching, until he had screwed the letter into a ball and thrown it on the ground. He told her not to be afraid; he said he would protect her. He too regarded her as his wife. The only thing that mattered was how she saw herself from now on. She said nothing, just went on sobbing, broken as she was with exhaustion, alarm, headache. She got undressed, and went to bed: her teeth were chattering with fever. He darkened the room a little by drawing the curtains and told her to go to sleep. His voice was angry and she thought he was angry at her dithering. She sobbed herself to sleep. But in her sleep she felt the terror in herself and the inexorable pressure. As she slept she dreamt of what she might reply, if she wrote to Brox. But she was not clear what; she got no further than a vague plea for mercy. When she woke, she saw Duco near her bed. She took his hand and there was calmness in her. But she had no hope. She had no confidence in the days to come … She looked at him, and saw his gloom, the way he was locked in himself, as she had never seen him … Oh, their happiness was over! That fateful day when he had seen her off at the station in Rome, they had said farewell to their happiness. Gone, gone! Gone the sweet walks through ruins and museums, the trips to Frascati, Naples, Amalfi! Gone the dear sweet intimacy of their poverty in the big studio, amid the flickering colours of the old brocades and chasubles, the old silvers and bronzes! Gone their peering together at the watercolour *Banners*, she with her head on his shoulder, in his arms, living his art together with him, enjoying his work with him! Gone the ecstasy of the night in the pergola, in the star-sprinkled night, the sacred lake at their feet! There was no more repeating life! They were trying in vain to repeat it here in this room, in Florence, in the Palazzo, in vain even for Memmi's holy angel, shooting its golden ray! They were repeating their life, their happiness, their love in vain; in vain they had forced together the lifelines that had sprung apart! They were still circling each other for a while, in a single despairing arabesque … It was gone, gone … ! He sat gloomy and severe beside her bed, and she knew, he felt powerless, because she did not feel herself his wife. His mistress … ! Oh, she had felt that involuntary rejection when she had spoken that word. Hadn't he wanted to marry her all along? But unconsciously she had always felt that it was impossible, that she had no right. Beneath the proliferation of acerbic slogans in her feminist phase that had been the unconscious truth. She, while inveighing against marriage, had deep down always felt married. Not according to the law or a signature, but according to an ancient law, a primeval right of man over

woman, a law and a right of blood and flesh and deepest
marrow! Oh, above that immovable physical truth her
soul had blossomed with white poppies and lilies, and
that blossoming too was the innermost truth, the exalted
truth of happiness and love. But the poppies and lilies
faded: the soul blossoms for only a single summer. The
soul does not blossom for a lifetime. It may blossom before
life, or it may blossom after life, but *in* life the soul blossoms
for only a single summer! She had blossomed, and it was
over! And in her body, which was alive, in her body that
survived, she felt the truth in her very marrow! He sat
beside her bed, but he had no right, now the lilies had
faded. She was devastated with pity for him … She took
his hand and kissed it tenderly and sobbed over it. He
said nothing. He could think of nothing to say. It would all
have been simple, if she had wanted to become his wife.
As it was he could not help her. As it was he could see his
happiness headed for destruction, and he stood and
watched: there was nothing to be done. Like a crumbling
ruin it was slowly collapsing … It was over! It was over!

She spent these days in bed, she slept, she dreamed,
woke again and could not shake off the sense of expectation. Now and then she had a slight fever and it was better
to stay in bed. Mostly he stayed with her. But once when
Duco had gone off to get something from the pharmacy,
there was a knock at the door. She jumped up in bed,
afraid, afraid to see *him*, the one she was constantly thinking of … Half faint with alarm, she opened the door a
fraction. But it was the postman with a registered letter.
From him! Even more brusquely than the last time, he
wrote that immediately on receipt of his letter, she must

314

send a telegram telling him the date she was arriving. And that if by such and such a day—he would work out which—he did not receive her telegram, he would take the night train to Florence and would shoot her lover like a dog at her feet. That he would not hesitate for a moment. That he did not give a damn about the consequences. The passion and rage that this short letter exuded struck her in the face like a red storm. She knew him and knew that he would do it. As in a flash she saw the dreadful scene, saw the murdered Duco fall, bathed in blood. And she was no longer in control of herself. At a distance, because of the red rage of that letter, she had become completely his object, his thing. She had hurriedly torn the letter open, even before she had signed the postman's book. The man was waiting in the hall. It flashed through at dizzying speed, it swirled before her like a whirlpool. If she hesitated another moment, it would be too late, too late for Duco … And she asked the postman, nervously,

"Can you deliver a telegram for me straightaway?"

No, he couldn't: it wasn't on his way.

But she begged him to do it. She said she was sick, that she must send the telegram at once. And in her purse she found a ten-franc gold coin and gave it to him as a tip. She also gave him money for the telegram, And the man promised. And she wrote the telegram: Leaving tomorrow, express.

It was a vague telegram. She did not know what express; she had not been able to look up the timetable. Would it be in the evening or very early in the morning? She had no idea. How could she leave? She had no idea. But she thought the telegram would calm him down. And she would go. There was nothing to be done. Now she had fled in desperation, she saw clearly: if he wanted her back, back as his wife, she had to go. If he had not wanted this, she could have stayed, anywhere, despite her sense that she belonged to him. But now that he wanted it, she had to go back. But how, how was she to tell Duco! She was not thinking of herself, she was thinking of Duco.

She saw him in front of her in a pool of blood. She forgot that she had no money left. Should she ask him? Oh God, what was she to do? She could not go tomorrow, despite her telegram! She could not tell Duco she was going … She had wanted to sneak off to the station while he was out … Or should she tell him … What would be the least hurtful? Or … should she tell Duco everything and … run away … together with him, run away somewhere, and tell no one where … But if *he* discovered them! And he would find them! And then … he would … murder him!

She was almost delirious with fear, not knowing what to do, how and what … There was Duco's footstep on the stairs … He came in bringing her the pills … And as always, she told him everything, too weak, too tired to dissemble, and showed him the letter … He snorted in fury, hatred, but she fell down at his feet and grasped his hands. She said that she had already replied … He became suddenly cool, as if overwhelmed by the inevitable. He said he had no money to pay her fare. Then, once more he took her in his arms, kissed her, begged to be his wife, said he would kill her husband, just as he was threatening to kill him. But she sobbed and refused, although she remained clinging desperately to him. Then he resigned himself to the fateful omnipotence of the silent pressure of life. He felt himself dying inside. But he wanted to stay calm for her sake. He said that he forgave her. He held her, sobbing, in his arms, because the feeling of him calmed her. And he said that if she wanted to go back— she nodded dejectedly—it would be better to telegraph Brox and ask for the fare and give a clear date and time of arrival. He would do it for her. She looked at him in astonishment through her tears. He composed the telegram himself and left. My darling, my darling, she thought as he went, feeling the pain in his divided heart. She threw herself on the bed. When he returned he found her in hysterics. When he had tended to her, and tucked her in bed, he sat down beside her. And with a dead voice he said:

"My love, calm yourself. The day after tomorrow I shall take you to Genoa. We'll say goodbye there, for ever. If it can't be otherwise, that's how it must be. If you feel that that's how it must be, then that's what must be done. If you feel so strongly that you must go back to your husband, you may not be unhappy with him. Calm yourself, calm yourself, my love."

"Will you take me?"

"I'll take you as far as Genoa. I was able to borrow some money from a friend for that. But the main thing is that you try to be calm. Your husband wants you back; he won't want you back to beat you. He must have feelings for you, if he wants that. And if that's how it has to be … it may be good … for you. Although I can't see it …

He covered his face with his hands, and no longer able to control himself, burst out sobbing. She pulled him to her. She was calmer than he was now. While he sobbed with his head resting on her pounding heart, she calmly stroked his forehead, her eyes distant, looking through the walls of the room ...

LIV

NOW SHE SAT ALONE in the train. By tipping gener-
ously they had been able to travel alone at night and
no one had disturbed them in their compartment. They
had not spoken, but had sat close together, hand in hand,
eyes focused far ahead, as if staring at the approaching
point of separation. The gloomy thought of that separation
did not leave them, but raced along with the rattling
train. Sometimes she thought of a train crash, and of how
welcome it would be to die together. But inexorably the
lights of Genoa had appeared. The train had come to a
halt. And he had opened his arms and they had kissed,
for the last time. As she clung to him, she had felt his
pain. Then he had let go of her and hurried away without looking round. She watched him go, but he had not
looked round and she saw him disappear into the morning fog, shot through with points of light that hung about
the station. She had seen him disappear among the other
people, seen him dissolve into the haze of fog. Then her
silent despair and desolation had grown so great that she
had not even been able to cry. Her head slumped forward, her arms went limp. Like an inert thing she allowed
the roaring, rattling train to carry her further.

A white pre-dawn had risen on the left over the mirror-
like sea and as the first daylight imparted a blue colour to
the water, the horizon became discernible. The train
continued for hours, while she sat motionless, looking out

to sea and feeling almost numb with desolation and irre-
sponsibility. She was now going to allow life, her husband, the train to do as they wanted with her. As if in a
weary dream she thought of the gradualness of everything, and of her own unconscious self, of the first rebellion against her husband's dominance, of the illusion of
her independence, the pride of her sense of self and all
the happiness of the gentle ecstasy, all the gladness of harmony achieved … Now it was over; now all question of
free will was vain. The train was taking her to where
Rudolf was calling her, and life had been around her, not
very roughly, with a gentle pressure of ghostlike hands,
which pushed and guided and pointed …

And she stopped thinking. The weary dream dissolved
in the increasing blue of the day and she felt that she was
approaching Nice. She was returning to a small reality.
She felt that she looked a little travel-worn and sensing
unconsciously that it would be better if Rudolf's first
glimpse of her were not so unappealing, she slowly opened
her bag, washed herself with a handkerchief sprinkled
with eau-de-Cologne, combed her hair, powdered her
face, brushed herself off and carefully drew a white veil
over her face, and put on a pair of new gloves. At a station
she bought a couple of yellow roses and stuck them in her
belt. She did all this unconsciously, without thinking that
it was right, sensible to do so, for Rudolf to see her again
with that aura of a beautiful woman. She felt that from
now on her main task was to be beautiful, and that nothing
else really mattered. And when the train rumbled into the
station, when she recognised Nice, she was calm, because
the conflict was over, because she was submitting to all

the superior forces. The carriage door was pulled open, and in the station, which at that hour was not very full, she saw him at once: large, sturdy, with an easy manner, with his ruddy male face, his light summer suit, straw hat, yellow shoes. He gave an impression of healthy solidity and mainly of broad-shouldered masculinity and not-withstanding that broadness a 'gentleman' from head to toe, immaculately turned out without a suggestion of the dandy. And the ironically smiling moustache and the firm gaze of his handsome grey eyes, always on the look out for women gave him a powerful and certain air of being able to do what he wanted, of being able to domi-nate, if he so wished. An ironic pride in his handsome strength, with a hint of contempt for the others who were not so handsome and powerful, so healthily animal and yet aristocratic, and in particular a sarcastic condescen-sion towards all women, since he knew women and knew what they really counted for—this was expressed by his eyes, his bearing, his gestures. That was how she knew him. In the past it had often sparked rebellion in her, but now she felt resigned, and a little frightened too.

He had come over to her and helped her alight. She could see that he was angry, that he intended to give her a rough reception; then that his moustache curled into a smile, as if scoffing because he was the strongest … But she said nothing, calmly took his hand and got off the train. He took her out of the station and in the carriage she waited a moment for the suitcase. His eyes surveyed her. She was wearing an old blue linen skirt and a blue linen jacket, but despite the old clothes and the weary resignation she looked like an elegant, beautiful woman.

"I'm pleased you've finally seen the virtue of following my wishes," he said at last.

"I thought it was best," she said softly.

He was struck by her tone and he observed her closely from the side. He did not understand her, but he was pleased she had come. She was tired now from the emotion and from the train, but he thought she looked most charming, even though she was not as glamorous as at Mrs Uxeley's ball, when he had spoken to his ex-wife for the first time.

"Are you tired?" he asked.

"I've had a bit of a temperature for a few days, and of course I did not sleep last night," she said, as if apologising.

The suitcase had been loaded and they drove off, to the Hôtel Continental. They said nothing else in the carriage. They were also silent as they entered the hotel and the lift and he took her to his room. It was an ordinary hotel room, but she found it strange to see his brushes lying on the table, to see his jackets and trousers hanging on the hooks, things with a shape and creases that she remembered from before, with which she seemed familiar. In a corner she recognised his suitcase.

He opened the windows wide. She had sat down on a chair, in an attitude of wait and see. She felt slightly faint and closed her eyes, dazzled by the stream of sunlight.

"I expect you're hungry," he said. "What shall I order for you?"

"I'd like some tea and bread and butter."

Her suitcase was brought in and he ordered her breakfast.

"Take your hat off," he said.

She got up. She took off her jacket. Her cotton blouse was creased and she did not like it. In front of the mirror she pulled the pin out of her hat and very naturally combed her hair with his comb, which she saw lying on the table. And she folded the silk ribbon round her linen collar. He had lit up a cigar and was calmly standing smoking. A waiter brought breakfast. Silently she had something to eat and drank a cup of tea.

"Have you already had breakfast?" she asked.

"Yes."

They fell silent again and she ate.

"Shall we talk a bit now?" he asked, standing smoking.

"Very well."

"I don't want to talk about your running off," he said. "At first I was going to give you a piece of my mind: it was a damn idiotic thing for you to do … "

She said nothing. She just looked up at him and her lovely eyes took on a new expression—one of gentle resignation. Again he was silent, obviously restraining himself, choosing his words.

"As I say, I don't want to talk about it again. For a moment you didn't know what you were doing, you weren't responsible for your actions. But there's got to be an end to it now: that's how I want it. Of course I know that in the eyes of the law I haven't the slightest claim on you. But we've already talked about that, and I've already written to you. You were my wife, and now I see you again I feel very clearly that, despite everything, I look on you as my wife. You must have had the same impression of our reunion here in Nice."

"Yes," she said calmly.

"You admit it?"

"Yes," she repeated.

"That's all right then. That's all I want from you. From now on don't let's think about the past, our divorce, the things you did afterwards. From now on we'll blot all that out. I look on you as my wife and you'll be my wife again. According to the law we can't remarry, but that doesn't matter. I regard our legal divorce as an interlude, a formality that as far as possible we shall render null and void. If we have children, we shall legitimise them. I'll consult a lawyer about all that and take all the necessary steps, including financial ones. So our divorce will be nothing but a formality, with no force at all for us and only minimal force for the world and the law. And then I shall leave the army. I wouldn't have wanted to stay in for ever anyway, and so I can leave sooner than I planned. Besides, you won't enjoy living in Holland, and it doesn't appeal to me either."

"No," she murmured.

"Where would you like to live?"

"I don't know … "

"In Italy?"

"No … " the tone was pleading.

"Shall we stay here?"

"I'd rather not … to begin with."

"I was thinking of Paris. Would you like to live in Paris?"

"Fine … "

"That's agreed then. We'll go to Paris as soon as possible, look for an apartment and get settled in. It'll soon be spring and that'll make a good start in Paris."

"Fine … "

He threw himself into an armchair, which groaned under him.

"Tell me, what are you thinking, deep down?"

"What do you mean?"

"I wanted to know what you were thinking about this husband of yours. Did you think he was ridiculous?"

"No … "

"Come and sit on my knee."

She got up and went over to him. She did as he wanted and sat on his knee, and he pulled her towards him. He put his hand on her head: that gesture that left her unable to think. She closed her eyes and snuggled up to him, resting her head against his cheek.

"You didn't forget me completely, did you?"

She shook her head.

"We should never have divorced, should we?"

Again she shook her head.

"We were hot-headed back then, both of us. You mustn't be hot-headed any more. It makes you nasty and ugly. You're much sweeter and more beautiful as you are now."

She smiled faintly.

"I'm glad to have you back," he whispered, giving her a long kiss on the mouth.

She closed her eyes as he kissed her, while his moustache bristled against her skin and his lips pressed on hers.

"Are you still tired?" he asked. "Do you want to rest a little?"

"Yes," she said. "I want to put on something more comfortable."

"You should go to bed for a bit," he said. "Oh, and I

was going to tell you: your friend the princess is coming here this evening."

"Isn't Urania angry … ?"

"No. I've told her everything, she knows the whole story."

She was glad that Urania wasn't angry, that she still had a friend.

"And I saw Mrs Uxeley too."

"She *is* angry with me, I expect."

He laughed.

"Poor old thing! No, not angry. She's put out that she'll have to do without you. She was very fond of you. She likes beautiful people around her, she told me. She can't stand an ugly lady's companion, with no class. Come on, get undressed and lie down for a bit. I'll leave you alone and find somewhere to sit downstairs."

They had got up. His eyes had a golden sparkle and an ironic smile played beneath his moustache. He swept her into his arms.

"Corrie," he said hoarsely. "It's wonderful to have you back. Tell me, are you mine, are you mine?"

He hugged her to him, almost stifling her, both arms around her, weighing on her.

"Tell me, are you mine?"

"Yes … "

"What was your name for me—when you loved me?"

She hesitated.

"What did you call me?" he insisted, gripping her still tighter. Pushing at his shoulders she fought for breath.

"My Rudy … " she murmured. "My beautiful, gorgeous Rudy … "

Mechanically she cradled his head in her arm. With what seemed a great effort, he let go of her.

"You undress," he said, "and try to get some sleep. I'll come back later."

He left, while she undressed and brushed her hair with his brush, and put some drops of the toilet water he used into the bowl. She closed the top curtains, behind which the afternoon sun was shining, plunging the room into a downy, wine-red gloom. And she crept into the big bed and waited for him, trembling. Her head was empty of thoughts. There was no pain and no memory in her. All that was in her was a single expectation of the slow but inexorable course of life. She felt nothing but a bride, though not an ignorant bride, and in her deepest core she felt herself the wife, in her deepest core the wife of the man she was waiting for. In her mind's eye, dreamlike, she saw the figures of children … If she were to be truly his wife, she wanted to be not only his lover, but also the mother of his children … She knew that despite his rough manners, he loved the softness of children, and she would want them in her second marriage, as a precious consolation in the times when she was no longer beautiful, no longer young … In her mind's eye, dreamlike, she saw the figures of children … And she waited for him, listened for his step, longed for him to come, her body quivering in expectation. When he came in and approached her, her arms closed round him in a gesture of deep and conscious certainty, and without a doubt, against his chest, in his arms, she had a sure sense of his male dominance, while the dream of her life Rome, Duco, the studio— submerged in a vortex of black melancholy …

AFTERWORD

LOUIS COUPERUS was born in The Hague in 1863 into a family with a distinguished tradition of government service in the Netherlands East Indies, where he spent part of his childhood. Returning to Europe, he obtained a teaching qualification in Dutch, but his real ambitions lay elsewhere. After his early poetry was ridiculed by the literary avant-garde, he turned to fiction with *Eline Vere* (1889), creating a rich Tolstoyan panorama of upper-class Hague life, against which is set the downfall of his hypersensitive and maladjusted heroine. This was the beginning of a prolific and successful career, in the course of which he produced over twenty novels, as well as numerous collections of stories and travelogues.

In 1891 Couperus married his cousin Elisabeth Baud, a lover of literature and occasional translator, who gave him lifelong companionship and loyal emotional as well as practical support. The marriage remained childless, and much in Couperus' work is strongly suggestive of a homosexual or at least bisexual orientation. On occasion his prose style betrays his thwarted poetic aspirations, leading one commentator to lament a tendency to overwrite:

> He powdered his style as he did his face, he manicured his sentences as he did his nails, he dressed up his novels in the same way as he dressed up his body. This dressing up and embellishing is one of his most conspicuous weaknesses, and together with his tendency to longwindedness

and his fatal urge to continue a book beyond its logical ending prevented him from becoming a second Tolstoy, Flaubert or Henry James, in whose class he potentially belonged.

Nevertheless Couperus' wide and continuing appeal to readers is easy to understand: his great gift for narrative, characterisation and dialogue is allied to a compelling fatalistic vision.

The outbreak of World War I brought four years of enforced confinement within the neutral borders of his native Netherlands, and put a brake on Couperus' growing reputation in the English-speaking world, where since the 1890s he had enjoyed critical and popular success with a string of translations. As early as 1891 *Footsteps of Fate* (Noodlot, 1890) had appealed to Oscar Wilde and his circle, *Old People and the Things that Pass* (*Van oude mensen de dingen die voorbijgaan*, 1906) was praised, albeit faintly, by D H Lawrence, and the ambitious four-novel cycle *The Books of the Small Souls* (*De boeken der kleine zielen*, 1901–1903) won the endorsement of Katherine Mansfield.

Once hostilities ceased the priority was his reintroduction to an international audience. Deciding which of his books was best suited to inaugurate such a relaunch was no easy task: both the brilliant and perceptive colonial novel *De stille kracht* (*The Hidden Force*, 1901) and the explicit homosexuality of *De berg van licht* (*The Mountain of Light*, 1905–1906), centring on the downfall of the androgynous boy-emperor Heliogabalus, were too controversial for the contemporary moral and political climate in the target countries. Though *The Hidden Force* eventually appeared with some success in a slightly censored version in the UK in 1922 and in 1924 in the US, where the film rights were also sold, the latter novel, in some ways the fictional counterpart of the languid classical tableaux of the painter Lawrence Alma-Tadema (1836–1912) and cited in Mario Praz's classic study *The Romantic Agony* as an exemplary decadent novel, remains untranslated.

The final choice was the 1900 novel *Langs lijnen van gelei-delijkheid*, which was published first in America as *Inevitable* in 1920, in the version by Couperus' regular translator Alexander Teixeira de Mattos, and the following year in the UK under the (even more) portentous title *The Law Inevitable*. This study of a young upper-class divorcée's attempt to build a new, emancipated and culturally fulfilling life in Italy and her eventual return to her ex-husband received rapturous reviews in the US, where the author's skill, power and versatility and his creation of a 'beautiful and passionate' protagonist were widely admired. In Britain, however, the reception was more mixed. There were two main reservations: firstly, the novel's erotic explicitness and specifically the concluding bedroom scene (which was discreetly bowdlerised in the UK edition); secondly, the title's suggestion that Cornélie's story is exemplary and universal. The latter stricture stems from a misapprehension caused by the English title, particularly in its expanded form. In fact Couperus' Dutch title means something more like 'slowly but surely' or 'little by little', highlighting the specific, slow-acting chemistry between the heroine and her (ex-)husband.

On a literary level, *Inevitable* represents an interesting variation on some of Couperus' major themes, including the complex underlying factors determining human character and action, and the contrast between Northern and Southern Europe—the former representing grey gloom, repression and convention, the latter sunshine, warmth and self-fulfilment. Present-day readers may detect echoes of Henry James (especially the story *Daisy Miller* of 1878) in both setting and tone, and be reminded of E M Forster's evocations of Italian boarding-house life in *A Room with a View* (1908). Aspects of the ending suggest a comparison with D H Lawrence. The vagaries of a woman's attempt at self-liberation recall a novel like H G Wells' *Ann Veronica* (1909), though the optimism of the latter book is lacking.

Contemporary Dutch readers will have inevitably recognised the novel's allusions to real life in the shape of the aristocratic women's rights activist and writer Cecile Goekoop-de Jong van Beek en Donk (1866–1944), one of the principal organisers of the epoch-making Dutch National Exhibition of Women's Labour held in The Hague in 1898. The heroine of her militantly feminist novel *Hilda van Suylenburg* (1897) combines a happy marriage with a successful career as a lawyer. The author's own life fell somewhat short of this emancipated ideal: having left her rich husband in 1898 and fled to Italy, she was briefly reconciled with him after he followed her abroad, but was divorced in 1899, later remarrying and converting to Catholicism.

This biographical and literary link with contemporary feminism raises the question whether Couperus' book is to be read as a fictional counterblast to *Hilda van Suylenburg* and its message that women 'can have it all'. A commentator like Marianne Braun, for example, in her study of the first wave of feminism in the Netherlands, sees Couperus's novel as an 'antipode' to the earlier book. This, though, would seem a rather crude reading of a generally empathetic and balanced work. Certainly it would be simplistic to view Cornélie's final submission to Brox as a pre-Lawrentian recipe for 'sexual bliss ever after'; there is a heavy price to pay for Couperus' character: her independence, her political engagement, and the cultural and intellectual affinity as well as the love she had shared in Rome with Duco. The Dutch critic Herman Verhaar has pointed to Couperus's debt to *Madeleine Férat* (1868), an early novel by his revered model Zola, while stressing the Dutch writer's commitment to individual psychology over the deterministic theories of 'first impregnation' that loom large in Zola's vision. Ton Anbeek stresses the fact that Couperus' fatalism is never crudely physical or psychological, but has from the outset a mystical dimension, for most of his career classical in flavour, though in his last period coloured increasingly by oriental beliefs. Anbeek quotes a passage early in the novel (Chapter II), which seems to present Cornélie one-dimensionally as a product of her social class:

> This woman was a child of her time but particularly of her environment, which was why she was so immature: conflict against conflict, a balance of contradiction, which might be either her downfall or her salvation, but was certainly her fate.

Certainly, the socio-economic consequences of an up bringing that has left her unfit for 'menial' shop work in

Rome are clearly spelt out (for example in Chapter XLII). It is no accident that Mrs Holt, the English feminist who urges Cornélie, as the author of an influential pamphlet, to rejoin the struggle, should be wealthy (Chapter XLVI). But realistic elements can be contrasted with a less tangible expression of her quandary when she is forced to leave Duco (Chapter XLIII):

> There was absolutely no reason to leave him. He did not want her to either, he would never want it. And they held each other tight, as if they could feel something that might separate them, an inexorable necessity, as if hands were floating around them, pushing, guiding, restraining and defending, a battle of hands, like a cloud around the two of them; hands trying to sunder violently their glistening lifeline, their merged lifeline, though too narrow for both their feet, and the hands would wrest them apart, making the single great line spiral split apart into two.

Couperus is too great an artist to content himself with a purely programmatic treatment of his heroine's predicament, though such charged passages, of which there are many in the novel, may seem to border on mystification. Today's reader may wish to supply his or her own question mark to the English title (which, it must be stressed, was not the author's choice).

PAUL VINCENT